DEADLY
SECRETS

A Novel

DEADLY SECRETS

Frank Richardson

Covenant Communications, Inc.

Covenant®

Cover image: *Man Walking Down Corridor* © Gremlin, courtesy of iStockphoto.com

Cover design copyright © 2015 by Covenant Communications, Inc.

Published by Covenant Communications, Inc.
American Fork, Utah

Printed in the United States of America
First Printing: January 2015

21 20 19 18 17 16 15   10 9 8 7 6 5 4 3 2 1

ISBN 978-1-62108-905-6

Acknowledgments

NOVELS ARE TEAM PRODUCTS.

My sweetheart, Diane, was first to read each draft. She endured endless discussions about story, plot, characters, and marketing the book, always with a smile and words of encouragement.

Brad Richardson, courtroom attorney and partner in the Eagle, Idaho, law firm of Garrett Richardson, provided valued guidance on legal terms and procedures for Rick Street's three appearances in Judge Springer's Third District Court.

Jim Hunter reviewed military aspects of the story for accuracy and authenticity. Jim's thirty-year military career began with the 3rd Marine Division in Vietnam. His experiences in the 19th Special Forces Group were especially relevant to circumstances surrounding Ryan Tate's unfortunate death in Afghanistan.

Brian Law retired recently as deputy to the Davis County (Utah) Sheriff and now nurses in the ER at Ogden Utah's McKay-Dee Hospital. Brian helped me tackle practical aspects of law enforcement procedure that arose as I tried to depict Rick Street's interactions with the SLCPD detective division.

Thanks and congratulations to Lloyd Pendleton, director of the Utah Homeless Task Force, and the many others who contribute to Utah's Housing First initiative and help to end homelessness in Utah.

Gregg and Nick Richardson, Alan Last, and the guys from the Ponds Park Ward fathers and sons group helped early on with plot and character development in a fantastic campfire brainstorming session. Nick proposed the oft-considered "glue his hands to his butt" strategy for punishing the story's villain.

Further thanks to managing editor, Kathryn Gordon; Stacey Owen; and other members of the Covenant Communications acquisition, editorial, and design teams who bring Rick Street and his friends to you.

Lastly, thanks to you, the reader. Your pleasurable reading experience is the aim toward which all our effort and countless happy hours of imagination, discussion, and keyboard tinkering is focused. Enjoy!

Chapter 1

RICK STREET WATCHED THE RAGGED girl leave the Rescue Mission, hands in pockets, walking north with Slice into the freezing darkness. Instinct and experience told Rick that, without his help, this girl wouldn't survive the night.

Stupid!

Icy tracks and the jetsam of passing snowplows and street traffic littered the sidewalk. Rick slipped his hands into the pockets of the military field jacket he had picked out of the Rescue Mission's donated-clothing bin just hours earlier. He hunched his shoulders against the cold, pushing the stiff collar up tight around his neck.

She probably can't help being on the street, but she should go to the women's shelter or some other safe place.

The couple disappeared into the dark beyond the streetlamp ahead of him. Rick followed slowly.

Why can't I just let her go to whatever fate a stupid girl deserves?

The girl and Slice walked along like a couple of teens under the spell of forbidden romance. They rounded the corner and crossed the busy street without waiting for the pedestrian signal. Once on the south end of Pioneer Park, they faded into the landscape along a leafless tree-lined walk, heading toward the interior.

She's crazy to hook up with Slice. He's twisted. Dangerous.

Rick waited for the light. He continued north along the west side of the park, watching for glimpses of the couple without looking directly at them.

She doesn't know it, but she needs me.

He moaned.

If the staff finds out about this, I'm out. And I want to be in so bad.

He fingered the little penknife in his pocket given him by the old grandfather of his last foster family. Rick's only enduring possession. But it was too small to help him tonight.

Need to find me a weapon.

Searching the frozen, snow-covered ground for anything that might extend his reach or deflect a blow, he spied a section of two-by-four lying frozen into the ice along the edge of the sidewalk. This he kicked at until it loosened a little. He stooped and tried to pry it up with his bare hands. The ice-bound board taunted him. He kicked it again. Finally, the piece came loose, still armed along the edges with wicked shards of ice, looking like some primitive club. The thing was freezing to the touch, and Rick's hands were numbed to near uselessness.

Putting the board under his arm so he could warm his hands a little with his hot breath, he circled through the trees and made his way back toward the point where he'd last seen the couple. He moved slowly, scanning the inky areas between park lamps for any sign of the two. He could see other walkers at a distance but nothing of the couple.

Slowly, he circled toward the restroom and park maintenance building, careful to stay on new-fallen snow that muffled the sound of his steps. The couple had disappeared. Rick stood still, partially enveloped by the boughs of a massive evergreen.

He thought he could see a slight movement in the recessed doorway of the restroom building, now closed for the season. He moved closer.

There.

The nearest lamp cast an irregular beam into the opening, lighting one of Slice's legs from the waist to midcalf and a section of his back clasped by the girl's arm. The picture changed constantly as the couple writhed, locked in a lustful embrace.

I don't wanna see this.

Normally, Rick would look the other way and pass by. This time he held his ground.

Minutes passed.

Though he couldn't see either figure clearly, it looked like Slice's hand dropped below the back of his tattered coat, reaching for something concealed in his waistband. Whatever the object was, it would be hidden from the unsuspecting girl. Rick's pulse quickened. He held his breath and strained to see all he could in the poor light.

As Slice's hand passed through the sliver of light, Rick clearly saw the glint of something metallic.

A knife.

Was it a knife?

Rick couldn't be sure. But the stakes were high. No time to take a chance.

Without further thought, Rick lunged toward the doorway, yelling Slice's name. He raised the board, ready to strike in the girl's defense.

Four long strides brought him to the doorway. Both Slice and the girl had turned to see who'd shouted. Slice backed into the recess, ready to ward off the impending blow.

In midstride, Rick sensed—more than heard—movement behind him. Before he could turn to look, he felt a sudden searing pain in the back of both knees. Instantly, his legs buckled. Powerful, unseen hands wrenched him backward by the collar of his new jacket. He landed flat on his back, the impact driving the air from his lungs. His unprotected head struck the ice-covered walkway. His ears rang. Lazy lights swam in his vision.

Rolled onto his stomach, his arms forced behind him, a knee in the small of his back pinning him to the frigid snow, Rick Street was being cuffed.

Above him, a powerful voice rumbled.

"All right, scumbag, show's over. You're under arrest for attempted assault with a deadly weapon. You have the right to remain silent. Anything you say can be used against you in a court of law . . ."

Chapter 2

RICK SAT ON A MISERABLY hard chair in a barren interrogation room of the Salt Lake County Metro Jail. He couldn't be sure what time it was. He put his head down on his arms folded on the tabletop in front of him and closed his eyes. Processing his arrest had taken hours, waiting first at one desk and then another. He'd spent a couple hours in a holding cell with no beds—just a hard bench attached to the wall.

At some point he'd surrendered his few personal effects and received a receipt, the only thing now in his pocket.

When the door opened at last, two men entered. Rick recognized them. They were the arresting officers from the night before. Both looked freshly showered. Their tidiness accentuated Rick's chaotic appearance. Their energy highlighted his exhaustion. Both men carried coffee cups.

I am so beat.

Rick's eyes burned. His butt bones smarted from too many hours on hard chairs. After an initial glance at his captors, he rested his face in his hands, propped up from the table by his elbows. He ran his fingers through his long hair, reasonably clean because he'd showered the night before last. The hair hung like a curtain around his down-turned face, blocking out some of the harsh fluorescent light. He waited.

I just want this to be over. Please be over!

One of the police officers identified himself as Detective Warner. He sat across the table, placing his notepad and Styrofoam coffee cup between him and Rick. Rick's stare fixed on the cup.

That smells so good. Bet you're not gonna offer me any of that.

Warner was wiry, maybe in his forties, and had a heavily scarred complexion. The other detective, whose name Rick couldn't remember, stood silently behind Warner. He was a larger man. His stomach hung far over his belt. When he spoke, it was in a too-loud volume. He leaned against the wall, twizzling his coffee.

"Richard Street." Warner reminded Rick of his rights then began reading from a rap sheet lying on the note pad in front of him. "Age twenty-eight. No known residence. Nevada driver's license. Three arrests, two for public intoxication, one DUI."

Rick said nothing.

"Look at me, Street."

Rick looked up through his fingers. Warner had shaved since bringing Rick in late last night. He now sat forward, rubbing his chin, his eyes boring into Rick.

"What were you doing in the park last night?"

"I . . ." Rick shook his head.

"Street, what were you doing in the park?"

"I was following somebody."

"Who?"

"A street guy. We call him Slice. And a girl."

"Who was the girl?"

"I don't know her name. Just a girl. I've seen her around."

"Why were you following them?"

Rick looked from one detective to the other.

"The guy in the doorway—Slice—has a bad rep."

"So?"

"So I thought the girl was in danger. I thought I would . . . like, protect her, you know? If she needed it."

Detective Warner shook his head slowly. Then he turned toward the larger detective, who simply rolled his eyes.

"Yeah. Right." Warner turned back toward Rick. "We're not buying it. You're asking us to believe you were this girl's self-appointed guardian?"

"Weird but true," Rick mumbled, shifting his weight on the chair.

"What made you think the girl needed protecting?"

"This guy, Slice, is violent and abusive. The girl was vulnerable. She was asking for trouble. I thought—and I know I'm right on this—she was in danger. Three women have been murdered near the park. Everybody over there thinks it's a serial killer. If anybody on the street is capable of that, it's Slice. Word on the street is that Slice did it."

"The last of those killings was four months ago. What made you think this girl was in danger last night?"

"She's helpless. Pathetic. You know? No way she could take care of herself."

With Rick's pronouncement, a hint of a smile crossed Warner's face, and both detectives glanced instinctively toward a one-way window in the wall to Rick's left. Rick's eyes followed the officers' glance.

"Street, look at me," Detective Warner demanded.

"Why did you try to club this Slice? Were you jealous? He cutting in on your territory?"

"No," replied Rick. "Nothing like that. Slice has a knife. He was gonna kill the girl. I was just trying to save her."

"Just trying to save her." Warner's voice dripped sarcasm. "Well, Street, the guy you were stalking didn't have a knife. He was unarmed. You followed him there with the intent to kill him. And you're going to jail for trying to bash his head in."

"He's vicious," said Rick. "I've seen him cut people before. I think he killed those three women. He would have killed the girl last night. If you didn't arrest him, you made a big mistake."

Warner shook his head.

"You're our man, Street. Not him."

"No," Rick moaned. "I'm not that kind of person."

"So you say," said Warner. "What you tried to do last night proves otherwise."

"Ask anybody on the street. At the Mission. At the shelter. I've never hurt anybody."

"We just came from there. We asked," said Warner. "People down there tell us you're a fighter."

"No," said Rick. "Well, yeah, I've been in a few fights. But only to help people who can't take care of themselves. I mean, I'm not like a bully or anything."

"Can't buy it, Street. We saw what you did last night. You were out to kill."

"No. I'm not a killer. I'm trying to make something of myself. If the people down at the Mission find out about this, they're gonna throw me out. I'm trying to get into their rehab program. I need it."

Rick dropped his gaze and shook his head in despair.

"Too late for that," said Warner. "We already told 'em."

"Ohhhhh, man!" howled Rick.

"Sounds like you wanted that pretty bad, but you must have wanted to hurt Slice more."

"I didn't wanna hurt him. I was just trying to save the girl. Slice is your guy. You gotta believe me."

Warner shook his head.

"I *know* he's your guy. Why don't you check *him* out?"

"We're checking everybody out," said Warner. "If your guy, Slice, was our killer, we'll never know, will we? Because you interfered. You broke the law, Street."

Rick looked from one detective to the other and then to the two-way.

"The whole thing last night was a sting? That's how you happened to be there at just the right time? You were trying to lure the killer in?"

"We're asking the questions here, Street. Not you."

Rick's head dropped into his hands.

"Tell me it's not true," he moaned. "You can't know how much this has cost me."

The room was silent except for the grating of the big detective's swizzle stick against the sides of his coffee cup.

Warner smiled at Rick, not kindly. "You can't even imagine how much this is *going* to cost you. Attempted assault is a class B misdemeanor. Ninety days. You also interfered with a police investigation. Another ninety. Street, we won't see you at the park again until next summer."

Chapter 3

RICK STREET PACED HIS HOLDING cell. The only other person in the cell was an older man who nodded, glassy-eyed, when Rick first entered and had said nothing since. He sat silently in the corner with his feet up on the bench.

Gradually, the cellmate began following Rick's movements, a sign that he was sobering. Eventually, he spoke. His breath whistled through a gap left by two missing front teeth.

"Time goes slow in here, don't it?"

Rick kept pacing. "It do," he answered but didn't want to talk.

A long silence ensued.

"You been in before?" asked the cellmate.

"Couple times," answered Rick. He glanced over at the older man. The man's age was indiscernible—long gray hair; weathered face; worn, soiled clothes. Doubtlessly from the street, but Rick didn't recognize him.

"Jail ain't no good for a guy," said the drunk, his gaze drifting up toward the ceiling. "But you can get some purty long days on the street too."

Rick nodded.

"And nights," said the older man.

Rick's cellmate was warming up to become a thoroughgoing conversationalist. Rick had experienced this same pattern a million times.

"Oh yeah," replied Rick. "Nights can get long."

"Ever done time in the Big House?"

"Nope. Don't ever want to."

"That's right, you don't want to. Time do go slow in the Big House."

Rick shuddered.

"I only spent one day in the pen," Rick's cellmate said with a laugh. "The day started when I was about twenty and ended when I turned thirty. That were a long day."

He shook his head as he laughed, grinning up at Rick.

It was Rick's turn to talk. Not returning this stranger's self-revelation would be cold rejection. Rick sighed. "I spent my longest night under the Jordan River bridge down by 3300 South," Rick told him.

"A guy named Scotty and I crawled underneath trying to get out of the wind. We smoked a couple of his joints. That helped for a while. After that, the night ate us alive. The ground was froze. The concrete was cold against our backs. Me and Scotty sat together, sharing body heat. Wasn't much of that. The place was too small to stretch. The wind was too cold to go outside. That were a long night."

"I hear you," the old man whistled through his teeth. "Scotty shared his stash with you? I guess you owe him, huh?"

"Yeah. I owe him."

"And you was glad Scotty was there. I hear you." The cellmate nodded his understanding.

I spent most of that night wishing Scotty was someplace else. He talked nonstop. Complained about his life, about the accommodations, about his step-father, about his aching tooth, about Mexicans that take the best jobs. Scotty never worked a day since I knew him, so I took that complaint for what it was worth.

"Yeah," mumbled Rick. "Glad he was there. "

"Got a name?" asked Rick's stranger.

"Name's Rick."

"Friends call me Shark," laughed the older man. "Cuz of my teeth."

Rick acknowledged the introduction with a nod. The cell went silent again.

"Got any plans?" asked Shark eventually.

Rick shrugged. "Get me a car. Have my own place, maybe with a big screen and a wet bar. But I need to get some school first."

"Me too," replied Shark. "Same here. And I wanna get me an ol' lady. Things can get kinda lonely."

"I hear you." Rick nodded.

The conversation with Shark drifted meaninglessly. Rick continued to pace until he'd worn himself completely out.

Chapter 4

MIRANDA MARTINEZ WAS IN HER last week with the Detective Division. She listened as Detectives Taylor and Warner briefed their supervisor, Lieutenant Stack, on the botched sting of the night before and the questioning of Rick Street.

"Much as I'd like to pin this thing on Street, the guy's not a killer," said Taylor. "If anything, he's a crusader. But he interfered with a police operation. If he hadn't bungled it for us, we might have gotten our killer. I say we push for prosecution on the attempted assault charge."

Stack was a little man, mid- to late-fifties, approaching retirement. Taylor towered over him. Stack turned to Warner.

"How about you, Nate?"

Warner wagged his head.

"These operations are always unpredictable," said Warner. "If it hadn't been Street, it could have been somebody else. The thing about Street is that he broke the rules of the street, you know? Don't ask. Don't tell. Don't get involved. These people see everything but don't get involved. Here we have a guy who was ready to act. He doesn't fit the street profile—regardless of his name.

"He claims he wants to rehab," Warner continued. "If he's headed for rehab and we prosecute, we just derail him. I don't know."

"A good, decisive answer." Stack sighed, removing his glasses and rubbing his eyes.

Warner shrugged. "You asked me; I told you."

"Right. I'm just not sure *what* you told me."

"I told you it's not clear cut. You can go either way."

"Okay." Stack sighed again. "M, you got anything to add?"

Miranda Martinez looked at the two detectives—both her seniors—then back at Stack.

"My gut reaction?" she asked.

"Yeah, give it to me."

"I say prosecute if you can. I think Warner's right. Street's just hiding out down here. He's found a comfort zone, but he's capable of more. Going to jail won't be good for his record, but it might jolt him. Get him off his dime. It could be good for him in the long run."

"That'll be the day, when jail is actually good for somebody," replied Stack. "Just to be sure we're all reading from the same sheet of music, assure me there's no evidence linking Street to the murders."

Silence.

Taylor was first to speak. "No evidence."

Warner and Martinez both shook their heads.

"Okay, I'll talk to the city prosecutor's people. If they're willing to prosecute, we'll hold him. Otherwise, we've got until midnight to put him back on the street. I'm betting the prosecutor will tell us to turn him loose. They've got too many other irons in the fire. I'll let you know."

As an afterthought, he added, "By the way, M, get yourself some breath mints."

Miranda Martinez stood and stretched.

"Thanks for your compassion," she said. "I need to get back to the street. I love your company, but every time we meet, it ups the chances that my cover will get blown."

"How many days have you been out there?" asked Stack.

"Eighteen," she said. "Three to go."

"Gonna miss us?" asked Taylor.

"Not gonna miss this assignment," said Miranda.

"Didn't like last night's make-out session?"

Miranda shuddered. "His touch, his taste, his smell—they all made me slightly ill," she said. "But I knew it wouldn't all be roses when I signed up. It's important work, and it was something I could do."

"Not very comforting to hear Street call him Slice," said Taylor.

"I didn't have any trouble buying Street's story," Miranda replied.

"You might run into some of these same characters in your new job," said Taylor.

"No doubt," she said. "At least with the DCC, I can be me."

"Street's description of you wasn't all that flattering," laughed Warner. "Helpless. Pathetic. Can't take care of herself," Warner mimicked Rick's words.

"Yeah, well, Street's no Greek god," Miranda scoffed.

Miranda crept carefully from the building, taking her time to scan the street before moving outside.

Pathetic? Helpless? I don't think so.

Miranda tasted the inside of her mouth. She definitely needed some breath mints.

Chapter 5

RICK STREET AND HIS PUBLIC defender entered just as court convened on Monday morning. Rick had been arraigned two days after his arrest and then waited in jail almost two weeks for a hearing before the judge. The courtroom was mostly empty. The Third District Court judge handling Rick's arraignment, Judge Springer, was a woman in her midforties.

They waited through a series of arraignments of other defendants on various charges. When Rick's turn arrived, he stepped to the defendant's table and pled guilty to the charges of attempted assault and interference with a police investigation, as the attorney had advised him.

Once his plea was entered, the judge pronounced her finding without further questions or discussion. She was neither severe nor condescending. She simply removed her reading glasses and spoke directly to Rick. "The court finds you, Richard Harrison Street, guilty of attempted aggravated assault and sentences you to six months in jail."

Rick placed his hands on the table in front of him to steady himself.

The judge was silent while the impact of the sentence seeped into every molecule of Rick's being. He grew sick to his stomach. He closed his eyes and tried to swallow, but the swallow stuck in his throat.

"Now, Mr. Street," Judge Springer continued. "The court is suspending your sentence and placing you on electronically monitored probation for a period of one year and on continuing supervised probation for an additional year. I'm placing you under supervision of a specially appointed probation counselor from the State Department of Community and Culture. Mr. Street, if you successfully complete probation and meet the rehabilitation criteria set by the Homeless Task Force, this arrest and conviction will be expunged from your record. In effect, if you keep your nose clean for two years and transform yourself into a contributing member of society, this action by the court will not prejudice future opportunities.

"However, Mr. Street, if you violate probation at any time in those two years, you will go to prison and serve your full sentence minus the two weeks already served. Do you understand the magnitude of the choice facing you?"

Rick cleared his throat and answered as evenly as he could. "Yes, Your Honor."

"Speak up, Mr. Street. The court can't hear you."

"Yes, Your Honor."

Judge Springer brought her gavel down on the sound block with a sharp bang. "Next case," she ordered.

Before leaving the courtroom, Rick's public defender leaned in. "Somebody's trying to do you a favor. I'll meet you back at the jail and explain what this means."

"Yeah. Thanks," Rick replied half consciously.

At County Metro Jail, Rick traded his handcuffs for an ankle bracelet that he would wear 24 hours a day for 365 days, part of his electronically monitored probation.

He changed into his street clothes and stopped at the personal-effects window before finally being discharged. His personal effects were few: a battered wallet with his driver's license, his pocket knife, a ball-point pen, a few scraps of paper he had scribbled notes on, and a few sheets of folded and dog-eared stationery. He didn't recognize the stationery. He mentioned it to the officer who passed him a form requiring his signature.

"These are the items you signed in," replied the officer, matter-of-factly. "Now you're signing 'em out."

Rick shrugged, replaced the items in his coat pockets, and stepped out the door toward freedom—or at least to that part of freedom he could still claim.

His public defender waited across the jail lobby. He was talking with a classy woman somewhat younger than Rick. Rick walked toward them.

The defender didn't offer a hand. The same professional distance and cool reserve that existed between them in each of their consultations still prevailed. The attorney gestured toward the young woman standing beside him.

"Street, meet Miranda Martinez of the DCC."

Rick nodded as Miranda extended her hand. Though Rick couldn't remember ever meeting Miranda, her dark eyes seemed familiar.

Chapter 6

MIRANDA MARTINEZ GLANCED AT STREET from time to time in the front seat of her sporty Nissan Altima coupe. He was taller than she and a few years older. Thin enough to look gaunt. His jet-black hair hung to his shoulders. Street hunched slightly forward, briefly closing his piercing blue eyes.

You could be handsome—even better than handsome—if you put on some muscle. The big question is whether you're all there in the head.

Street didn't seem zoned out, but only time would tell.

The man had several noticeable scars on his face, one about two inches long starting in the brow over his left eye and extending down to his cheek. Another, about half as long, was at the corner of his mouth on the same side. He'd either been in an accident or a bad fight.

The knuckles of Street's bony hands were also heavily scarred. As Miranda drove, Street's hands rested loosely on the legs of his worn denims.

In her effort to engage Street in a conversation—something she had failed to do so far—Miranda asked him about his army field jacket. "I'm interested in your jacket," she said. "Who's Tate?"

Street glanced down at the embroidered name over the jacket's chest pocket but said nothing.

"A friend?"

No answer.

"A relative?" Miranda smiled with a pleading shrug.

No answer.

The jacket must have been a loaner or a donation. It was newer and cleaner than the rest of Street's clothes, made from standard desert camo worn by U.S. troops in the Middle East. It still bore the military markings of its owner, including a single black bar to indicate rank. The jacket hung loosely on Street.

He was clearly uncomfortable being alone with Miranda. There was nothing of the bravado in him that she encountered in other guys his age. He looked uneasy, even frightened, maybe intimidated by her official position. He reminded her of a stray dog—one that had been homeless, hungry, and hard put for too long.

I wonder what you'd be like if you'd grown up in favorable circumstances.

"You don't really have much choice here," she said, pulling up in front of an old three-story apartment building. "The court remanded you to supervised probation. You can't go anywhere since your location is monitored. Instead of reporting to a probation officer every week, you'll report to me. My job is to help you. We're really trying to do you a favor."

Street was still silent, looking straight ahead. He hadn't turned his eyes toward her once during the short drive from the county jail. He also hadn't spoken.

Miranda looked down at her car keys, which she now held in her hand.

"Look," she said. "There are hundreds of guys on the street who would love this opportunity. I'll try to help you make the best of it. But we can't do much if you won't talk to me."

Street responded with a barely perceptible nod of his head.

"Okay." Miranda sighed heavily, opening her door against a stiff winter wind. The day was gray. Small snowflakes blew horizontally past, like little bullets.

"Let's go look at this place and see where we go from there." She got out of the car and stood for half a minute with her back to the wind, her dark hair whipping about her face. Street made no move to follow.

"Okay, loser," she groused, shrugging and walking toward the building. By the time she reached the entry, sheltered only by a small porch roof, she could hear the passenger door of her Nissan close. She turned to see Street walking toward her, the collar of his jacket turned up, his hands in the jacket's waist pockets, and his shoulders turned in against the biting wind.

Miranda opened the entry door, stepped across the small foyer, and started up the steep stairs. As she rounded the landing and began the second flight, she heard Street close the outside door.

Just what I need—a prima donna.

By the time she unlocked and opened the door to apartment 2B, Street had caught up to her. The apartment was nearly as cold as the outdoors.

She turned to look at Street, who stood still, hands in his pockets, face ashen from the cold or from his day in court—or both.

She raised her hands from her sides, gesturing to the sparsely furnished interior. "What do you think?" she asked him.

Street looked around, moving only his head and eyes. When he had seen all he could see from his stationary vantage point, he shrugged and made no effort to move.

"Is it all right if I sit down?" Miranda asked.

Street looked at her for the first time. "It's your place," he muttered.

Miranda stepped to an armchair and sat. After looking around for a few seconds, she glanced back at Street, who still hadn't moved. "Thank you," she said. "And, no, this isn't my place, Mr. Street. This is your place."

Street continued to survey the room, not as though he had any particular interest in it but because it clearly seemed preferable to interacting with Miranda. Finally he looked over his shoulder to the door that had been left open as he entered. Slowly, he turned and pushed the door shut.

Glancing at Miranda again, who made no effort to either move or speak, Street looked toward the curtained window on the opposite wall. He walked cautiously to the window and looked out, parting the simple curtains with the back of his hand. Miranda could see that the windowpanes were frosted. Street probably couldn't see anything outside. Still, he stood looking at them as though he could.

Miranda sighed. *Street, are you impossibly dense? Do you even know what it means to be grateful? Or cooperative?*

She folded her hands in her lap, closed her eyes, and decided to listen to, rather than watch, Street. She could hear the traffic passing on Redwood Road. She could also hear the old building creaking as it withstood the blasts of winter wind. From the floor above came distant sounds. A woman was raising her voice—Miranda guessed she was angry. Then there was a mighty whack on the floor above, as though something heavy had been dropped.

After a time, Miranda heard Street exhale. His muffled footsteps crossed in front of her, and the springs in the sofa facing her chair squeaked under Street's weight.

Miranda opened her eyes and found Street looking in her direction without looking directly at her.

She nodded and tried to smile, but her face felt stiff. *Well, I'm not exactly enjoying this. It's not what I imagined.*

"So what's the deal?" Street finally asked. Miranda could barely hear him.

"The deal is that this is your apartment," she answered. "We'll sign a rental agreement; we'll pay most of the rent—at least for a time. At the end of six months, we'll see how you're doing and decide what to do from there."

Street considered this. Though he was sitting, he still had his hands in his jacket pockets, his shoulders still raised against the cold. "Who's we?" he asked.

"The State Division of Community and Culture under the auspices of the governor's task force on homelessness."

"Why?" he asked.

"Why what?" replied Miranda.

"Why are you doing this?"

"You need a place to stay, a place you can call your own."

Street shook his head.

"What?" asked Miranda and waited for a response.

"There's lots of people out there who need a place of their own. They don't get one. Nobody just gives you a place."

Street stood again and returned to the window. There was still nothing to see.

"Is this like witness protection? Do I know something the cops don't want to get out? Why would you put me up?"

"In any year, there are as many as thirteen thousand homeless people in Utah," she said. "Fewer than a thousand of those are chronically homeless. You know some of them personally. You were one of them. It costs the state a lot to take care of some of those people. Two-thirds are men. Half, or a little more, are addicts. A quarter have mental illnesses. The other quarter haven't found a spot in society where they fit yet."

Miranda corrected herself. "That's really not true. They're filling a spot in society. It's just not a spot that many of them are happy with."

She paused. "You know all this," she finally continued. "About 15 percent of the homeless use 60 percent of the available shelter time. They need to be fed, housed, educated, and protected. Some get sick or injured. Some OD. It's more efficient to provide housing to as many as possible so they're protected and have a base to work from."

"Not a very flattering picture," said Street. "What you're saying is that we're burdens on society, and it's cheaper to put us in a cage."

"No, I'm saying we're trying to help as many as possible. But we can't help all."

"Just so you know," his voice grew a little stronger and was tinged with defensiveness, "the picture isn't very rosy from our side either."

Gee, thanks. You really are dense, aren't you? "Don't lecture me," she snapped back at him deliberately. "I know it's not a rosy picture. I'm not condemning you or anybody else. You asked why the state is willing to provide housing. I tried to answer your question."

Street's gaze dropped. "Sorry," he replied.

Chapter 7

RICK'S FIRST WEEKS IN HIS apartment passed slowly. The apartment had four rooms—a living room, a bedroom, a bathroom, and a kitchenette. Furniture was scarce. Each morning he made his bed and straightened everything in the apartment. Then he swept the floor with a used broom he'd purchased at Deseret Industries with his voucher. Miranda Martinez had given him the voucher with the understanding that he could have another later on if he needed it.

In addition to the broom, Rick purchased two shirts, two pairs of casual pants, a robe, an assortment of kitchen utensils, and a picture to hang on the living room wall—all used. The picture was a drawing of the head of Jesus, rendered in subdued colors on a piece of black velvet and framed in rustic wood.

Among the drastic changes in Rick's lifestyle was making food choices. Eating at the Mission, Rick's choices were limited to yes or no—yes, I'll eat that; no, I won't. Now he shopped at a supermarket two blocks from the apartment. He had a few hundred dollars in food stamps. He arranged his purchases in the refrigerator and a pantry cupboard so that he knew exactly where to find each item. He didn't want to let food spoil.

Rick sat on the bedroom chair, putting on his shoes. He was ready to go job hunting. He'd already been through his daily straightening ritual. The only possessions he hadn't yet straightened were those in the bedroom dresser. Once he had his shoes on, he stood beside the dresser and opened the drawers one at a time, starting on the bottom.

Reaching the top drawer, he moved the little packet of personal effects he'd brought with him from jail to the other side of the drawer. There were no other items in the drawer. As he lifted items, he left lying in place the sheets of stationery. He had never opened the sheets, reasoning that since they didn't belong to him, it was none of his business what might be written on them.

On this morning, Rick unfolded the stationery. There were three sheets of what seemed like quality paper. Faint blue lines showed through the dusty-rose color. Handwriting filled two of the pages completely, the third page about halfway.

It appeared to be a personal letter, dated about eleven months earlier and written in a very precise hand.

No name was given, just a street address on E. Harvard Avenue, Salt Lake City, Utah. Thinking about this address for a second, Rick could almost picture the location of the street.

Before he could close the letter again, his eyes fell to the first lines of text.

Dear Mother,
I'm still alive.

Chapter 8

DEAR MOTHER,

I'm still alive.

I wish I could say the same for the men we lost. It makes my heart ache. For the most part, these were my friends, my brothers. My wounds are serious but no longer life threatening. I feel sure I'll recover. I Skyped Nicole two nights ago. I'm sure she's already told you everything there is to say, but I thought I'd write you a personal note so I can express my love for you. That wouldn't be easy to do out loud in a hospital bay surrounded by other soldiers.

According to our CO, it's a toss-up at this point whether I'll be sent back to the States before our deployment ends. If the wounds heal and I can avoid infection, I should be able to return to my unit. Though I miss Nicole and Trevor terribly, I feel like I need to be with my men, especially now that four are dead. I feel like I have a score to settle. I can handle my share of tragedy, but I can't tolerate treachery.

I wonder if you could do me a favor. Could you write down the information Nicole has told you? I told her all I could, but I can't really write it out on paper. Military security rules are pretty strict. If you could write it down and add it to my personal history stuff that you have, I would really appreciate that.

I love you, Mom. You know how I feel about Nicole. She's the greatest. And you know how I feel about you as a mother. You're the best. No man ever had a better mom. The same goes for Dad. No matter how long or short I live, I'll always know that the best thing that could ever happen to a baby boy was to come into your home. You're my friend and my hero. I miss you so much. Thanks for taking care of Nicole and Trevor.

Know that I love you, and please give my love to Dad.

Ryan

Rick reread the short letter several times before putting it back in the drawer. Its intimate tone touched a tender spot in his imagination. He found himself reflecting on the letter throughout the day, trying to picture Ryan and his parents, wondering about Nicole and Trevor.

Chapter 9

IN THE WEEKS AFTER INTRODUCING Rick Street to his apartment, Miranda Martinez made regular scheduled visits. They agreed that she would visit him each Tuesday afternoon unless Street found work that conflicted. The visiting schedule would be regular but flexible.

As she did each week, Miranda checked with the Department of Corrections to make sure Street hadn't strayed from his allowance zone or entered any of the exclusion zones Miranda had mapped out for him.

So far, so good.

Her knock at Street's door brought an immediate answer. Framed in the apartment doorway, Street seemed taller. He was standing upright and wearing clean clothes. His hair was newly washed and combed. He was shaven, and if anything, there was a hint of a smile on his face.

Miranda jokingly stepped back and looked around her. "Wow," she said. "Did I knock on the right door?"

She had overdone the greeting. Street's face turned scarlet with embarrassment.

"Hi," he said quietly and stepped back into the room, opening the door so she could enter.

"No offense intended," she said. "You look better. How does it feel to have your own place?"

Street motioned her toward the seat from which she had earlier watched his reaction to his new home.

There were a few personal things in view. A little glass mug stood on the single lamp table next to the sofa. A copy of the daily newspaper lay partially unfolded beneath the mug. The room was still cool but not uncomfortably cold.

"I see you learned how to turn up the heat," Miranda said spontaneously. "It feels better in here."

Again, Street blushed and fidgeted nervously, still standing while Miranda sat. "I've lived in a house before," Street answered quietly. "I know what a thermostat is."

Miranda exhaled and shrugged. "Listen, Street, I'm just trying to help. Please don't take offense at every word I say. I haven't been doing this job very long, and I'm still learning. Maybe you can help me while I'm trying to help you."

"Yeah, sorry," he replied. "Anyway, I've been a good boy." He pointed to the ankle where the monitor was strapped.

"Good for you," Miranda nodded. "Looks like you tried out the thrift store voucher."

"Yeah. Got me some new duds."

"You look . . . nice clothes," she said, feeling a sudden, unwelcome flash of attraction.

Street seemed uncertain. "Don't like 'em?" he asked.

"No, no." Miranda laughed. "They look great. You're . . ." She stopped short again.

"The woman at the thrift store, Cheryl, helped me pick 'em. She liked 'em. Said I looked hot." Street raised his eyebrows a little.

"She's right," Miranda said with a little laugh, self-consciously reaching up to straighten her hair. "How did the food card work?"

"Worked great," Street replied cautiously. "We're in a good place here. I can walk to the market and over to the community center. They have a little loaner library with some paperbacks. Got myself a paperback."

"Good for you," said Miranda.

Though Street was carrying on something of a conversation, he still fidgeted, clearly uncomfortable.

"What can I do to help you?" she asked.

Street looked directly at her.

Whoa, you really have blue eyes.

"I'm thirsty," he replied. "The food card doesn't work for booze or cigarettes."

"How can I help?" she asked.

Rick nodded like he understood that she couldn't change the rule. "I need two things to get where I wanna go," he said with unexpected forcefulness.

"What are those?" she asked.

"A job and an education."

Chapter 10

As Rick's search persisted, finding a job didn't get any easier. In fact, each rejection took a toll on his courage and determination. He found himself outside each prospective employer's door, lecturing himself to toughen up.

It's not personal. These are hard times. Lots of people outta work. Besides you don't have great references. Just keep goin'. It only takes one yes.

He kept track of each attempt in a little journal he'd bought at the thrift store. The journal's previous owner had only written on the first few pages then apparently abandoned the task. Rick didn't tear the used pages out when he bought the journal. *No reason both of us can't keep track of our lives in the same book.*

When the number of rejection entries in his journal reached twenty-five, Rick felt alarm. At forty, he felt despair. At fifty, he was sure there was something seriously wrong with him.

Everybody can see I have a problem but me.

Approaching each new employer took more vigorous self-talk.

It must be the felony conviction. Nothing I can do about that.

He had been convicted. Should he lie about it? When he tried to explain how it happened, he could tell that his listeners thought he was lying.

Who wants to hire a liar and a criminal?

On Tuesday morning, Rick knew that Miranda would be by to see him late in the afternoon. It would be great to have something positive to report. He could ask Miranda for help finding a job, but the woman had already given him a place to live, food to eat, and clothes to wear. Pride wouldn't let him ask for more help.

Following the morning's straightening ritual, he stood facing the picture of Jesus on his living room wall. With no television or radio, and with no other people living in the apartment, Rick talked to Jesus from time to time. The picture was a little austere for Rick's taste, but at least Jesus was always there.

"Too bad you can't answer," Rick told Jesus. "I'd love to talk. I really need a listening ear right now."

Rick had noticed St. Ignatius Catholic Church on the backside of the same block as the community center. Because he had no exact plan for the morning's job search, he walked there. The weather had moderated somewhat, but by the time he reached St. Ignatius, Rick was still thoroughly chilled. He stepped into the foyer and tried to warm his hands as he looked about him.

The building featured modernistic architecture, unadorned block walls, and windows of brilliant stained glass. Straight ahead of Rick were double wooden doors leading into the sanctuary. To his right a door bore the sign *Fr. John*. Rick's rap on Father John's door brought a quick response. The door opened to reveal the priest.

"I'm Father John. How can I help you?"

Father John was somewhat shorter than Rick, probably five feet ten inches. He appeared to be in his fifties, light complexioned, graying hair displaying a mild case of male pattern baldness. He was stocky but not too heavy for his size. In fact, he looked robust. When he smiled, his eyes sparkled. He was smiling now.

"Father John, my name's Rick Street. Do you have a minute?"

Father John looked at his wristwatch.

"I have a few minutes, Rick. I have to go teach my class. But come in and tell me how I can help. Then if we need to, we'll meet later to talk more."

The office was just large enough for a desk and a couple of side chairs. Books lined the wall beside the desk. A crucifix hung near the door. Father John motioned Rick to one of the chairs then sat in the swivel chair at the desk and turned toward him.

"I'm all ears," he said with a smile. "Not much hair but a lot of ears."

Rick smiled. "Thanks. It feels good to talk to somebody. I moved in nearby a few weeks ago and don't know anybody around here. I guess I'm missing my friends from the street," said Rick, scratching a spot over his ear.

"Loneliness can be dangerous," said Father John. "You're lucky you've had friends to miss."

"Yeah. I guess I didn't have a lot of friends, but I always had somebody to talk to until . . ." He shrugged, leaning forward in the chair, his hands clasped between his knees. "Father, I just need a little advice. I'm a convict trying to find a job. Nobody wants to hire a convict. I've tried fifty businesses, and I'm getting way discouraged. Any advice?"

Father John leaned back in his chair, steepling his hands in front of his face.

"That must be very discouraging. It sounds like you're doing all you can do."

Rick nodded.

"Would an employer have anything to fear from you?" asked the priest. "Are you violent? Are you a thief? Do you have a good work ethic?"

Rick paused before answering. This was no time to shade the truth. "I'm not violent," he replied. "An employer wouldn't have anything to fear that way. I've stolen from some past employers, but I don't do that anymore. I've served the evil masters—alcohol and drugs—but I'm really working to get free. Haven't had anything to drink for over a month. Problem is, I feel like I'm weakening. I gotta get a job. Gotta have someplace to go with my life."

After another pause, Rick continued. "My work ethic hasn't been real good. I work hard when I'm trying to make a good impression, but I have trouble sticking with it." Rick shrugged. "I could lie to you and tell you I'm better than I am. But I'm really trying to get myself straight. I really wanna make it this time."

Father John checked his watch. "Gotta go," he said. "Sorry to rush. Let me think about what advice I should give. Come back and see me Thursday, a little earlier in the morning."

The priest grabbed his overcoat and slipped an arm into it. Then, as if in afterthought, he spoke again. "In the meantime, go see Norm Pulsifer at the Home Depot down on Thirty-Third South. Norm's a friend of mine. I call him Norman the Mormon. He told me they're hiring sales help. Home Depot usually gives pretty good training. You could do worse. Tell Norm I sent you. See you on Thursday."

Father John was out the door.

Chapter 11

RICK COULD HARDLY SUPPRESS A smile. He finally had good news to share with Miranda that afternoon. It was the first time since moving into the apartment nearly a month earlier that he didn't struggle with the urge to binge.

Rick had never been much into drugs, though he'd tried a little of everything.

But he drank—sometimes a lot. He wasn't addicted in the sense that he suffered withdrawals; however, the urge to binge was a constant battle. It was an emotional thing. Parties broke up the monotony of day-to-day existence. They also provided an excuse to socialize. A person like Rick, alone in the world without family or friends, felt more connected to the rest of humanity swimming around in party interactions, superficial as they were.

Late in the morning, he made the long walk back from Home Depot. He showered and put his hair in a ponytail. He'd have changed clothes in honor of the occasion but didn't have anything better to wear.

Waiting for Miranda to arrive, Rick debated exactly what he was celebrating. That he had finally found a job?

Or that Miranda is coming?

He distracted himself by straightening the apartment, a task that would take anyone else three minutes. Rick dragged it out for an hour.

When he opened the top drawer of his dresser, he saw Ryan's letter once again. He'd read it many times—practically memorized it. Each time he read it, he chided himself for snooping in the world of another man.

Better if I built a world of my own.

How had the letter come to be in the pocket of a jacket donated to charity? Was the Ryan who wrote the letter the same as Tate who owned the jacket? There didn't seem to be another explanation, so Rick now thought of the writer as Ryan Tate.

Should he return the letter to the mailing address? If it was a letter to a mother from her son, wouldn't she want it as a keepsake?

When Miranda Martinez arrived at Rick's apartment, she seemed eager to talk. She had brought a series of documents to help Rick plan his future and was apparently determined to walk him through them. He'd been through similar planning drills with other agencies.

He already had a plan for his short-term future—get a job and get into school. That plan was simple enough for him to wrap his mind around and detailed enough to move him forward. He responded to Miranda's efforts politely but wasn't as enthusiastic as she appeared to be.

"Rick, setting goals, calendaring activities, and learning to budget resources are skills you need if you want to eventually become self-reliant." Miranda's voice betrayed a touch of impatience. "You don't seem to be taking this very seriously. You won't always have your own case manager. These are things you have to learn to do on your own."

Rick grinned a little self-consciously. "I like having my own case manager," he replied. "If I learn to do all this on my own, somebody will take away my caseworker."

Miranda looked at him for a moment as if trying to decide whether he was joking around. "Please be serious," she continued. "You know the state isn't going to take care of you forever. Then you'll be back on the street. Don't you want to learn to make it on your own?"

"I do want to make it on my own," he answered. "I'm sorry. I know you have a lot to do. I just enjoy visiting."

"Unfortunately that won't get you anywhere." Miranda shook her head.

Rick was seeing a different Miranda Martinez.

I thought you had some confidence in me. Obviously not much.

Rick's desire to tell Miranda about his new job gradually waned as their visit went on. Though he'd been talkative when Miranda arrived, he soon became silent.

"Street, what's wrong with you today?" Miranda asked in frustration. "Don't you want my help?"

Rick didn't have to think about his answer. If she was feeling frustrated with him, he was feeling a frustration of his own. "What I really need is not to always be reminded of my failures. Nobody's more aware of them than me. I don't need to learn to budget as bad as I just need somebody to talk to."

Rick stood up and walked over to the window. *How come I was singled out for this life? Are people always gonna be trying to fix me?*

"You know what?" he said, hoping there was room for him to be honest without seeming ungrateful. "I've been here for a while now. It's been great. I love it. I don't deserve it. Like you said before, hundreds of people would love this opportunity. But it's lonely. It's like everybody around here has been warned to stay away from me. I'm a bad person. I'm a convict.

"I was looking forward to your visit because . . ." He paused, searching for words. "Well, because you're the only person I know. The only person who visits me. And you only do it because it's your job."

Rick put his hands in his pockets, shrugged, and turned to face Miranda.

"Sorry," he said. "I'm not blaming you. You've been great. I know I don't deserve it."

Miranda didn't answer for a long moment.

"No," she said. "I'm sorry I pushed my own agenda today. I'm still learning my job, and I have a long way to go."

"I think you're doing great," he replied cautiously.

A long pause followed, Miranda taking a deep breath, Rick picking at his scarred knuckles.

"Could I ask one favor?" he asked.

Miranda cleared her throat. "What would that be?"

"Would it be all right if I just went down to the Mission for a visit? I miss those people. I mean, it's great to have a place of my own. And I haven't been hungry since I got here. It's the first time I've had regular meals in ten years. I'm real grateful . . . but I'm lonely. All I have to do here is fight to stay clean and sober. And, by the way, I've done that."

Before Miranda spoke, her look conveyed a measure of compassion for his plight. "Street," she said, "you're right. It's a mistake for someone to think they know more than the people they're trying to help. I hadn't even thought about loneliness as a problem. But I totally see it. Still"—she shook her head—"I can't authorize you to go to the Mission, Pioneer Park, or anywhere downtown. That was part of the deal with the court."

Rick finally replied. "I just want to hang out with somebody—anybody."

Miranda nodded. "Have you thought about AA?" she asked.

"Yeah," he replied. "The problem is that talking about alcohol increases my desire to binge. I know AA works for a lot of people. I'm weird. What I need is to take my mind off it."

"Of course, the ideal thing in that case might be to find a job," Miranda suggested.

"I've thought of that," Rick replied.

"Have you tried Workforce Services?" she asked.

"Tried them."

"Have you looked for Help Wanted signs?

"Done that."

"If you get turned down for a job, do you ask for referrals?"

"I've tried that."

Miranda made eye contact with Rick. Her eyes were a deep brown, nearly black. Rick felt his heart flutter as he looked silently at her, neither speaking. Miranda was the first to look away. Rick could see her swallow and squirm in her seat.

"Getting a job for you sounds like the big thing right now. Don't give up. I know it's hard, but it'll happen," Miranda offered with a cautious *let's be friends* smile.

"Yeah," replied Rick. "I believe you." This wasn't the right time to tell her he already had a job.

"Well, don't worry about me," said Rick, waiting for Miranda to stand and walking her to the door. He handed her the winter coat she'd yielded when she came in.

"You can see I make friends everywhere I go."

As Miranda stepped out the door into the stairwell, she turned and touched Rick on the arm.

"Street, you don't fool me," she said, her earlier impatience now gone. "Both of us know there's more to Rick Street than he likes to show."

Rick watched Miranda descend the stairs. Nothing she could say would have made Rick feel any better than her gentle touch had.

Chapter 12

RICK WALKED TWO MILES EACH way to work at Home Depot. The first snowy day, he discovered that Ryan Tate's field jacket was water repellent but not waterproof.

The store managers were excellent to work for. Rick would have understood their caution in placing trust in him because of his less-than-stellar work record, but they maintained an atmosphere of tolerance toward their nontraditional employees. Employees were trusted until they showed themselves unworthy of trust.

Before Rick left for work each morning, he stood in front of Jesus hanging there on his wall. *So far my record at the store is clean. Please help me keep it that way.*

When he returned each afternoon, he reported in. *Still clean.*

Rick received thirty-six hours of sales associate training. Because he didn't have any work experience in the trades like electrical, plumbing, or painting, his first assignment sent him to the building materials department. He learned the locations and specs on lumber, drywall, sacked concrete, and roofing materials.

At the beginning of March, Miranda brought Rick another voucher for the thrift store, and he picked up his food stamps. With his first paycheck, he had his hair trimmed and bought himself a pair of ankle-high hiking boots and a monthly bus pass. The daily trip to work now took five minutes instead of thirty-five.

His first real crisis occurred the afternoon following his first payday. Rick was mightily tempted to drop into the state liquor store and carry home a bottle. It would have wiped out the cash remaining from his paycheck, but he had done well staying sober, and he felt like celebrating.

The debate raged in him. He decided to jump off the bus at the stop adjacent to the liquor store. A bottle wouldn't help him, but he figured he could handle it. With wavering conviction, he stood to exit the bus.

As he did so, Father John, the Catholic priest from St. Ignatius, got onto the bus. The two men met in the doorway. Rick suddenly remembered that he'd promised to visit Father John a day or two following their first meeting. Rick had totally forgotten his commitment. Father John's referral had led directly to Rick's job. He should have returned to thank the affable priest.

"Rick, right?" Father John pointed a finger at Rick in recognition.

"Right," Rick replied. As he did so, the door closed, and the bus pulled away from the curb.

"How's it going?" Father John asked.

"Great," answered Rick looking back toward the liquor store. "The tip you gave me about the job at Home Depot panned out. I got the job. Yesterday was my first payday."

"Fabulous!" cried Father John, loudly enough for everyone on the bus to hear. "That's terrific. Good for you."

Rick smiled despite his guilty conscience. "Father, I told you I'd come back to visit, but when I got the job, I forgot all about my promise."

"It's never too late to come for a visit," replied the priest. "I'd like to get to know you better. Maybe we could think of something I can do to help."

"To be honest, Father, you just helped me." Rick laughed awkwardly. "When you got on the bus, I was just getting off to blow my last few bucks on a bottle. You saved me some money and probably a load of heartache."

Father John laughed again, clapping Rick on the shoulder. "Then, Rick, we did each other a favor. Just talking to you makes me feel better on a day that didn't start out too well. Thank you."

The pair continued to visit as they rode along. Rick was first to exit the bus.

As Rick pulled the cord and stood to leave, Father John spoke with his trademark smile. "Listen, Rick. Don't feel obligated. Just come visit when the time's right for you."

"Thanks, Father," Rick replied. "I'll be by if I manage to keep away from the liquor store."

Despite Rick's best intentions, weeks slipped by at an ever-accelerating pace, and he didn't go by to visit as promised, but he thought of Father John often.

In reality, Rick was settling into a routine that suited him. He felt little need to seek out the priest, and he couldn't imagine what he and Father John might have to talk about if Rick actually visited.

Chapter 13

MIRANDA MARTINEZ FELT SMUG. HER smugness arose, in part, from the realization that Rick Street no longer seemed like a homeless man. He worked steadily and had proven to be a model renter. He no longer fled from direct conversation by strolling over to the apartment window and offering short replies while his back was turned to her. At their latest meeting, he had actually remained seated—though fidgety—and had answered her questions directly. His gaze was often on the floor, his feet, or his hands, but he was clearly making progress.

Miranda noticed again how handsome Rick was. His shoulder-length hair definitely had more luster. His blue eyes were even more piercing, if possible, peering out of a healthier, more colorful face. At one point in their weekly interview, Rick told her he had just registered for classes at Salt Lake Community College. He actually smiled. His lips parted slightly so that his teeth showed through. His eyes definitely sparkled.

Miranda felt a flutter. She was distracted for a moment by the thought that more months of progress like the last few might turn this man into a magazine model. She wanted to hug him because she felt proud of him, though that would never do. She was sure that any overt show of affection would chase Rick back into the shadows from which he was just beginning to emerge.

Smug. That's what she was feeling. *Can things keep going this well?*

Chapter 14

RICK HAD FINALLY DECIDED WHAT to do with Ryan Tate's letter. At their weekly Tuesday meeting, he told Miranda about the letter and asked if he could travel to the east side of the city to the address showing on the letter, an address apparently belonging to Ryan's mother.

Miranda hesitated. "You're doing so well right now," she replied. "Are you sure you're ready for a change of routine?"

"It's only a bus trip with one transfer," Rick replied. "I think I can handle that."

"You know you can't go down to the Mission, right?" she asked.

"I know that."

"Can't go to the park? Can't visit any friends down there?"

"Yeah," Rick replied just cracking a cautious smile. "No fun. No excitement. Nothing that normal people would do."

"A few weeks ago," said Miranda, "you told me you were really lonely. How are you doing now?"

"Things are better," Rick answered. "I have friends at work. I've made a few friends here in the building." He smiled again but looked quickly away.

Miranda nodded. "Okay. What day do you think you'll go? I need to notify the Department of Corrections that you'll be on the move."

"I don't work on Thursday. I thought I'd go about noon. I'll be back before dinner."

"Okay, Street. It's up to you. But please don't let yourself down. You've worked too hard to make any mistakes now."

Rick was watching Miranda. When they made eye contact, he looked quickly down at his hands. He picked at the dead skin on his scarred knuckles while he was thinking. "Could I ask you a favor?" he said without looking at her.

"I'll help if I can," she replied.

Rick hesitated for a long moment. "Do you think you could call me Rick instead of Street? That always makes me feel like I'm talking to the police. Do you think anybody would care if you used my first name?"

Miranda blanched. She was clearly embarrassed either by the more intimate use of a first name or because he had put her in an awkward spot. But before he could apologize, Miranda nodded and replied without smiling. "Yes, Rick. That's a bad habit I fell into at my last job."

She paused. "I notice you never call me by my first name either. In fact, you never say my name at all. My name is Miranda. I'll call you Rick if you'll call me Miranda."

Rick nodded his consent.

Miranda smiled as if doubting he could bring himself to actually say her name anytime soon. And she was probably right.

Chapter 15

THURSDAY DAWNED COOL ENOUGH TO feel cold. Rick had gone two days in a row without work. That troubled him because if he wasn't at work, he truly had nothing to do with himself.

He slept in until about eight, though the sleep was tortured by dreams of his life on the street. After he showered and dressed in his best clothes, he straightened and restraightened his apartment through the remainder of the morning. He read Ryan Tate's letter to his mom again and again. He wondered if, by returning the letter, he might get a chance to meet Ryan or any of the other people named in the letter.

He was curious about Ryan. About Ryan's mom, his dad, Nicole, and Trevor.

Over the weeks, Rick had come to associate faces and personalities with the names in Ryan Tate's letter. But he doubted that he would have the courage to ask about them when the time really came to hand the letter over.

About noon, Rick boarded the 217 bus that would carry him down-town to the corner of State and 400 South. This was the first time in three months he had passed through the city center. He knew the sites inti-mately. He could almost smell the familiar locations as the bus sped past.

Several times, Rick saw faces he thought he recognized. But the weather had turned to a drizzle, and most of the pedestrians either walked under umbrellas or pulled hoods over their heads. He really didn't see anyone he knew. That disappointed him.

The stop at 400 South interrupted these reflections. Rick was pleased that he'd decided to wear Ryan Tate's jacket. He had debated that decision until the time for his departure. On the one hand, he didn't want to evoke any criticism from Ryan's family because he was wearing a castoff once belonging to their son. On the other, Rick felt that wearing the jacket might help to explain how he came to be in possession of the letter.

Because of the weather, Rick was doubly grateful for the jacket when the southbound bus stopped twenty yards from the corner of 1300 East and Harvard Avenue. It was a quick walk along the puddling sidewalk up Harvard Avenue to the house number on the letter. The home and surroundings were typical of mid–twentieth century upscale neighborhoods still kept in careful repair. The homes had probably cost forty thousand when they were built. Now they were likely worth ten times that much—or more.

The home Rick stopped in front of was redbrick, solid, and respectable in appearance. Standing at the front walk and peering past the established shrubs and trees, Rick suddenly felt entirely out of place. All of the worst scenarios he had imagined flooded back into his mind.

Maybe the thing to do was to keep walking past the home as though he were headed to another destination. But he hesitated. He really wanted to know who lived in this house. Stuffing his hands into his pants' pockets, he slowly proceeded up the walk. His hand felt leaden as he reached a finger toward the pearl button on the doorbell.

Again he hesitated, made a partial turn away, then stopped. With a quivering hand, he reached to the bell and pushed.

The deed was done. He had only to wait—assuming that anybody was home.

While he waited, he tried to remember his rehearsed greeting and explanation. Rick could hear the sound of footsteps approaching the other side of the door. His heart raced. He shook his head to flip the soaked hair away from his face.

A firing squad couldn't be any scarier than this.

The door opened slowly, revealing a friendly, smiling face. Female. Maybe midfifties. Light-colored hair with reverse highlights. Trim. A little matronly but generally very well tended. Refined features. She wore tailored pants, a warm sweater, and house slippers.

As Rick opened his mouth to speak, the color drained from the face before him. The smile vanished. A trembling hand covered the mouth as the eyes widened. A sharp catch in the breath. A little cry. The woman fell back from before the door as if viewing the living dead.

"No!" she cried. "No! No!"

Chapter 16

RICK ALSO FELL BACK FROM the door, startled by this horrific response. No reception he had imagined could possibly compare with what was happening. Of course, his first thought was for his own emotional preservation.

What'd I do? He fled from the door, stammering. "I'm sorry. I didn't mean to scare you."

Rick was halfway to the sidewalk before he heard the woman gasp.

"No. Stop! Please, stop." He turned to see her standing in the door again, steadying herself with a hand.

"I'm so sorry," she called. "Don't leave. Please, come back. Tell me who you are."

Rick fished in his coat pocket for Ryan Tate's letter. Holding the folded sheets in front of him like an offering, he slowly advanced toward the woman, who stood pale and quivering.

"I'm sorry," he said again. "I don't mean any harm. I just wanted to return this letter. I thought it might belong to you."

The woman reached out with her free hand and grasped the letter, but her eyes didn't move fractionally from Rick's face. She was searching him desperately.

"Oh, my. Oh, my!" That was all she could say.

Rick nodded. He'd done what he came to do. It was time to make tracks. As he began to turn, he felt the woman's touch on his coat sleeve. She was reaching out with her other hand, now freed from grasping the doorpost.

"Please," she said. "Just give me a few seconds to catch my breath. Please don't leave. I must talk to you. Come in out of the rain."

Rick had no idea what just happened to the woman—or to him. What if this woman was seriously ill or emotionally unstable? What kind of trouble could he get in?

"I can't," he lied. "I'm in kind of a hurry. Just wanted to bring that to you."

"No," she now said more forcibly. "I've frightened you. I'm sorry. You must think I'm crazy." She laughed apologetically, seeming to realize what impact her reaction might have on an unsuspecting stranger. "I can explain," she continued. "But please come in out of the weather. You've made the trip here. At least tell me who you are."

Rick hesitantly followed the woman into the entry. The closing door sounded like the bars of a jail cell slamming behind him. He shuddered. "I'm Rick Street. I guess somebody donated this coat to the Salt Lake Rescue Mission. They gave it to me."

Pointing at the letter that his hostess was now unfolding, he continued. "That letter was in the pocket. It has your address on it. I just wanted to return it. I won't bother you anymore."

The woman was now looking at the letter. When she looked back up at Rick, she shook her head again in disbelief.

"I'm so sorry I treated you like that," she said. "It's just that you remind me of someone else. Someone very dear to me." She gestured toward a formal living room just off the entry. "Won't you sit for a few minutes? I'd love to know a little about you."

Rick looked down at his clothes and shoes. "I'm all wet," he answered. "I'd get your furniture wet."

"Don't worry about the furniture," she replied. "Please stay a little. Let me take your wet coat. Don't worry about the furniture one bit. This is more important than furniture."

"I really shouldn't," Rick answered.

It wasn't so much that Rick was in a strange world. He'd been in nice houses before. The problem was he'd never had a *good* experience in a setting like this. All his past experiences in these sorts of settings were bad.

As a foster child, he'd never known how to behave around nice people with nice possessions. The families he lived with were poor. They had poor ways. Acting ignorantly or misbehaving brought a cuff to the head. Misbehaving sometimes even led to the worst punishment of all, being given back. *Given back* meant going back to not belonging to anyone.

This is dangerous territory. I have absolutely no idea what to do, what to say. Oh, Miranda. I wish you were here. I need you.

"Please," the woman asked once more.

Rick didn't know how to decline, so he drew down the husky zipper on his coat and let it slip off his shoulders into her hands.

"Please sit. Would you like a towel to dry your hair?"

"I . . ."

The woman took Rick's nonresponse as acquiescence. She walked from the room holding the dripping coat with a sort of endearing reverence. When she returned, Rick had seated himself in a single chair, sitting as far forward as possible, barely in contact with the seat cushion. She handed him a soft and heavy towel. He had never felt or used a towel like it. It smelled rich and inviting.

Rick patted the hair around his face and then rubbed the back of his head where water from his long hair dripped onto his neck and shoulders. His hostess watched him with great interest as though she had never seen anything so fascinating. Her intense interest only heightened his discomfort, if that were possible.

"I'm Linda Tate," the woman said. "Do you live nearby?"

At least Rick now had a confirmation that he was at the right house. Linda was obviously a member of Ryan Tate's family. Possibly Ryan's mother.

Knowing that allowed Rick to look at her a little less fearfully. "I live over on Redwood Road," Rick answered, clearing his throat.

"Did you say your name is Rick Street?" Linda asked.

"Yes."

"Do you mind if I ask who your parents are?"

Rick froze.

In a single question, Linda had leapt to Rick's greatest vulnerability. He thought about lying to her. He had lied to many others when asked the same question. Better to be a liar than someone unworthy of having parents.

He didn't want to lie to Linda. He remembered how much affection Ryan expressed for his mother. If this was Ryan's mother, maybe she was the kind of person Rick could trust with the truth.

His reply came slowly. "I don't really have any parents."

"I see," she said. Rick glanced up at her. She wore no disdain on her face, but neither did she show pity. She looked at Rick with more of what he read as understanding. "Am I being too nosey to ask how old you are?"

"I'm twenty-eight," Rick answered reaching for his Nevada driver's license. "I was born on Christmas Day."

Again, Linda caught her breath. Her startle was obvious. Again she shook her head as in disbelief.

"Did you grow up in Salt Lake City?"

"No, I had a bunch of foster families. Mostly in Nevada. But I also lived in Arizona and New Mexico." As an afterthought, he added, "The foster parents I lived with the longest moved there."

"Do you know who your birth mother was?" asked Linda.

Rick shook his head.

Linda looked around as if trying to decide what questions she should ask. "Rick, would you like something to eat?" This was asked in a kind and almost motherly manner.

"I really need to be going," Rick answered, making a move to rise.

"Rick, before you go, there's someone I'd like you to meet." Linda seemed to be picking her words carefully.

"Who's that?"

"My husband. His name is Dennis. Dennis Tate. When I went to get you a towel, I called him and asked him to come home to meet you."

Rick jerked involuntarily, unable to hide his alarm. Here he was, a convicted felon, alone in a man's home with his wife.

"I have to be going," Rick stood.

"Please, don't be frightened, Rick. Dennis will want to meet you. I promise nothing bad will happen to you in this house." Linda said this with certainty.

"Really, I don't want to get in the way," Rick replied.

"You're not in the way."

Again, her manner calmed Rick somewhat.

"Dennis is on his way. He'll be here any minute. Please sit down. Don't rush off." Tears shimmered in Linda's eyes. "I'm afraid if you leave, we'll never see you again."

What does that mean?

Rick sat slowly. He needed answers to a few questions of his own.

"The, uh, jacket I was wearing, it has the name Tate on it. Is that a member of your family?"

Linda's eyes were clearly tearing now. "Yes," she replied. "It belonged to our son."

"And you donated it to the Mission?" Rick asked.

"No," Linda answered. She reached for a tissue on the lamp table next to the sofa. "Ryan's wife, Nicole, must have donated it."

So in one answer, Linda had helped to build the family picture. She was Ryan's mom. Dennis was his dad. Nicole was Ryan's wife. The only person missing was Trevor.

A son?

A brother?

Rick was trying to think of a way to ask about Trevor when a door in the back of the house opened and closed. Linda rose and went to meet the newcomer. Rick could only guess that he was about to meet Ryan's father, Dennis Tate.

Chapter 17

RICK COULD TELL THAT DENNIS Tate was a big man just by listening to the approaching footsteps. Dennis, trailed by his wife, entered the formal sitting room where Rick waited. Dennis was larger than might be expected considering the stature of his wife, who was of medium height and a trim figure. Dennis was probably six feet two inches and built like a former football player—bulky and heavy.

However, the big man's reaction to Rick was similar to his wife's. Though not as extreme, Dennis's expression was a jaw-dropping, eye-popping gawk, but it lasted only a couple of seconds.

"Whoa," he exclaimed with a hearty laugh. "You took me off guard a little." He glanced over at his wife, rolling his eyes in astonishment. "Have a seat. When Linda called and said she had somebody she wanted me to meet, I didn't quite know what to expect."

He laughed again and shook his head in clear astonishment. "I'm Dennis Tate. Linda's husband. And you are?"

"My name's Rick Street."

"How did you find us?"

At this point, Linda stepped to a seat beside Dennis.

"You'll never believe the coincidence," she said to her husband. "Nicole apparently gave one of Ryan's army jackets to the Salt Lake Rescue Mission. It eventually reached Rick. There was a letter in the pocket addressed to us from Ryan. Rick was nice enough to bring it by."

At the mention of the Rescue Mission, Dennis's eyebrows raised in question. "Do you work at the Rescue Mission? Volunteer?"

Rick cleared his throat to answer, not surprised by the man's questioning tone. "I was staying there for a while, between jobs," Rick lied.

Dennis nodded his understanding. He understood that Rick was lying.

"What do you do for a living?"

Like his wife, Dennis had come directly to an issue that concerned Rick most. That was probably true whenever he met anyone for the first time.

Fortunately, Rick had an acceptable answer—or at least a truthful one. "I'm in building supply sales," he replied. "Right now I'm at Home Depot on Thirty-Third South and Redwood."

A little of the fire went out of Dennis's eyes, which wasn't necessarily a good thing. Rick knew that once suspicion was ignited, it couldn't be doused barely, it must be doused overwhelmingly. But Rick had used all the truth he could muster. He didn't want to fuel the flame with easily detected lies. He chose silence.

Linda came to the rescue. "Rick is twenty-eight. He was born on Christmas Day. Isn't that a fascinating coincidence?" she asked.

Dennis, who appeared to still be weighing the information about Rick's livelihood, took a few seconds to process this latest information. But when the significance of Linda's revelation soaked in, Dennis was startled, as his wife had been.

"Really?" was his only reply. It was said with an interest that promised he'd forgotten about Rick's stay at the Mission and modest career prospects, at least for the time being.

Dennis settled back to listen. Linda assumed the reins of the social encounter. "Rick, the reason we're acting so strangely is that you remind us both of our son Ryan. Would you like to see a picture of him?"

Rick did want to see a picture of the man who had worn the coat and written the letter—the man whose penmanship was so precise it looked like it had been printed on a machine. "Sure. I guess," answered Rick. "Where does Ryan live now?"

Neither parent answered. Linda rose and left the room, soon returning with a framed picture. Not a word passed between Rick and Dennis while she was away. Dennis looked at Rick without blinking, as though he was figuring the younger man out without being hampered by additional information.

Rick squirmed and looked down at his hands, picking some of the dead skin off his scarred knuckles with his longish but clean fingernails.

Linda walked directly to Rick, the framed picture held against her body, the image toward her. She glanced at her husband and then turned the picture, placing it in Rick's hands.

Chapter 18

It was Rick's turn to be startled.

Watching Linda Tate step toward him with a picture of Ryan in her hands, Rick hadn't known what to expect.

What she handed Rick was a picture of himself.

At least, very close.

What he saw was a military officer, somewhat younger than Rick when the photo was taken but nearly identical in appearance. The officer was standing in a full dress uniform in front of an American flag. The gold-piped epaulets on his shoulders bore single silver bars. On his chest were two rows of ribbons and a pair of jump wings. On his left shoulder he wore a Ranger tab and other patches Rick didn't recognize.

Rick couldn't tell the man's height, but he was more athletically built than Rick. His hair was the same ebony color, cropped close. His eyes were the same blue as Rick's.

In all, the man cut a striking image. His photograph conveyed an air of confidence and strength. Doubtlessly, women would find him very manly. He was attractive in an admiring sense, even to Rick.

No, this was not a picture of Rick. But if one considered only the face, an observer could easily come to the conclusion that Rick and the man in the picture were twins.

Rick shook his head. "That's Ryan?" he asked.

Both Linda and Dennis seemed to be awaiting Rick's verdict.

"That's Ryan," Linda confirmed.

Rick studied the photo again, this time realizing the amazing coincidence of arriving at the Tate home wearing their son's coat and looking almost identical to him. Now he understood their reactions to him.

"I see," he said simply.

Linda stepped to Rick's side so that they were both viewing the photo from similar angles. "But you know what, Rick? The thing that nearly made me faint is that your facial expressions, your voice, and your mannerisms are identical to Ryan's."

"No, I don't think so." Dennis spoke up from across the room.

"Yes, they are sweetie," Linda argued.

"Maybe," replied Dennis with an unconvinced shrug.

Rick wasn't sure what to say. How could he show his appreciation for their interest in him and this remarkable similarity?

"He looks like a good guy," he said with what he judged to be neither too much nor too little enthusiasm. "I'd like to meet him."

Both of Ryan's parents were silent.

"Could I take the towel and get you something to drink? Are you hungry? Would you like to stay and have dinner with us?"

"A little early in the day for dinner," observed Dennis.

She ignored her husband. "I'd be happy to fix you a sandwich," Linda continued.

"Thanks," answered Rick. "I'd better be getting back. But it was really nice to meet you." He stood.

"I'll get your coat."

Linda took the towel and returned with Ryan's—now Rick's—jacket, which Rick put on. The wet had soaked through, and the inside was damp and cold. He zipped it up. "Tell Ryan hello for me, and Nicole and Trevor."

Rick had lived with these names for several months and thought about them so often that he really didn't consider his comment until he realized that both Linda and Dennis were gazing at him in shock.

He had let the cat out of the bag. Awkwardly, he apologized. "I'm sorry. I read those names in your son's letter. That wasn't right of me to read it. I hope you'll forgive me."

Linda smiled sadly. Dennis's face showed harder lines.

"Anyway, thanks a lot." Rick nodded and turned to the door.

As he stepped into the entryway and reached for the inside door handle, Linda called from behind him. "Rick, will you give us your telephone number so we can call if we think of anything else?"

"I don't have a phone," Rick hesitated. "I guess you could reach me at the store if you need to."

"How about a mailing address? Could we send you a note?" she asked.

Dennis was shaking his head in disagreement but said nothing.

Linda handed Rick a card and a pen. He wrote down the mailing address for his apartment.

Back out in the rain, Rick waited at least twenty minutes for the next northbound bus. He was thoroughly soaked and cold.

Mostly, he was humiliated.

Other than answering a few important questions for Rick, the visit had gone terribly wrong.

By the time Rick reached home, a cough was developing. He stripped off his wet clothing and fell into bed, glad he didn't have to work the next day. Sleep came instantly.

The next morning Rick awoke sick with a cold and fever. All he could remember of the night's dreams was a long, recurring nightmare in which he was a soldier with broad shoulders and short hair, fighting for his life in a mountainous and arid land. The dream was filled with dark characters, including Dennis Tate. Its overall tone, one of treachery.

Chapter 19

MIRANDA'S JOB WAS GOING WELL. The state's Homeless Coordinating Council had been operative for a half dozen years. Local councils in various regions of the state were now established, all united in their effort to reach the governor's goal of abolishing homelessness. A major tool for achieving their aim was Housing First. The program was simple: provide free housing to selected homeless where the chances of stability were good.

Rick Street was one of those, the first that Miranda actually helped to place. While Rick looked like a success, not all of her clients were adjusting as easily. But she was hopeful.

Knowing she would be making another weekly visit to Rick the following afternoon, Miranda reviewed his case file and thought about what might be accomplished.

Late in the evening, as she worked, her cell phone rang. "Miranda Martinez," she answered.

No voice on the other end.

Again, Miranda announced her name.

She could hear indistinct background noises. She was certain someone was listening to her. Feeling an uneasy sense of alarm, Miranda checked the number of the incoming call. She didn't recognize it.

Not willing to play games, she punched the End button, severing the connection. She had the caller's number in her call log. She could have it traced if she needed to. She put the phone down and returned to her work.

It was a small thing. Those calls came occasionally. Sometimes a caller was too timid to announce that he or she had dialed a wrong number. Miranda tried to put the episode out of her mind, but there was something about being alone in an apartment at night that worked the psyche.

Following the call, she found herself having difficulty concentrating. She put the work aside and retired to the bedroom to get ready for bed.

Maybe half an hour had passed since the unresolved call when Miranda heard the phone ring again. She took a deep breath. She considered letting it ring. But one troubling call was no excuse for rejecting all calls. The caller might be a client in need. She glanced at the clock on her nightstand. Exactly 10:00 p.m. Late for business calls.

She slipped on a robe and sprinted to the kitchen by about the eighth ring, just before rolling over to voice mail. She had no time to even glance at the caller ID.

"Miranda Martinez," she answered breathlessly.

Again, no answer.

Miranda glanced at the ID. Different from the last call. "Who is this?" Miranda demanded.

On the other end, she heard a laugh.

"If you want to talk," Miranda announced hotly, "you'd better start doing it now. I don't play these games."

Again she heard a laugh. Then a male voice said in a barely audible whisper, "I'm watching you, Miranda, baby."

"And you can go straight to—" she began to answer but could tell that the call had been terminated. Miranda slammed the phone onto the counter.

"You're going to pay for this, sleezebag," she said aloud.

Grabbing the phone again, she redialed the number. The call didn't go to voice mail, and Miranda was determined to let it ring until there was an answer. The phone rang twenty or thirty times before she heard a woman's voice answering uncertainly. "Hello?"

Miranda fairly shouted into the phone. "Did you just make a call from that phone?"

"No," replied the woman. "The phone was on the ground by the back tire of our car when we came out of the movie. I don't know who it belongs to."

"Is anybody else around?"

"Nobody that we can see," came the answer.

"What kind of phone is it?"

There was a pause. Miranda could hear bits of a conversation between the woman and a man.

"We're not sure," the woman finally replied. "It looks like one of those prepaid phones, you know, the kind you use up and throw away."

Miranda tried to calm herself. "I'm sorry to be so demanding," she said more softly. "I just received a threatening phone call from that phone.

My name is Miranda Martinez. Can you tell me your name and how I can contact you?"

After a lengthy pause, the woman said meekly, "I don't think so."

"Please," pled Miranda. "It would really help me."

Listening again, Miranda could hear the ambient noise of what seemed to be a parking area. "Please," she spoke louder. "I want to take this to the police. You can help me."

No answer.

"Please," she cried once more.

This time Miranda heard a voice. Not the voice of the bewildered woman. It was the same whisper as the earlier call, sending ice through her veins.

"Yes, Miranda. That's right. I want to hear you beg."

The call went dead.

Miranda stood speechless in the dark of her kitchen, listening to the deafening silence.

Chapter 20

TUESDAY MORNING, BRIGHT AND EARLY, Miranda was on the phone to her friends in the Detective Division. Actually, it wasn't very bright, since the day had dawned gray and wet. And it wasn't especially early. Detectives Taylor and Warner were coming in after a late-evening shift. Miranda called three times before she reached Detective Taylor.

"Taylor, this is Miranda Martinez."

"Hi, M. Great to hear your voice."

"Great to hear yours," she replied. "I miss you guys. My new job is going great, but something happened that I hope you can help me with."

"Sure," replied Taylor. "What can we do?"

"Last night I got two threatening calls just before ten o'clock. I'm wondering if you can get a fix on the phone owner."

"Did they come from the same phone?"

"I don't think so. I've got two numbers. One may have been from a burner. Neither call sparked my caller ID."

"Any idea who the callers might have been?"

"Same caller. Male. He tried to disguise by using a whisper. He may also have a female accomplice."

"Anything in the calls you recognized?"

"Not really. One of the calls may have been made from the parking area at a movie complex. At least, the female said they were coming from a movie."

"Did the call come to your business or home phone?"

"Business."

"How many people have the number?"

"A couple of dozen, at least. I've given it to my bosses here. I know I've passed it on to the food bank, the Rescue Mission, the homeless shelter, and maybe a half dozen other agencies. Probably a dozen clients have it."

"Any guesses as to what's going on?"

"I can't be sure. The caller knew my name."

"That's bad. Sounds like you'd better switch phones."

"Yeah," Miranda replied. "That's not easy."

"No, but . . ." Taylor left the obvious unstated. "Any clients come to mind that might be making the calls?"

"Can't think of any," said Miranda.

"We'll look around," Taylor promised.

"Thanks. That's all I can ask. Whoever this guy is, he made a big mistake choosing me for his mark."

"That's my girl." Taylor laughed.

Miranda gave him the numbers, and he filled her in on the latest developments in the triple-murder investigation. The police had little to go on and still hadn't zeroed in on a suspect.

Chapter 21

RICK'S FIRST DAY OF SCHOOL at Salt Lake Community College dawned warm but wet, continuing a Salt Lake City spring that seemed would never dry out. He pulled his shift at Home Depot and headed for the Redwood campus of the community college full of anticipation but characteristically nervous.

With help from the student counseling center, Rick had secured a federal educational grant. Home Depot also kicked in a portion of his tuition so that when all fees were paid and textbooks purchased, Rick dipped only minimally into the little savings account he'd opened at a bank branch near his apartment. His first semester classes were basic math, a survey course in social problems, and a general ed health credit for strength training. All of the classes were held during afternoons or evenings throughout the week.

To Rick's delight, the survey of social problems course was taught by none other than Father John of St. Ignatius parish. As class ended and Rick stowed his binder and text in the backpack he'd picked up at the thrift store, Father John approached his desk and stood over him.

"Rick, my friend. You're looking well. I'm thrilled that we'll have a chance to get better acquainted after all. This is truly a pleasure."

"Father, you can't be as glad as I am. Any friendly face is a welcome sight. I feel like a freak here."

Father John considered Rick for a moment, sitting himself on the top of the nearest desk in the next row.

"I guess I don't understand, Rick. You look like you fit in perfectly here. Why do you think you're feeling out of place?"

Rick shrugged. "Don't know. That's the way I am."

"Rick, you're going to do great in school. Don't let your fears get the best of you." He stood and smiled as students in the next scheduled class began to enter the room. "I'll do everything I can to help," Father John said to Rick. "As for my class, all I ask is that you work hard and be here every day."

"I'll try," Rick said.

As Rick turned to leave, the priest caught him by the arm. The two men stood close. "Rick, promise me one thing," said Father John. "If the going gets tough, for whatever reason, promise me you'll come and talk to me. Promise that you won't simply disappear."

Rick didn't plan to disappear. He'd come to school because he wanted to be here. He planned to succeed. "Okay," Rick replied.

"Does that mean you promise?" asked Father John with a smile.

"Yeah."

They were standing in the middle of the hallway, students passing in both directions.

"Can you do me a favor?" Father John laughed. "Chalk it up to the insecurities of an old priest. Would you just say the words, *I promise?*" After another pause, he continued. "I just like to hear those words. They may be the most important words a man ever says." He continued to look at Rick expectantly.

Rick had to look away.

Saying the words was tough for Rick. Still, the priest wasn't asking anything difficult. He wasn't asking anything that Rick didn't already want to do. This was just another one of those moments when Rick had to decide whether to step up.

Rick turned to the priest, who stood unblinkingly awaiting an answer.

"I promise," he said.

"Good man." Father John slapped Rick on the back. With a toss of his head and a hearty laugh, the priest turned and strode away.

Chapter 22

SHORTLY AFTER STARTING SCHOOL, RICK completed his fourth month of uninterrupted employment at Home Depot. In addition to a meager pay increase, the store management moved Rick from new-hire to regular status. This routine shift occasioned a small celebration in Rick's honor among the employees in his department.

They were a reasonably close-knit group that included a couple of men with general contractor's licenses, three men and a woman who had previously been in construction trades but now needed less physically demanding work, and an assortment of part-time retired workers who came back to work when they realized they couldn't really afford to be retired.

The two department leads were career employees—Ron, who liked the work and his people, and Kelvin, a young college graduate on the Home Depot management-training track who seemed to care little about either building materials or the sales associates.

Rick tried his best to pull morning shifts when Ron was at work. In Ron's presence, Rick could relax a little, though he was ever watchful in meeting store standards. It wasn't always easy to pull mornings because of intense competition among sales associates to work during Ron's shifts instead of Kelvin's.

Rick could never relax around Kelvin. In contrast to Ron's practical approach to meeting complaints and solving problems, Kelvin let it be known that he expected a superior performance at all times. Any mistake by a sales associate reflected poorly on Kelvin. He would stand for no goofing off, or as he put it, horseplay.

Ron just shook his head. In private, he encouraged Rick not to let Kelvin's badgering upset him. "He'll only be here three or four months, six at most. Just keep doing your job and stay out of his way," Ron told Rick.

Ron set up a party in Rick's honor. "Don't worry about this," he told Rick. "It's no big deal. Punch and cookies in the back room at shift break. A dozen of us at most. Ten minutes. We just want you to know we're proud of you and like to work with you. The store managers won't come. No sweat. Bring a friend if you like. Some of the associates bring their spouses and kids. Since you don't have a family, bring somebody we can meet."

Rick invited Miranda.

They were still working well together. Their regular visits were the highlight of Rick's week. He thought of her often and, on some days, constantly. He'd noticed a shift in her mood in past weeks. At times she seemed more distant than she had early in their association. Rick couldn't blame her for sometimes being preoccupied with other concerns. He was sure that working closely with knuckleheads like him would wear on any woman in Miranda's position. But whatever the cause for her concerns, Rick was growing increasingly dependent on Miranda's steadiness. When she was doing well, Rick felt good. The opposite could also be true. He suspected that she recognized his reliance on her and that she tried to always be upbeat when they met, for his sake.

In his daydreams, Rick had imagined the little gathering at the store and thought it would feel good to share his success with Miranda. But as the hour approached, the prospect of her presence bumped up his anxiety level. He knew Kelvin would be there. For most of the sales associates, the punch and cookies were far more important than anything Rick had achieved. He began to worry that Miranda would see how meager his status really was in the working world.

Miranda was college trained. She had a full-time job with benefits. She worked for the governor's task force. How impressed was she going to be with his punch-and-cookie fest?

Still he thought he'd seen a light in her eyes when she accepted his invitation. He crossed his fingers and hoped he wouldn't foul it up by anything he said.

During the shift before the party, Rick walked into the back room repeatedly. Each time, he did a little straightening. As the shift end neared, he swept the bare concrete floor and straightened the OSHA posters on the bulletin board.

Rick waited near the front door of the store for Miranda to arrive. He still had his orange apron on with its hand-lettered name tag. The apron sported the pin presented to him when he completed his new-hire status. He stroked his long hair to make sure the braid was still tight.

The day was warm and cloudless. Across the parking lot, he saw Miranda's sport coupe pull into a stall. She was right on time, though a few minutes one way or the other wouldn't matter much to the casual gathering.

Miranda emerged from the auto and walked toward the store in the bright sunlight.

Miranda always wore pants to work. Rick had never seen her dressed any other way. But today she was wearing a dress of rich, blue silky fabric and complementary high heels. Her lustrous black hair was down on her shoulders and swayed from side to side in rhythm with the hem of her dress as she approached him. She wore dark glasses, and the high-gloss color on her lips grabbed the eye.

First of all, Rick was stunned.

Second, he was breathless.

Finally, he was mortified.

He wanted to run.

It was too late to run. He stiffened and swallowed hard. His entire system had been hijacked by his insecurities. He could already imagine the ridicule the appearance of this gorgeous woman would occasion.

Hey, Bozo. How did a looser like you ever hook up with that?

She sure is hot. She must be blind.

All right, dude. When she comes to her senses, send her my way.

Rick tried to move forward through the open doors to greet her, but his feet wouldn't move. Miranda stepped confidently forward and stopped within a foot of him. She removed her stylish sunglasses and folded them in her hand.

When they made eye contact, Rick was sure that at any second he would disintegrate. Only the extreme tension gripping his body could possibly hold together all the supercharged molecules waiting to explode in a million different directions. He could feel his heart beating in his neck and temples and knew that his face must be scarlet.

Miranda smiled. It wasn't a romantic smile. It wasn't seductive. It wasn't pleading. This smile was simply *confident*.

"Hi, Rick. Am I on time?" she asked.

Rick nodded in the slight jerking motion of one who has no control over muscle movements.

"I wasn't sure what to wear. Do I look okay?"

"Ah . . . yeah. Yeah! You look . . . Wow!" Rick's brain had stopped working, and his mouth didn't know where to go for words.

The greeting, the party, Rick's entire life would have ended in irreversible disaster but for one thing. Miranda's smile sharpened, and her eyes conveyed to Rick a message sent without words. *Relax, Rick. You're going to be okay. Show me where you work. I'd like to meet your friends.*

Rick did relax—gradually. There was no explosion. There was no meltdown. He felt every eye in the universe on him—on them, on *her*—as he walked Miranda to the back room. He gestured awkwardly toward the shelves, showing her the store—his domain. And though he stumbled through the introductions to the small group of coworkers, though he endured looks of astonishment, envy, and amusement at his expense, he made it. Rick survived.

Furthermore, Rick was a man who knew the meaning of *owing*. On the street, when one streetie gave out, stood up, stuck his neck out, did a favor, the other—the recipient—knew instinctively and acknowledged openly that he or she *owed*.

You owe me, dude.

I owe you. Thanks, man.

How many times each day did that exchange occur on the street? It was the economy of the street. The commodity of exchange in a moneyless society. The process of contracting that gave a measure of stability to an entire social class.

Rick knew how to owe. When the party was over, when Miranda Martinez dropped Rick at his apartment and thanked him for inviting her, Rick *owed*.

He already owed Miranda everything he had, practically his entire life. But now he owed in a far more personal, more intimate way. He realized that Miranda knew exactly what she was doing. She hadn't been shaken by Rick's awkwardness, his embarrassment at her eye-popping appearance. She'd expected it. It was as though she'd known in advance all that would happen.

Miranda carried it off flawlessly. She had charmed them all. She wasn't hard with anyone, not even Kelvin. Her focus was on them. Her interest was in their work and their world. She was relaxed, pleasant, wonderful.

Rick Street sat on the front porch for a long time, rethinking all that had happened. Miranda had turned something that started as *no big deal* into a *very big deal.* Each of his coworkers had gone away admiring, envying, or resenting.

Rick owed. He owed Miranda more than he could ever repay. He couldn't even think of how to begin repaying.

Above all, Rick Street was in love.

Chapter 23

"MIRANDA, YOU HAVE ME WORRIED," said Danny Komatsu as gently as he could. He caught up to Miranda on her way to the door following her workout at the dojo.

"You're hitting harder, but you're slowing down. You're angry. When you get angry, you get stiff. You're beaten before the contest begins."

"I know," she replied. "I feel it. I just can't do anything about it."

"You still getting calls?" asked Danny.

"I haven't had a call since my birthday," she answered. "But my stalker left a note under my apartment door."

Danny shook his head, commiserating with his star student.

Miranda wore a deliberately cheerful face.

"Let's talk," said Danny. He grasped Miranda by the arm and steered her toward the office.

The wall behind Danny's desk was papered with pictures of his wife, Heiko, and their boys, all now grown to manhood. A business license, trophies, and photos of Danny with many of his students over the years gave testimony to the master's lifetime of devotion to the Bushido code.

As always, on entering the office, Miranda's eyes shot to the oversized photo of her and Danny following her victory in the grand championship at the US Open in San Diego the summer before she turned eighteen. Danny's face in the photo showed a mixture of exhilaration and pain, doubtlessly because his facial muscles hadn't formed a smile in decades. But even in the photo, the affection between the master and his student was obvious.

Danny was a second father to Miranda. Though there was probably nothing Danny could do to help, just knowing he was aware gave Miranda added confidence in herself. "I'm angry," she confessed.

"It's so unfair, so cowardly, so maddening. Our homes are private. I don't want anybody or anything to invade my home. For this pervert to keep calling and then to come right up to the door and shove a note under it is a personal insult. His persistence is infuriating. I just want to get my hands on him."

"Are you afraid?" asked Danny.

"No," answered Miranda too quickly. "Why would I be afraid?"

Danny didn't look like he was buying the answer.

"I'm not afraid of a fight," she corrected. "If anything is frightening, it's that this stalker seems to be smart. Very smart. So far, he hasn't made a mistake. My friends at SLCPD have gotten forensics involved. No traceable cell phones. No matching voiceprints. No fingerprints. No traceable stationery. Nobody has seen him. No patterns. Stalkers are usually ruled by their emotions instead of by reason. They make mistakes. Sometimes lots of mistakes. And many of them want to be caught. Most stalking incidents become obsessions. They're over within days or weeks. This stalker seems to feel no hurry. Possibly because he's stalking more than one victim. So I have to just accept the fact that he's following me, watching me, maybe listening in on my conversations." Miranda closed her eyes and sighed deeply.

"Any idea who it is?"

"No. There are too many possibilities."

"Anybody else know?"

"No!" she replied as if the possibility was unthinkable.

"Anything I can do to help?" asked Danny.

"No," she answered. "Just keep talking to me. I've got to stay sane."

Miranda allowed the conversation to move to other topics of mutual interest. Danny, as always, asked the standard question. "Got a guy on the line yet?"

"No." Miranda laughed. "What man could hold his own with me?"

"Somebody will come along," said Danny gruffly. "It's usually the one you least expect."

"You'll be the first to know." Miranda smiled.

The pair parted, Danny turning his attention to the coming week's class schedule, Miranda heading to the car, intent on stopping at the market on her way home.

She slid in behind the steering wheel, reaching the key into the ignition. As she did so, she noticed a slip of paper under the windshield wiper arm. That wasn't unusual. The dojo was in a strip mall next to a larger shopping center where small-time merchants often tried to harvest a little cheap advertising by putting a flier on each vehicle in the parking area.

Miranda reached around the doorpost and retrieved the slip, intending to crumple it and toss it in the next trash receptacle she encountered. She didn't like the practice of leaving paper on windshields, much of which would eventually end up on the ground—adding to the clutter already evident in these downscale areas.

Before she could get rid of it, however, she noticed that the slip was handwritten rather than printed. Without thinking further, she held it up in the dimming light and read the short message: *Miranda, baby, I've missed you. I love watching you work out.*

Here, the language became lurid. There was no signature on the note. No signature was necessary.

In rage, Miranda crushed the note in her fist, squeezing it again and again as if she could crush all the life out of it—all the evil. Then, contrary to her own code, she tossed the crumpled paper to the ground, slammed the door, and pulled her car toward the street.

Miranda had reached a new threshold. She would not allow her enemy the pleasure of stalking her any longer. She would go after him. Find him. She would crush him as she had crushed his message.

She gunned the engine. Her tires squealed as she entered the stream of traffic on the street.

The crushed note lay on the asphalt, too heavy in its compacted form to move under the force of the slight breeze that swept along some of the debris usual to public areas.

*   *   *

Miranda was gone several minutes when a hand reached down to the asphalt and gathered in the irregular paper ball she had discarded. The hand belonged to a man. He lifted the ball between his fingers, smelling it, then letting it brush his cheek lightly.

Chapter 24

A FEW WEEKS INTO SCHOOL found Rick at the bus stop near dinnertime, headed home to do his homework. The weather was warm. Rick wore his work clothes, in which he also attended class. His backpack was at his feet. He was proofing a math problem in his notebook, glancing up only occasionally to see if his bus was approaching.

During one of those perfunctory glances, Rick noticed a figure approaching slowly from down the street. The man was too far away to be recognizable, but his manner was undeniable—he shuffled along, head down, glancing from the curb to the parking areas across the sidewalk, searching for any dropped coin, any bargainable object, any cigarette butt worth picking up. Rick knew the man immediately. He might wear any of a thousand faces, he could have any name ever known, his birthplace and the particulars of his past might vary widely, but his present circumstance was perfectly obvious. The man was a streetie.

He was broke. He was hungry. He was dirty and itching in the hot afternoon sun. He was humming to himself a fragment of a favorite melody. He was taking comfort from the realization that he was nearly invisible to the privileged world. When glimpsed briefly, he knew himself to be a source of annoyance to the beholder. But he had bigger problems to worry about. A toothache. Shoes that pinched his toes. A rash, a wound that wouldn't heal, a thirst that couldn't possibly be satisfied. A mind devoid of anything that mattered to the outside world and a future devoid of any hope.

Rick watched the man approaching, hair blown by the passing traffic, carrying a bag of possessions over his shoulder, stooping to peer into a public trash receptacle at the intersection. Then with a turn of the man's head, Rick did recognize him. The man was Scotty, a street acquaintance

Rick had known off and on for a half dozen years. In the course of their wanderings, Rick and Scotty had shared a miserable, unforgettable night under a bridge. Nearly freezing to death, the two men had connected in a way that only a life-or-death experience could.

Worst of all, Rick instantly recalled that he owed Scotty. Scotty had shared his stash; Rick had never repaid. Rick owed.

Rick partially turned his back in hopes that Scotty wouldn't recognize him. He was weaseling on Scotty. Weaseling on one of his own. Nobody likes a weasel. But Rick's world had changed. He reasoned that he wasn't in complete control of his life. He couldn't imagine what an encounter with Scotty might bring.

Once again he glanced down the street, hoping to see his bus. No bus.

Rick kept looking at his notebook, but the figures on the page just swam before his eyes. His pulse raced. What was he supposed to do?

His next glance showed that Scotty was nearing. Several streets beyond, a bus finally came into view. Scotty was now looking up. Had he recognized Rick?

Rick forced himself to look down at his notes and keep his gaze fixed there. The race was on, between the bus pulling up and a sure collision between two worlds that Rick wasn't sure he could survive.

Come on, bus. Dang! What's taking you so long?

A final glance. Scotty was ten feet away, the bus still a lousy block away. Scotty had seen him. He raised his hand in a feeble gesture—big enough to signal that he knew Rick, little enough that if Rick weaseled on him completely, Scotty could save a little face by consoling himself that Rick probably hadn't seen him.

Rick raised his head in acknowledgment and returned the hand gesture, all the while cursing the tardy bus that could have spared him this encounter.

"Street. That you?"

"Hey, man. How's it goin'?"

"It's goin'. We thought you wuz dead or put away. Heard the word that you got in a fight and was knifed. Where you been?"

The bus was pulling up.

"I gotta get on this bus," Rick said lamely.

"Wait," Scotty pled. "Things been lookin' up for you?" He inspected Rick from head to foot. Rick knew the routine. *Scotty's saying, "You've come into some stuff and you owe me. Time to pay up."*

Rick wavered. He knew he owed Scotty, and when push came to shove, he couldn't let himself weasel out.

"Things have been lookin' up," he replied.

The two men were about twenty blocks from Rick's apartment. Before the next bus came, Rick told Scotty what had happened to him, giving as little detail as possible.

Scotty kept shaking his head in disbelief. "How do I get on that program?" he asked about ten times.

When the bus arrived, Rick flashed his pass and paid Scotty's fare in cash. Scotty watched everything Rick did with microscopic care. There were no secrets on the street. When Rick tried to wrap up the conversation and move to another topic, Scotty would have none of it. He pumped Rick for additional information.

In twenty-four hours every detail of my life will be out on the street.

Scotty could have ridden the bus on to the city center when Rick got off. Rick prayed that the man would go on. But without invitation, Scotty followed Rick off the bus and to his apartment. He followed Rick inside and gave himself a tour.

"This is yours?" Scotty asked. "Man, I can't believe it. This is one sweet deal. I am so hungry I could eat the wallpaper. Got anything to eat?"

Rick fed Scotty, hoping that would suffice to repay what he owed. Scotty could not be filled. He went back to the refrigerator over and over until Rick's closely budgeted food supply for the week was nearly exhausted.

"Could I stay with you for one night?" Scotty asked, looking around the apartment again, shaking his head in utter disbelief. "This is way better than the night we spent under the bridge, isn't it?" Scotty smiled, showing badly decayed teeth. He was reminding Rick of a social debt. There was no way Rick could gracefully decline.

"I don't think I can have anybody here overnight," Rick replied tentatively. "It's in the contract."

"Who's going to know?" Scotty raised his voice a little and with it raised the stakes in what was sure to be a dispute.

Rick gestured for him to keep it down, but Scotty spoke even louder. "I can sleep on the couch. It's only one night. You know what it's like out there. One night and maybe a shower would sure make up for our night under the bridge."

"I got work tomorrow morning and then school," Rick countered.

"It's okay. I can let myself out," Scotty smiled.

Finally Rick conceded. Scotty showered. He helped himself to whatever he wanted. With each encroachment, he asked with phony politeness for Rick's permission.

By the time Rick crawled into bed, his normally spotless apartment—and his life—had suddenly plummeted into disarray. What worse fortune could have befallen him than to bump into Scotty, of all people?

He thought about how Scotty smelled, about Scotty's manners, about the immense chasm that existed between his world and Scotty's world after just six months. Maybe a night with Scotty at this point wasn't all bad. Rick reasoned that the unwanted encounter at least gave him a visible measure of the progress in his life.

But one question kept begging an answer.

Where will this lead?

Chapter 25

When Rick left for work the following morning, Scotty was still asleep on the couch. The day was miserable for Rick. Before he left home, he put all of his valuables into his backpack. He suspected that Scotty would go through everything in the place before departing, but there was nothing he could do about that now.

The hours at work crept by. Rick could hardly concentrate in class. His notes were muddled, and when the hour ended, he could scarcely remember a thing that had been said. He wanted to get home and see how much damage had been done to his world.

The minute class was dismissed, Rick rushed from the building and fairly sprinted to the bus stop. Afraid but hoping for the best, he entered the apartment building and took the stairs two at a time, arriving to find his front door open. His heart sank. He could tell by the sounds within that Scotty was still there.

Stepping inside, he placed his backpack carefully at the entry then closed the door. Walking into the kitchenette, he found Scotty sitting on the lone stool at the bar, dressed only in his soiled trousers, eating cold cereal from the box. Scotty's weathered skin hung like fabric on his bony frame, and his naked torso exposed several large open sores.

"Hey!" Scotty greeted Rick.

"Hey," was Rick's subdued reply.

Rick glanced around. There were dirty dishes in the sink. An empty bread sack lay on the counter next to a dinner knife with remnants of butter and jelly on the blade. Rick knew the place so well he could instantly see a hundred things awry.

"I didn't expect you to still be here," Rick said.

"You mean you hoped I wouldn't be here." Scotty stretched his arms over his head and gave a lazy yawn. "I thought about leaving," he said, "but I just couldn't bring myself to do it." He smiled, his rotting teeth drawing Rick's immediate gaze. "Nope. Couldn't do it. This is such a sweet deal you've got. A lot better than that night we spent underneath the bridge, isn't it?"

Scotty was confronting Rick openly. In effect, he was saying, *I'm not leaving until somebody makes me. You'll have to throw me out physically.*

"A sweet deal like this can't last forever," Scotty continued when Rick failed to answer. "It won't last forever, but a guy would be a fool not to take advantage of it while he can." He smiled again.

The image of a hungry hyena came into Rick's mind. He didn't know what to say.

"But, hey," said Scotty, "we need to go shopping. We're about out of food, and I just can't get full."

Rick and Scotty went shopping. Scotty was shameless in his demands, including his demand that Rick buy him a carton of cigarettes.

"Can't smoke in the apartment," Rick remonstrated.

"Who says?"

"The landlord. It's in the contract."

"I'll smoke outside," Scotty assured him.

The next day was the same. Rick went to work. Went to school. Couldn't think about anything but his intruder.

The problem was he could see this situation through Scotty's eyes. Rick could never bring himself to be so openly confronting, so openly demanding as Scotty was. It wasn't in Rick's nature. He didn't know Scotty well. Spending one miserable, freezing night with the guy under a bridge didn't make Rick an expert. But he was continually surprised by Scotty's aggressive imposition.

If Rick was expert at anything, it was in understanding street mentality. He knew what Scotty was doing. And in truth, Rick could hardly blame him. The choice between living in the apartment and living on the street was easy to make. The small debt Rick owed Scotty could easily be reframed into an obligation to share everything he had. Rick didn't like it, but he understood it. And he wasn't inclined to fight with a hungry man over a few bucks worth of food.

So Rick did what he always did—he bided his time.

After finishing his shift at Home Depot on the third day of Scotty's tenure, a Saturday, then rushing over to the college to work on his weight training goals, Rick returned to the apartment with more than apprehension—something bordering on dread.

Ascending the stairs to the second floor, Rick again found the door to his apartment standing open. Pausing just inside, he could hear voices coming from his bedroom. Stepping that way, he found Scotty, fully clothed, stretched out on the bed, his fingers interlaced behind his head, staring contentedly up at the ceiling. Lying next to Scotty in similar posture was an older man with a full gray beard. His long oily hair splayed across Rick's pillow.

Scotty's eyes moved to Rick, a cheesy smile washing across his face. "Hey!" Scotty gave his customary greeting, making no effort to move from his luxuriant repose. "I've got to get me one of these," he said.

"Come on, guys," Rick half pleaded, half demanded, the irritation obvious in his voice. "Get off the bed."

Scotty rose slowly to his elbows, looking across at his bedmate. "Soapy," he said, "looks like the landlord is evicting us."

Rick stood guard, making sure his two unwanted guests complied. When Scotty got onto his feet, he gestured toward his companion, whose face was familiar, though Rick didn't recall ever having met the man.

"Street, this is Soapy Hess, my good friend. Soapy needed a place to hang, and I was getting kind of lonely here by myself, so I invited him in."

Soapy glanced at Rick and then turned quickly away, putting one of Scotty's cigarettes to his lips. As Rick studied Soapy, he noted that one of the man's eyes was glazed over with a silvery film, obviously a blinded eye.

Scotty noticed Rick's lingering gaze. "Soapy got a little lye in his eye when he was a kid," said Scotty. "Blinded him. That's how he got his name."

Like Soapy, everybody on the street had a story. Most were eager to tell anyone who would listen.

With Soapy's arrival, Rick began wondering how far this unfolding drama would carry him. He now faced two desperately homeless refugees. How many more would there be at the end of a week?

Chapter 26

RICK WAS JUST WRAPPING UP his Sunday morning shift when a customer asked him where to find prefab storage shelves. Those weren't building materials, but Rick knew where they were. "I'll show you," Rick offered and walked the customer to the spot.

On the way back to his own department, Rick thought he saw Miranda at the head of one of the cross aisles moving in the same direction he was. It didn't seem likely, but he picked up his step to be sure he would be in his department if she arrived.

As he rounded the lumber, he saw her approaching. She didn't look happy.

"Hi." He smiled.

"Rick," she said, "we need to talk. How long until you finish your shift?"

Rick's thinking about Miranda had undergone a transformation since the day she'd attended his work party. Where he had previously thought of her only as *the law*, he now began to see her as a woman—a very desirable woman. But her demeanor as she stood before him at the moment was definitely the law. The law had arrived, not the woman. This transformation added to the emotional turmoil he had been enduring since Scotty and Soapy moved in.

When Rick clocked out, Miranda walked briskly to her sporty coupe, Rick trailing along behind. He winced at the recollection of himself as a boy following his teacher—who had walked at about the same pace as Miranda, with the same determined demeanor—toward the principal's office.

Seated in the car, securely seat-belted, Rick awaited Miranda's assault. Her black eyes flashed. "What are you thinking?"

Rick shrugged and looked away without answering.

"Your landlord called and said that your *buddies* are partying in the apartment. Noise. Smoke. People traipsing in and out half naked. You're violating the terms of the rental contract, and you're casting a bad light on the program. We need that apartment, and we need the cooperation of our landlords." The volume of Miranda's voice rose as she listed the offenses, so did the rate of her speech. Her whole body was alive. She gestured with her hands, open palms toward the heavens as if pleading with some higher omniscience to understand how God could have created creatures as stupid as Rick.

In the face of the verbal and emotional onslaught, all Rick could do was pull into his shell. He could only shake his head slightly.

Finally, Miranda took a deep breath. She made an obvious effort to let her shoulders relax and calm herself. She looked directly at Rick, her tone plaintive. "How could you do this, Rick? I thought things were going so well. You caught me completely by surprise. The last thing I expected was for you to violate your probation at this point."

She paused.

Rick made no effort to answer.

"Please. Talk to me. Where did you find these guys? Are you so lonely that you decided to throw it all away? After all your effort? You know, I don't think I have any choice at this point. I have to turn you in. I hope you've enjoyed this little fling because tonight you'll be sleeping in a cell."

Rick's head was down. He had reverted to picking at the skin on his knuckles.

"Please. Tell me how this happened," Miranda pled once more. "Did you find a way around the ankle bracelet? Did you go down to the Rescue Mission? Down to the park?"

Rick shook his head in answer. "I didn't go down. I didn't find them. They found me." His spoke so softly that he couldn't have been overheard even in the quiet of a church sanctuary.

At first haltingly, Rick relayed the sequence of events leading to his present dilemma.

"Oh, oh, oh," Miranda moaned. "I wish you'd have called me."

"I don't have a phone."

"I know, Rick. But there are phones around. You like to joke about having your own case manager. But this is not the first time something important has happened and I find out about it later. In this case, probably *too* late. If you trust me, why won't you talk to me?"

Again Rick shook his head and tried two or three times to formulate an explanation of how he felt whenever he had to face the law. He couldn't quite put it into words.

"Okay, Humpty," said Miranda more tenderly as the storm began to pass. "Why don't we see if we can put the pieces back together again."

They neared his apartment.

"Can you explain why you didn't tell these guys to get lost if you didn't want them there in the first place? Why didn't you just say so?"

Rick reflected on this question for a moment. "I know this will sound lame, but I guess I didn't want to hurt 'em."

"They're big boys," replied Miranda. "They'll get over it."

"No," said Rick, shaking his head. "No. They'll go on, all right. But they won't get over it. People who have been turned away don't get over it. They push the hurt down deeper inside. It piles up until there isn't anything else but hurt. Even guys like Scotty—the one I told you about—who act like the world owes them, are hurtin' bad." Rick shrugged and fell silent.

They parked on the street in front of the apartment. Turning the ignition off, Miranda craned her neck to look up at Rick's second-story window. "Well, Mr. Street," she said in a resigned tone, "I'm sorry for all that. I truly am. But right now, *you* are my first concern. This isn't a matter of social justice. You're on court-ordered probation. Right now, the law comes first.

"The only way I can face the judge and plead clemency in this violation of your probation is for you to go up and tell those guys—how ever many there may be—that they have to leave and leave now. It's got to come from you. That's how the judge will know, when the chips are down, that you're really committed to carry through this probation.

"If I have to kick them out, she'll rule that I—the program—is just carrying you along. It won't work. She'll terminate the probation. You go to jail. These guys are out on the street again anyway."

She looked at Rick, who was gazing straight ahead.

"Do you understand me?"

His answer, a barely perceptible nod.

"I'll give you ten minutes," she said in a harder voice. "If they come out that door in ten minutes, I've got something I can go back to the judge with.

"If they don't come out," she paused as if allowing this all to sink in with Rick, "then I'll come up. I guarantee you they'll be on their way. It may not be pretty."

"Be careful of Scotty," Rick warned. "He can be a loose cannon."

Miranda seemed unafraid. "I can take care of myself," she told him.

"Maybe so," Rick shrugged. "I'm just putting you on notice."

"I'm not worried," she replied. "Because you are going to go in there, and they will come out. It's between you and them."

Rick opened the door and walked toward the building with all the eagerness of a prisoner on his way to the gallows.

Chapter 27

MIRANDA MARTINEZ GLANCED REPEATEDLY UP at Rick's window, all the while watching the clock. She crossed her fingers. She tried to imagine Rick not as he was but as she knew he could and eventually would become.

Ten minutes passed. No one emerged. Miranda's hopes sank. She waited a couple of extra minutes for good measure. Then shaking her head sadly, she got out to do what had to be done.

Rick's door was open a crack. Miranda walked in without knocking. There she found Rick sitting on the only chair in the living room, facing a man on the couch who was big but, like Rick, thin and drawn. This man had obviously not left the apartment and didn't appear to have any immediate plans for doing so. He sat back with his arm along the top of the sofa, bare-chested, bare-footed, wearing only his trousers.

Rick cut his characteristic pose. He sat forward on the chair, elbows on knees, his head down, looking at this hands. Neither man spoke. Miranda could hear another person in the kitchenette.

Seeing Miranda, Rick arose but appeared reluctant to look at her. The other man, who Miranda supposed to be Scotty from Rick's earlier description, appeared startled by her arrival.

Miranda couldn't be sure what had passed between the men before she arrived. All she knew for sure was that the intruders hadn't gotten the message. She walked directly to the man on the couch and stopped, hands on hips, locking her gaze directly on his eyes.

"Sir," she said, "you and your companion or companions need to get dressed and leave."

The man glanced at her briefly, then looked toward Rick, who was behind her.

Miranda continued. "Mr. Street is serving a court-ordered probation. He's living in state housing under very strict conditions. He may not have guests here—and he certainly may not have anyone living with him."

Again there was no reply.

Miranda could tell that if this man were standing, he would be two full heads taller than she. "Do you understand me, sir?" she asked.

At that question, Scotty looked up at her with a defiant grin that showcased his teeth, but still he said nothing.

Adrenalin began coursing through her limbs. "Sir, are you going to leave on your own, or do you need some help?" Miranda kept her tone level to avoid fueling a conflict, but she could hear the edge in her own voice.

Finally the man on the couch raised himself lethargically to a standing position. He was indeed two heads taller than Miranda. Even in his malnourished state, he would easily be twice her weight. He leered down at her. "You ain't no cop, and you ain't my mom. I'll go. But I'll go when I git good and ready." His voice was not as casual as his posture suggested.

Miranda couldn't see Rick behind her, but she felt his approach and judged that he might be standing an arm's length away.

As if to punctuate the end of his statement, Miranda's opponent reached toward her shoulder, probably intending to push her aside. She could easily sidestep this minimal threat and ground him in the blink of an eye. But she wanted him to assault her before she acted, if that became necessary. Any violent actions on his part would strengthen her case before the judge, contending that Rick had not invited the probationary violation but had been victimized by it.

Before the man's hand could reach Miranda's shoulder, Rick moved suddenly forward, filling her peripheral vision. His arm flashed; his hand intercepted her assailant's wrist with such force that it made an audible *thwack*.

Twisting the arm downward, he brought Scotty down to his knees, extracting a howl. Rick looked down at the man now helpless before him. When he spoke, his tone was more vicious than Miranda could ever have imagined escaping Rick's lips. "Scotty, the woman asked you nice. She's in my place. Nobody's goin' to be pushing her around. Not now. Not ever. Get your stuff and get out. Don't come back."

Then, without easing the twisting pressure on Scotty's arm, Rick roared, "Soapy, get dressed and get gone—before we tangle bad. Now!"

With that, he released Scotty's wrist. The big man backed away, moving toward a pile of his personal possessions in a corner of the living room.

"That's the Street we all know and love," Scotty mumbled, rubbing his wrist. His voice was thick with sarcasm. "Always watching over the women."

Soapy came out of the kitchenette with a sandwich in his hand. Without looking at either Miranda or Rick, he moved directly to his little pile of valuables, which he snatched up, and followed Scotty out the door. Scotty had slipped his feet into his shoes without socks and reached one arm into his shirt, which he was still pulling on while grasping his bundle with the other hand. The two disappeared out the door.

The tension in the room began to dissipate. Miranda looked at Rick, who was searching her face, apparently looking for a sign of her approval.

She smiled.

Rick shrugged and backed into the kitchenette, probably wanting to assess the damages.

"I'll see if I can reach the judge before the marshal gets here," she called after him.

"Thank you, Miranda," she heard from the kitchenette.

Miranda Martinez couldn't suppress a smile as she heard her name spoken by Rick for the first time.

Maybe he can't break completely out of his shell yet, but Rick really put a crack in it today.

Chapter 28

RICK HAD A MAILBOX, AS did all the tenants in the apartment building. The mailboxes were located just inside the main entryway in a small foyer at the foot of the stairs. With the same regularity that Rick pursued all the other patterns in his life, he checked the mail daily. He tossed the junk mail addressed to *Resident* in the recycling basket placed below the boxes.

Each day, when Rick finished sorting through his mail and discarding all but that addressed to him personally, he ascended the stairs to his apartment empty-handed. Since moving into his apartment in January, he had never once received a piece of mail addressed to Rick Street.

Miranda hand delivered anything from the court. He had thought of asking her to have his official mail forwarded to him just to reward his daily visit to the mailbox.

On one early June day, he flipped through the daily mail with perfunctory attention and nearly discarded the entire bundle. At the last second, he noticed a small, colored envelope sandwiched between a department store mailer and the weekly grocery store bargain sheet. Dropping the remaining mail into the recycling basket, he flipped the envelope over. To his delight, he found his name and mailing address carefully handwritten on the envelope's face. Written in the upper-left corner was merely the surname *Tate*.

Rick guessed immediately that the envelope and its contents were from Ryan Tate's mother, Linda. He judged the handwriting to be too intricate and precise to have been produced by Dennis Tate's beefy hand. Whipping his head to the side to clear his long hair from his eyes, Rick slit the envelope open with his long thumbnail. It was a habit he'd formed on the street and never discarded because of its ready convenience. He was too impatient to fish the penknife out of his pocket.

Inside the envelope was a note written on a single stationery sheet and dated two days earlier.

Dear Rick,

We have thought of you almost constantly since your visit to our home nearly four months ago. We have hoped to see you again. We trust that all is going well with you. I (we) have a special favor to ask and pray you will not decline. It is a matter of utmost importance that we wish to discuss with you.

Please call me so we can find a time to visit. If for any reason you have difficulty reaching us by telephone, we invite you to come by the home any afternoon. You are always welcome. In fact, we will be deeply disappointed if we do not see you again.

With affectionate regard,

Linda Tate

The Tate's telephone number followed.

Still standing by his mailbox, Rick read the note several times to be sure he understood Linda Tate's intent. Back in the apartment, he again read and reconsidered nearly every word.

This invitation to visit was new ground for Rick. He sat for many minutes trying to remember whether he had ever truly been invited to anything during his adult life. In the end, he couldn't think of a single instance.

At the same time, he was unsure whether visiting, or even responding to the note, would be appropriate. Having been recently dressed down by Miranda for failing to consult her in making major decisions and having barely escaped what he considered to be sheer disaster in the Scotty and Soapy affair, Rick hesitated to launch out in any new adventures at this point.

He decided to tuck the invitation away until he could discuss it with Miranda. Walking to the dresser in his bedroom, he slipped the note into the top drawer recently restored to order since the sudden, welcome departure of his two houseguests.

Miranda's next visit distracted Rick's intention to show the invitation to her. She suggested that—despite the recent wrinkle in Rick's progress—they could probably reduce the frequency of their scheduled appointments to two per month. The prospect disappointed Rick. Miranda's visit was the highlight of each week.

Conceding, as he always did, he remembered the invitation at the last moment and rushed to retrieve it from its honored spot in his drawer.

Miranda read the note with interest, nodding as she inspected the paper, turning it over in her hands to see if anything was written on the back.

"Well," she said finally, "you must have made a very good impression. They seem really eager to see you again. Sounds to me like the similarity between you and their son is propping open the door to some tender attachments from their past."

"What do you think?" asked Rick.

Miranda smiled but hesitated. "If the letter had come two weeks ago," she finally replied, "I'd probably have said, 'Yeah! Sounds great. Go for it. Have a good time.' But now, I guess my advice would be to let a little time pass while the Scotty and Soapy thing blows over. That has posed a few questions being discussed among our program administrators. We think we may need to create some kind of protocol to share with clients when they come into the program under a court order."

"I'll hold on to it." Rick nodded. "We'll see how it goes."

"That would probably be best," replied Miranda.

In a consoling gesture, Miranda touched Rick on his bare arm—the second time she had touched him. The touch probably meant little to Miranda, but it meant much to Rick. He felt a definite thrill.

I'll never wash that spot again.

Chapter 29

Rick spared no effort trying to let his schoolwork reflect excellence. He was always punctual, always attentive, always studying like he couldn't bear to see a drop of education wasted.

In like fashion, he invested himself in his weight-training course. When the semester began, he could barely bench a hundred pounds. By midterm, he had already benched two hundred pounds.

In consequence, his physique filled out noticeably. Every day's workout seemed to strengthen him.

Returning to his apartment on a midsummer evening after one of his workouts, Rick noticed a late-model luxury sedan parked on the curb near the apartment building. He didn't look closely but was fairly certain it was a Mercedes. At least two people were in the car.

As he turned up the walk to his entry, he heard a car door closing and a woman's voice calling, "Rick. Rick."

He turned to see Linda Tate waving and hurrying after him. At least, he thought it was Linda. He'd seen her only once, and that was indoors on a miserably wet spring day.

The woman wore a light summer dress, her face partially obscured by sunglasses. Nevertheless, she seemed familiar to Rick. And besides that, Rick couldn't think of anyone else her age who might know his name.

As she approached Rick, the driver also emerged from the Mercedes. Clearly, that was Dennis Tate. The big man would require a large auto to travel in any degree of comfort.

In an instant, Rick realized that Linda had dragged her husband down from their east Salt Lake home when she'd received no answer to her note. The man's expression clearly proclaimed that he didn't want to be there.

"Oh, Rick," said Linda Tate, "I'm so glad we caught you. We've been waiting a little while. Would it be okay if we come in for a visit?"

Rick felt trapped.

According to his agreement with Miranda, he wouldn't pursue his acquaintance with the Tates until she gave him a green light. At the same time, he couldn't turn his back on this woman. To do so would be impolite, even rude. He could think of no explanation he could give her. "I . . . " Rick stammered. "I . . ."

Linda walked directly up to Rick. Standing beside him, she put her hand on his arm. "Please, Rick," she said. "This is very important."

By that time, Dennis had muscled his way up to where they stood. He nodded his greeting.

"Hi, Mr. Tate," Rick said in return.

Rick feared this might lead to another confrontation with Miranda. He distinctly remembered Miranda telling Scotty that Rick wasn't free to have guests in his apartment without prior authorization. He didn't know whether she had said that as a matter of policy or just to get rid of the two intruders.

Though Rick hadn't thought as much about the Tates since visiting their home, he still wanted answers to some questions about Ryan Tate's family. And he liked Mrs. Tate. She seemed to like him. Certainly she had extended a vigorous invitation to him for a return visit.

Rick made a decision.

He would do the right thing. He'd have to work it out with Miranda later. He turned and gestured toward the door. "Please. Come in."

Another part of Rick's reluctance to have anyone visit sprang from the embarrassment of ushering guests into a residence so meagerly furnished. Yet, if meager furnishings caused him embarrassment, he hoped his spotless housekeeping would be as readily noticed.

Rick gestured the Tates toward the couch. Dennis Tate said he preferred to stand. Rick retrieved the chair from his bedroom, brought it out, and placed it next to the sofa, thinking that maybe Dennis didn't sit because the sofa appeared difficult to get out of. Dennis acknowledged this hospitable gesture and sat. So did Rick.

"Thank you, Rick," said Linda Tate genuinely. "I—we—haven't been able to get you out of our thoughts since you came to visit."

She paused. Rick could see tears welling in the corners of her eyes. She carried a small clutch bag from which she removed a handkerchief and dabbed the corners of her eyes before she continued. "It's like there's already a place for you in our lives," she said.

Rick had never expected to hear those words from anyone. He swallowed and continued to look at Mrs. Tate.

She was a pretty lady. Very proper in demeanor and dress. She didn't give Rick the impression that she judged others or that she would look down upon others of lesser social or material standing. Her eyes showed kindness. She had aged gracefully in such a way that the increasing wrinkles in her face seemed to turn upward in a perpetually pleasing smile.

Rick wanted to reciprocate Mrs. Tate's kind efforts to maintain contact with him. Though it felt awkward and sounded terribly insincere to his own ears, he croaked, "Thank you, Mrs. Tate. I've been thinking a lot about you too." He nodded toward Mr. Tate to make sure that his words were applied to the couple. Mr. Tate's eyes were closed, but he gave a partial nod in return.

"Please don't be angry with me," Linda Tate said again. "Sometimes mothers do things that seem pushy. I guess"—she looked over at her husband—"no one can really understand why those things seem so important to mothers unless they've been one. In my case, the mother of just two children. A son and a daughter, both of whom came into our lives by adoption."

This was new information for Rick.

Mrs. Tate glanced over at her husband again. Dennis wore a partial scowl and shook his head, clearly not in favor of going on with the discussion. Nevertheless, the woman seemed determined, and she pushed forward. "Rick, our son Ryan was killed violently in Afghanistan. He was a soldier. There's some question about whether his death was even necessary." She sighed deeply. "But he's gone. There's nothing we can do to bring him back. Ryan was a wonderful boy who grew to become a wonderful man. He was a very devoted husband and father. He left behind a lovely wife, Nicole, and a darling son, Trevor.

"I can only speak for myself, but I'm sure it's true for all members of the family," she said, glancing again at Mr. Tate. "Ryan's death broke my heart. I've missed him so deeply. I can't even begin to explain how that feels."

Not knowing what to say, Rick merely nodded his acknowledgment.

"Ryan had only been dead for about nine months when you came to visit," continued Linda Tate. "I was grieving his loss. The similarity between you and Ryan shook me thoroughly, as you may recall." Mrs. Tate cleared her throat delicately. She smiled in a pleading fashion, obviously hoping Rick would feel some of what she was trying to relate to him.

"After you left," she said, "I did something I'm very ashamed of. But having said that, I'm also glad I did it. The day you came to visit, it was raining outside. Your hair was wet, and I handed you a towel. You wiped your face and then rubbed the hair on the back of your head." She blushed as she continued. "After you were gone, I . . . well, I looked the towel over carefully to find some of your hair, which I kept. I didn't think you would miss the hair. If the results didn't turn out as expected, no harm would have been done.

"I phoned a friend whose son works in a medical lab here in town. Getting his number from her, I called him and asked how to go about getting a DNA test done. Do you know what a DNA test is?"

"Yes," Rick replied, though he'd only heard about use of DNA testing for two purposes—to establish the presence of a suspect at a crime scene and to establish the paternity of a child.

"I learned from this young man that hair samples contain DNA if the follicle is still attached," Mrs. Tate explained. "So I searched through the hair I'd collected and found one with its attached follicle. I went back to the towel and found a second. I needed three, but I could only find two. That would have to do." She smiled.

"So I'm sorry to say I sent samples of your hair to a lab for testing without your permission. I also sent samples that we were sure contained Ryan's DNA."

While she gave this more technical information, Linda Tate had been watching Rick closely. She looked once more at her husband and then squared her shoulders as though she were about to take a big leap. As for Dennis Tate, Rick could clearly see the husband wanted no part in this revelation—whatever it was to be.

Linda Tate shifted her position on the couch. "Rick," she said speaking so softly that Rick had to lean forward, "the results of that test—in fact, two tests—showed that you and our son Ryan have identical DNA. No one can tell which of you was born first, but it is absolutely certain that you both have the same mother and the same father. You were identical twins."

Chapter 30

THE ROOM WAS SILENT. RICK arose and opened his front window, hoping that any stir in the air would ease the uncomfortably hot temperature of the summer afternoon. He could hear a motorcycle accelerating out on Redwood Road. A dog barked somewhere in the neighborhood. Otherwise, all Rick could hear was his own breathing.

He returned to his seat, shaking his head, aware that Mrs. Tate's eyes were following his every move. "What does that mean?" Rick asked her.

Before answering his question, Mrs. Tate asked a question of her own. "Are you terribly angry with me for stepping into your private life without your permission?"

"No," answered Rick. "No, I'm not."

"I couldn't help myself," she said. "Can you understand that?"

"I think so," he replied. Though Rick had many questions, one demanded an immediate answer. "Um . . . do you know who Ryan's mother was?" Rick had no sooner asked the question than he wished he hadn't.

Mrs. Tate nodded solemnly. "We know."

Oh no!

On one hand, Rick desperately wanted to know who his parents were—more than he wanted anything, even to breathe. On the other, he feared the answer.

Finding out who his parents were might mean coming face-to-face with the real reasons they had given him up, cast him away, abandoned him in a chaotic and uncaring world. He wasn't sure he could stand to know those reasons.

Rick felt suddenly faint. Maybe it was the heat. Maybe it was exhaustion from the workout he'd just completed. Maybe it was coping with Mr. Tate's obvious dislike.

He rose again.

"I really don't know what to say. I need to think about this."

"I know you'll have many questions," replied Linda Tate. "We need to talk again when you've had a chance to think about it."

"Yeah," answered Rick. "That'd be real good."

Mrs. Tate turned to her husband. "Sweetheart, did you bring that journal in with you?" she asked.

"Nope." Dennis sighed visibly and grunted.

Mrs. Tate smiled at him. "Sweetie, will you please go out to the car and bring it up? I'd like to show it to Rick." There was a hint of scolding in her tone.

Dennis got up and left the room like a teenage boy following his mother's instructions.

"I know this is all very sudden," said Mrs. Tate in a confidential tone when her husband had left. "I think when it's all sorted out and you've had a chance to see all the pieces, you'll be glad this happened to you—to us, to everyone involved." Her persistent smile and soothing voice calmed Rick a little.

"I've shared this with Nicole," Mrs. Tate said. "I think she has a right to know that her husband had a brother. Their little Trevor is an angel. He doesn't know yet, but when the time comes to tell him, I think you'll find that you have a wonderful little friend and nephew."

Rick remained silent in a whirlwind of swirling emotions.

Dennis hadn't yet returned with the journal.

"Nicole didn't really receive the news happily," said Linda. "I think I can understand why. I wish I'd waited to tell her. She was doubtful about the results of the test since it was based on just two samples of your hair. Still, the lab assured me . . . How would you feel," she asked, "if we have an additional test run so that Nicole—and really all of us—can go forward with absolute confidence?"

"Sure," Rick shrugged slowly. "That sounds okay to me."

Mrs. Tate took from her clutch a long plastic tube with a couple of cotton swabs in it. Mrs. Tate removed the cotton swabs and handed them to Rick.

"Could you rub those around on the inside of your mouth so we can get some cheek cells? That will tell us for sure."

Rick did so and returned the swabs to her.

A minute or two later, Dennis entered through the door that he'd left ajar. Walking to his wife, he handed her a leather-bound volume with a ribbon marker showing on one end.

Mrs. Tate leafed through the book and then held the heavy volume out to Rick with both hands. "Rick, this journal belonged to Ryan, our son—your brother. Since he was a tiny boy, even before he started school, Ryan was driven to keep a record of his life. We let him draw during church meetings. He never drew cars or dinosaurs or anything like that. He always drew scenes from his own life. And he never wanted these thrown away. He wanted his name written on each, and the date, so that he could always remember when he had drawn them. Before he even learned to write, he would ask me to make journal entries for him. The dear little fellow would dictate to me, and I would write for him.

"When we could see that this was more than a passing interest, we bought him this journal, maybe twenty years ago. He looked over my shoulder while I copied into this book the journal we had written on separate sheets. When he began to write, he started journaling by himself— in this book. As you can see, the book is nearly three inches thick. Ryan filled it about the time he graduated from high school. Then he moved on to another volume. He left this one with us. I think Nicole has the other one.

"In addition to this journal, we have boxes of photographs, mementos, things Ryan wanted to keep so there would be a complete record of his life. I never understood this passion Ryan had for recording his life. It was a curiosity. I think we felt at times that he might want to show everything to his natural parents if he ever had contact with them. It was so like Ryan. He was exceptionally thoughtful of others.

"But when your DNA test came back positive and we realized that Ryan had an identical twin brother, I finally understood why this was so important to him.

"You may think I'm just a silly old lady." She smiled through her tears, reaching for Dennis, who was again sitting beside her. "I'm sorry about that. But I believe that mothers have a sense about these things."

She sighed. "At any rate, if you'd like to start getting acquainted with your brother, this journal is the place to begin."

Chapter 31

MONTHS HAD PASSED SINCE MIRANDA Martinez last visited the offices of SLCPD. Though she enjoyed her present work with the homeless task force, she missed the urgency and poignancy of her days with the Detective Division.

She sat in Lieutenant Stack's office, where newly promoted Lieutenant Taylor now presided. Stack had retired; Taylor now supervised. Nate Warner, promoted to senior detective, now taught the ropes to Dirk Patton, his new junior partner.

Because Taylor was a big man and fairly lumpy, he sometimes gave the impression of not being mentally swift. Miranda knew the opposite to be the case. Taylor was bright and unusually adept at keeping the big picture in mind while sorting through small pieces of information that related to a crime under investigation.

Miranda had received a call the previous day from Lieutenant Taylor. "Miranda, it looks like we can finally help out with your stalker problem. We think we've got the guy. Come down and take a look."

Miranda arrived just in time for a blind lineup. She watched through a one-way as each of six men stepped forward, stated his name and occupation, turned a profile, and stepped back into line. Taylor told her that another potential stalking victim had already been in and fingered the suspect.

Miranda recognized several of the faces from her undercover days in the street community. She didn't recall seeing any of the men in a suspicious pattern of encounters that would suggest they were stalking her. She had come downtown feeling hopeful that this arrest might be the beginning of the end of what had been an achingly tense and unpleasant season of her life.

"I don't see anything that pops for me," she said to Lieutenant Taylor. "But I think I'd recognize the voice first. Can you have them talk some more?"

Taylor gave the word. The officer managing the lineup instructed each of the men to tell a little about his past life and to explain where he had been on the previous Saturday evening. Miranda listened carefully but found nothing helpful.

"Numbers one and three both look like the kind of people I would imagine as stalkers," she told Taylor. "But I couldn't say for certain that any of them is my guy. Sorry!"

"Hey, no need to apologize. That's why we do this." Taylor shook his head.

"Which one is the suspect?" asked Miranda.

Taylor pointed at the men still standing in line.

"Number two. He was showing photos of some women, and word started to get around. We got a warrant to search his personal possessions since he doesn't have a regular place. He carries a medium-sized duffle. In there, we found pictures of a dozen women, including you. Also an address book with locations and some intimate personal information, for example, your parents' names and where you work out. How many guys know that kind of information?"

"Not many," Miranda replied. "Was there a link between those photos and any violent crimes?"

"Not yet," answered Taylor. "But we have another body from the street. A woman. Late twenties or early thirties. We haven't ID'd her yet. We're looking for a DNA match."

"You think she was a homicide?"

"Definitely. Sexual assault. Stabbed. Same MO as the murders last year."

"Why do you think there was such a long stretch between the last one in October and this one in July? Where has the killer been for eight months?"

"Just what we'd like to know," answered Taylor. "Though we're not sure he's been away or been inactive. A woman can go missing on the street. If nobody reports it, she can just disappear. There could be a half dozen bodies out there we just haven't found yet. Our present Jane Doe was found by a cleaning lady in a Dumpster behind a motel. Otherwise, she'd have gone to the landfill, and we wouldn't even know there was a murder."

"Sounds like your killer—if it's the same guy—has learned from his earlier mistakes. Do you think it's a serial killing?"

"My gut says yes."

"And you think number two is your killer? He doesn't look like he could pull that off."

"What makes you think that?" asked Taylor.

"He doesn't look strong enough to drag a body into an alley and heave it into a dumpster," replied Miranda. "And frankly, he doesn't look bright enough to learn from his mistakes."

Taylor remained silent, watching the lineup, possibly considering her comment.

"Did number two confess to stalking?"

"No. He claims he stole a bag from the Rescue Mission's storage area. All the incriminating evidence was in the bag."

"Can you trace it to an earlier owner?"

Lieutenant Taylor laughed. "Nobody has come forward to claim the stuff, naturally. We're fingerprinting it all now."

"You said he had pictures of other women? Can you ID them?"

"Not yet. We're working on that."

"Any other suspects at the moment?"

"Not really," replied Taylor. "You know how these things go. We just have to wait for mistakes. If the guy is really smart, that could take a long time."

"I don't understand why he would want to stalk me. I don't fit the victim profile. I don't feel like I'm next in line for a serial killing."

"No. All of these have been street people. You were at risk while you were undercover, but you should be in the clear now. Still, your picture and info were in the mix. Don't relax your guard until we find this guy. Besides," Taylor added, "the pattern could evolve. We have no way of knowing whether he's only satisfying periodic thirst or has some ultimate goal in mind."

"Well, sorry," said Miranda. "Number two doesn't look the part, and I don't hear my caller in his voice."

"Okay," Taylor shrugged. "It was worth a try. We're going to hold him while we do some more digging. The judge should buy that since the suspect is transient and a definite flight risk. We'll keep digging."

"If I think of anything, I'll let you know," Miranda promised as she turned to leave. "Taylor," she said, "thanks for your help. I want this guy.

I can't even tell you how much I want to get my hands on him. Tell me what I can do. I'll do anything."

Taylor nodded. "The guy must not know he's got a tiger by the tail. If I was him, I'd be running for cover instead of stalking. But be careful. These things don't always go down the way you wish they would."

"I'll be careful," she replied. "But I hate this waiting game. He's making all the moves. He's calling all the shots. I feel like I should be taking the fight to him. If I'm chasing him, he's a lot more likely to make a mistake. Right?"

Taylor nodded but said nothing.

"Remember the homeless guy over at the Rescue Mission that they called Slice?" asked Miranda. "Where's he these days?"

"Not sure," said Taylor. "I'm a little out of the picture. I'll ask Warner. Why?"

"He used to creep me out so bad," said Miranda. "Sometimes when I try to imagine my guy, Slice comes to mind."

"Yeah, he was no angel. Have you seen him since?"

"No."

"Any reason to think he's our guy?"

"He was on the street," said Miranda, "and he was capable."

"A lot of guys fit those criteria," answered Taylor. "What about Street? Is he still around?"

"He's one of my clients."

"Could he be your stalker?" asked Taylor.

"No. I don't think so."

"What should we do?" Taylor asked.

"Can we try to find Slice and put a little heat on him? Enough to push him out of his comfort zone? If we push on Slice and my stalker reacts, I'd say there's got to be a connection."

"Makes sense. I'll see what we can do."

*   *   *

A man of medium build wearing civilian clothes concealed himself behind a police van to watch Miranda as she headed toward her coupe in the parking garage. He was dark complexioned with shoulder-length brown hair. His face twisted into a sinister smile, the result of a large scar that pulled one corner of his mouth up toward his cheekbone.

Chapter 32

FOLLOWING THE VISIT FROM DENNIS and Linda Tate, Rick began lamenting that his life had become so much more complex than it was out on the street. There he focused on finding his next meal. Here he focused on making sense of his existence.

He thought long about Linda's revelation. It seemed nearly unbelievable that he could have been living for so many years in the same city as a twin brother he didn't know about.

What kind of prank is fate playing on me?

Even more strange was the unlikely coincidence of picking up a military jacket that had belonged to that brother. *What are the chances of that happening?*

Aside from this reflection, Rick tried to shelve further contemplation, preferring instead to dive into his studies. School was generally going well, though it brought emotional ups and downs. A good grade on an assignment or exam could send Rick's spirits soaring. Disappointments caused the same spirits to plunge.

At one point, two-thirds of the way through the summer, Rick seriously questioned whether he was cut out for school. Arising one morning after a long night of studies and a short night of sleep, Rick wasn't sure he could face another day. He thought for the first time about calling in sick to work and then skipping his classes, a pattern he feared. In the end, the only thing that kept him from turning his back on school was the promise Father John had extracted from him at the beginning of the semester. He had promised not to walk away. He didn't want to try explaining his surrender to the priest.

Near semester's end, Rick drew no shift for a Saturday. The day was intensely hot, but he needed to study. He decided to take the bus down to the college and study in the library, with its delicious air conditioning. Preparing to leave the apartment, he loaded his backpack and made himself a lunch.

Walking out of the building, he met the postal carrier sorting mail into the boxes on the wall of the entryway. Greeting her, Rick stood silently by while she finished sorting, shifted her bag on her shoulder, and left with a pleasant nod. Rick unlocked his box, retrieved the usual junk mail, and searched for anything personal. As had been the case several weeks earlier, he found a letter from Linda Tate. He decided to read it on the bus since standing in the entryway was already unpleasantly warm despite the early hour.

Once he was seated comfortably at the back of the bus, Rick opened the envelope.

Dear Rick,

Thanks again for our lovely visit at your apartment. Dennis and I have talked about you often. We hope school and work are still going well. Maybe after school is out we could find a time to visit again.

The DNA sample you let me take has been analyzed. According to the lab, there can be no doubt that you and Ryan were identical twins. They have given me a legal document verifying their findings.

I hope that discovery is comforting to you, as it is to me. I have many other things from Ryan's boyhood that you might be interested in seeing. I would also like to tell you what I know about your mother and father.

Please come by anytime. As far as we're concerned, you're one of the family.

With warmest regards,

Linda

Until now, Rick had successfully resisted the desire to read in Ryan's journal, but the receipt of this confirming news somehow removed a barrier. Rick exited the bus at the next stop, crossed the street, and fifteen minutes later returned to the apartment, where he withdrew the journal from his top drawer and placed it in his backpack.

Chapter 33

MY NAME IS RYAN TATE. I am four years old. My mommy is Linda. My daddy is Dennis. My baby sister is Lizzie. We live in Salt Lake City. My hair is black. My eyes are blue. I like to play catch, and I like to play soccer. My best friend's name is Tubby Barton. His real name is Tim. His daddy calls him Tubby, so I do too.

My favorite color is red. My favorite food is pizza. I like cookies and peanut butter. I hate spinach. I hate mush. I hate sour milk. I like to watch the Whiz Kids and Scooby Doo. My favorite holiday is Christmas. I was born on Christmas.

Rick hadn't made it to the library. He was sitting on the lawn beneath a tree, leafing through the journal. The early entries were made in an adult's hand, likely Linda's, obviously written while Ryan was dictating to her. There followed many pages written in a child's sprawling print, the *d*'s, *b*'s, and *p*'s often in reverse direction, the spelling of some words barely recognizable. Interspersed were many photos of Ryan in his youth, his little sister Lizzie, and his mom and dad. Also included were Ryan's hand-drawn pictures.

Rick needed to get to his homework, but he found himself unable to set the journal aside. He read a little farther.

Mommy and Daddy gave us a puppy for my birthday. He is a cocker spaniel. I wanted to name him Lightning, but Lizzie wanted to name him Spot, so I let her.

Farther still: *Lizzie got the flu. She almost died. She got to stay in the hospital. They fed her punch and jello. Lizzie is 4. I am 8 . . .*

Today I'm sad. I got invited to Tubby's birthday party. Lots of friends got invited. I didn't pick up the toys on the back porch like I should, so Daddy said I couldn't go to the party. I stayed home. I cried all day . . .

I can read good now. My teacher is Mrs. Bidaman. She says I'm the best reader in the class. I like to be best. I read a story about a boy in Scotland who was kidnapped. His uncle stole his money, and he was kidnapped in a ship that wrecked. . .

By the time Rick had reached Ryan's tenth birthday in the journal, he'd burned through much of the morning. The homework was still waiting. Rick placed the journal in his pack and turned to his studies.

He struggled to concentrate on preparation for the upcoming exams. His flagging spirits weren't the result of anything Ryan had written. Rather, they resulted from the obvious question that had taken up lodging in Rick's mind and couldn't be dispelled. *How could two halves of the same egg end up with such completely different lives?*

Ryan was a happy, well-adjusted kid, eager to learn, surrounded by friends, belonging to a stable family where important lessons were being taught. Rick's life at the same age had been dramatically and sadly different—though he reminded himself that it hadn't been all bad.

Twins. Two people couldn't possibly start out on a more even footing. *Why did one rise and the other fall?*

Rick couldn't study. It was impossible. Questions whirled in his mind.

If he'd started reading the journal on a weekday instead of Saturday, he would have sought out Father John on campus. Thinking about the priest, Rick realized there was probably a Saturday evening mass at St. Ignatius. Maybe he could catch Father John before or after that.

As five o'clock neared, Rick hopped a bus to the stop near the community center and church. By the time he reached the church, mass was already underway. When it ended, he sat until most of the congregants had departed. Father John had acknowledged Rick with a nod, so Rick waited to see if a visit were possible. In the meantime, he enjoyed the peaceful atmosphere.

Father John returned to the sanctuary after bidding the worshippers good-bye and removing his robes. He sat down next to Rick. "Whew," he said. "It's not hard work, but it does take something out of me every time. Hopefully, what it takes out is my pride. How are you doing, Rick?"

Rick nodded.

"*What* are you doing?" the priest continued when he saw that Rick would not speak.

"I was doing a little homework," Rick replied.

"That's good."

"Father, something is bothering me. Can I ask you a question?"

"Never ask a priest a question unless you're ready to accept the answer," Father John replied stoutly. He smiled warmly.

Rick could see that the good-natured cleric was trying to help him relax. "I'm not sure where to begin," said Rick. "Do you have time for me to tell you a story?"

"I have all the time you need, Rick. Tell away."

Rick gave the priest an abbreviated version of his story, including the recent revelation about Ryan Tate. Then he told him a little about what he'd learned from the journal.

When he finished, Father John put his hand on Rick's knee as they sat together. "No wonder you have questions. That's a fascinating story. I've never heard anything quite like it." Father John shook his head in wonder.

"My question is this . . ." Rick paused, trying to mentally organize his words before speaking. "Do you think I'm being punished for something I did before I was born? Why has my life been . . . well, hard, when my brother's life seemed to be so . . . I don't know, blessed? Why was he placed on the upper road while I was placed on a lower one?"

The priest leaned forward, his elbows on his knees. His face was in his hands. He shook his head and sighed. "I don't know, Rick. I can understand why you'd ask. I think I would too."

Both men sat silently for a while. Father John was first to speak. "I don't think you're being punished," said Father John. "I'm not sure what the dogma of the church would say about your particular situation. But a story comes to mind from the Bible. Jesus and his disciples saw a man who was blind from birth. The disciples asked, 'Master, who sinned, this man or his parents, that caused him to be born blind?' Jesus answered, 'Neither this man nor his parents have sinned. He was born blind so that the power of God could show forth in him.'

"Rick, I don't believe that your circumstances are the result of any sin on your part. And I don't believe the most important part of your life is behind you. The important part lies ahead. Like you said before, it seems like you've been rescued. I have no doubt that you've been rescued so that the power of God can show forth in you.

"I'm sorry you didn't share some of your life with me earlier. But know this, Rick, you are a person of power. The power is in you to do a lot of good. You haven't had much education yet, but you're bright. More importantly, you have a disciplined spirit. You have all the qualities of good character. Your challenge is to not let the misfortunes of your past life drag you down.

"Fortunately, you're not doing that now. You're finally on the high road. Keep going. I believe in time you'll see that God wants to show forth his power through you."

He chuckled. "That doesn't mean you have to become a priest or minister or anything like that. The strength of Christ's church is the strength of the private lives of the lay members. Whatever you do with your life, God can use you to lift the lives of those around you."

He paused for a moment, seeming lost in thought. Finally he spoke again. "No. This isn't about sin. This is about miracles. God is showing forth a miracle—His power—in your life and maybe in the life of your brother. So cheer up, brother." He gripped Rick's shoulder at the base of his neck and gave him a friendly shake. "Try to remember that some people are born to trouble but meant for higher things. I think Jesus is looking down on you, expecting you to do great things."

He laughed again. "Start by acing the final in our class."

Chapter 34

Semester's end was a blur.

Most of Rick's hours away from work were spent at school, studying or working out at the gym. The air-conditioned buildings on campus were infinitely preferable to his apartment. Additionally, Rick felt he was less likely to have any further encounters with people from his past life there. Consequently, he was almost never home.

About once each week, he found a note in the mail from Linda Tate. All were encouraging. One note invited him to their home on Labor Day for a barbecue with the entire family, including Ryan's sister, Lizzie, and her family; along with Ryan's widow, Nicole, and son, Trevor.

Rick immediately felt anxious at the prospect of meeting these family members. Just seeing Dennis again would be frightening enough. Rick would need to think about the invitation before responding. He would need to talk to Miranda about it.

Miranda.

The only real problem in Rick's life at the moment was his separation from Miranda. The new schedule of bimonthly interviews had distanced the pair seriously. Rick missed her. He wondered if she ever missed him.

The modicum of self-confidence growing within Rick allowed him to secretly nurture occasional romantic fantasies. He realized he could actually function, and even succeed, in the world of privilege. He had far to go, but he admitted to himself that one day he might finish college. One day he might have a full-time job that paid a living wage. One day, if he didn't screw up, he might actually have a wife, a home, a car, a family.

When he tried to imagine the unimaginable—himself in such a world—Miranda was always there. But he couldn't talk to her about it. Sending his hopes out into the open might invite Miranda to slay them. He couldn't do that now. Still, he missed her.

Chapter 35

Tubby gets into trouble a lot. When I am with him, I get in trouble too. He brought some cigarettes that his uncle left when he came to their house. I told him I didn't want to smoke. He called me a chicken and a yellow belly. I said I would try one. We hid behind the Morris's garden shed and smoked some. Tubby smoked three. I only smoked one. It tasted gross.

Mrs. Morris came around the shed and caught us. Then she told my mom. When Dad got home from work, he was going to beat me with his belt. He waved it in front of me and told me he'd use it on me if I ever smoked again. When I told him I was sorry and promised, he decided not to beat me . . .

Tubby wanted to spy on Gail Anderson. I knew it was wrong. I shouldn't let Tubby talk me into trouble. But I don't like it when people say I'm scared. Tubby dares me all the time. I'm stupid to let him do it. But sometimes I do.

We snuck behind the big bushes on the side of Gail's house and watched her window. We didn't see Gail, but her mom came over and pulled down the blind. So we just went home. Tubby was telling me that someday he was going to kidnap Gail. When I got home, I got in trouble for being out after dark . . .

I like Tubby. He's my good friend. But he gets me in a lot of trouble.

Chapter 36

RICK PUSHED BACK FROM THE computer and raised his fists in the victory signal.

Yes!

He had an A, an A-, and a B: the A from weight training, the A- from Father John's social problems class, and the B from math. The B was a huge relief. Likely, the instructor had rounded the grade up generously to encourage him to stay in school.

I've gotta show my grades to Miranda.

During the semester break, Rick devoted his free time to Ryan's journal, reading every word and returning to some sections to reread them. The photos in the journal also entranced Rick. He studied them, imagining himself standing next to his brother, indistinguishable in appearance.

One photo in particular drew Rick's attention repeatedly. Someone had slipped it into the back of the journal. Ryan looked older, perhaps in his midtwenties, clean cut, in uniform, standing ramrod straight.

One evening, after spending the nonwork portion of his day with Ryan's journal, Rick stood in front of his bathroom mirror looking at himself, comparing himself to Ryan's photo. His missing tooth upset his facial balance. He had two noticeable scars that were missing on Ryan. His complexion was weathered and hardened. Ryan's was smooth and colorful.

Most of all, Rick's long hair cast his face in a completely different context. His hair definitely proclaimed him as an inhabitant of some world other than Ryan's. Rick wondered how his life might be different if he made one small adjustment to his appearance—a haircut.

But that was impossible. Rick's hair had always been his trademark. It made a statement. His hair had been long since elementary school. Since the days when Ryan and Tubby were getting into trouble together.

Chapter 37

TUBBY BARTON AND I GOT in a fight today. I called him Tubby at school. He's always been Tubby to me. Now that we're in middle school, he doesn't want to be called Tubby. The fight was pretty bad. I apologized, but he wanted to fight. His girlfriend, Gail Anderson, was watching. I think he was just trying to impress her. It was my first real fight. Mostly we were pushing and shoving, but when other kids started to collect around, we wrestled on the ground. I told him I had enough, but he kept coming at me. Then he hit me in the face.

Something in me snapped. I've never been that mad before. I started punching him, going for his face. I got really winded. So did he. After a while, my anger kind of blew over, and the whole fight seemed real stupid to me. I started to laugh. Then he got madder. We beat each other up pretty much. By then, a teacher found out and took us to the principal's office. I got in real trouble when I got home. It's not fair. I get in bad trouble at home, but he never gets in trouble with his parents. They always understand him.

Tubby. Tubby. Tubby. He's Tubby. I don't care. And he's not my friend anymore . . .

Rick laughed. It was easy for him to imagine being dragged to the principal's office. He'd been there. Done that. A lot. To read that his perfect brother had also been in the principal's office made him laugh. Rick laughed out loud. It must have been Ryan's voice laughing. Rick never did that.

I made the seventh-grade basketball team. I'm pretty tall for my age. I like basketball. I want to play in front of the school and have everybody cheer when I score . . .

Basketball season has started again. This year I'm the power forward on the team. Coach Stevens says if I work real hard, I might get to play with the ninth graders some of the time. I also have a big part in the Christmas program. I'm the Ghost of Christmas Past . . .

Gail Anderson, a girl my age who goes to our church and lives one street away from us, is missing. Everybody at school is talking about it. Mom and Dad think she ran away because her parents are too strict. Her parents still remember what it was like when there were hippies. Lots of kids ran away from home and went to California.

But I talked to Gail a lot. She's a really nice girl but real quiet. She doesn't have many friends. As a student body officer, I try to talk to everybody. She told me she feels like a nerd magnet. The only boys who pay attention to her are the nerds. She said Tubby was one of those. She told me, 'Tim is always nice to me. He's always giving me things. He's kind of cute, but he's too intense. Sometimes I just want to be left alone, and he won't leave me alone.' It reminded me of all the times when Tubby used to tell me that he was going to kidnap her. But I guess she ran away. I hope she comes back home soon . . .

Tonight we lost the state 4A high school basketball championship, 87 to 83. I scored 14 points. We played at the Univ. of Utah Huntsman Center. It was exciting to play in front of so many people. The noise was deafening. I loved it. Next year . . .

I took Nicole Underwood to the prom. Four couples group dated. Before the dance, we ate at Sandy Haversham's house. Her mom's so cool. She's a way good cook. The dinner was better than a restaurant. But the evening was kind of ruined by Tub Barton.

Sometimes we're really good friends. Sometimes we're the worst enemies. He can be really nice, but he can also be really mean. Whenever something good happens to me, Tub gets mean. That's especially true with girls.

Nicole is pretty hot, and she's, like, way popular. She likes me. I can tell Tub is jealous. So all night at the dance, he was, like, jumping between me and her. We couldn't get away from him. I felt embarrassed for Sandy, Tub's date. It's like he was ignoring her, and I could tell it hurt her feelings. When we were getting ready to go, I told him he should pay attention to his own date, cuz she's really a cute girl. He got mad and wanted to fight.

Everybody told him to cool his jets. That just made him madder. So he says to me, 'Don't turn your back on me, fishbait. Someday I'll slice you.' That was really a downer. From then on, everybody in our group could hardly wait to drop him off. We used to be really good friends, but now he's a butt . . .

Nicole told me she's afraid of Tub. He keeps watching her, and she's way nervous about it . . .

Today was graduation. It was at the concert hall downtown. My whole family was there. Lizzy came up and kissed me. She told me I was the best brother ever. That was pretty special. I love her.

We went to our graduation party in Memory Grove. *The school sponsored it so that all the seniors wouldn't be going up the canyons for keggers. Nicole and I went to support the school. It was pretty fun. We were pretty close, like kissing in public. We talked about maybe getting married someday. Not now, but when we finish college. We'll keep dating till then. I'm pretty lucky cuz she's the coolest girl in the whole school.*

Chapter 38

MIRANDA MARTINEZ GLANCED AT THE date on her cell phone screen. August 7. It was her eight-month anniversary of employment with the state. A lot had happened in those eight months.

Miranda's life was going according to plan. She worked. She worked out. She saw her parents a couple of times each week. The only real detractor had been the anger and frustration of being stalked. She wanted to push back on the stalker and get the thing over with. She hadn't heard anything from her stalker since she asked Lieutenant Taylor to put some heat on Slice, the only man she could connect with her stalker in any way.

She was on her way to meet Rick Street. She met him every other Tuesday evening to review his plans and progress. During their previous meeting, Rick suggested that they meet at a local Chinese restaurant the next time.

"I'll buy," he had offered.

"If you can afford to take people out to dinner," Miranda teased, "maybe we'd better talk about you picking up more of your rent payment." She had meant the comment to be playful, but she should have known better. Rick wasn't a person to joke with. He immediately apologized for the burden he was to the state and wanted to make arrangements to pay more of his own way.

"I was joking," laughed Miranda, holding up her hands. "Okay? Rick? Relax. You're doing great. You're meeting and exceeding all of our best hopes for you. I'll be happy to meet you for dinner instead of at your apartment. But we'll go Dutch. You pay for your meal; I'll pay for mine."

So they agreed to meet.

Miranda pulled into the parking area at the side of the Canton Star and walked to the entry. The interior was small but well lit and nicely appointed with what appeared to be authentic Chinese art. Two rows of booths lined the interior walls. Tables to seat four filled the center section. A young Asian woman in a cheongsam greeted and seated her in a booth.

Miranda glanced around at the few diners but didn't see Rick. This was surprising because Rick had always been extremely punctual. In fact, Miranda had never known him to be late by even a minute. She decided to sit and wait.

She glanced at her watch repeatedly, wondering if she had misunderstood the agreed-upon time. As the minutes passed, she began to feel a little alarm. *What if something has happened?*

She had come to trust him so thoroughly that any deviation in his schedule or behavior seemed unimaginable.

Where are you, Rick? Her concern was professional, but it was also personal. Very personal.

She couldn't reach him by phone. Her only option was to drive to his apartment. She decided to do that, thinking he might have missed a bus.

Reaching down for her handbag lying on the seat beside her, she noticed that another of the guests, a man in a booth across and behind her, stood and moved toward her.

"Hello, Miranda. Didn't you want to sit with me?" It was Rick's soft voice.

Miranda was startled. She looked up at Rick standing over her. He smiled slightly then moved to the other side of the booth and sat. She blinked.

Miranda was speechless.

"I was sitting over there." Rick pointed to the other booth. "I was hoping you'd join me."

Miranda stared at Rick. It was certainly Rick. His voice was unmistakable. Miranda swallowed so loudly that she could hear the swallow and was certain Rick could too. "I . . . Hi, Rick," she stammered. "Sorry, I didn't recognize you."

She could see Rick's color change and knew she had embarrassed him. *Say something positive. Tell him how fantastic he looks.*

Again she swallowed and caught her breath. She started to speak just as Rick did. Both waited; then both started again. Miranda laughed awkwardly.

The sight of Rick awakened tender feelings inside Miranda. She felt tears welling in the corners of her eyes. Not tears of sadness but the kind of tears that sometimes accompany an inner thrill. "Rick. I didn't see you. You look fantastic." Miranda was feeling slightly breathless. "You cut your hair."

The man sitting across from Miranda was no longer the Rick Street she had coached for months. He was somebody else. She didn't know who he was, but he looked like he had stepped out of *Gentlemen's Quarterly*. His jet-black hair was styled short and glistened from whatever product the stylist had put on it.

He was clean-shaven. His face, though still rugged, was somehow softer. His lips were moister. He wore a pair of stylish sunglasses. She involuntarily put her hand to her face, staring at him in disbelief. At that moment, she knew what it meant to be *aflutter*.

"Sorry," he said. "I didn't mean to startle you."

Miranda laughed. "Don't apologize. And don't talk for a second. You'll wake me from a dream."

Rick didn't have to say anything.

Did you do this for me? To please me? To impress me? Does this mean you like me?

Miranda threw all caution to the wind. "Wow, Rick, you look gorgeous."

Again, Rick blushed, but she could see pleasure written in the lines of his face. Miranda Martinez had a problem.

Unthinkable as it was, she was falling for a client. Falling hard.

"You didn't like my long hair," he said softly.

"No, Rick. I loved your hair. You have great hair." She didn't know how far to go with this. "It's just that your hair didn't really seem to be you." She smiled tentatively.

"Why didn't you tell me?" he asked.

"Some things take time," she answered softly.

Rick looked around the room, obviously trying to distance himself a little from the intimate feelings that had engulfed them both. "Um, want to order some dinner?" he asked.

Miranda reached across the table and put her hand on Rick's. "Rick, let's not get lost in food. We can do that anytime. Tell me what you're feeling."

Rick shuddered visibly. He looked away but didn't try to withdraw his hand. When he finally looked back, it was his turn to swallow hard. "I miss you," he said. "I'd like to go back to meeting every week."

Miranda wanted to shout.

Another huge crack had just appeared in Rick's shell. He had finally voiced a feeling. He had taken an immense risk. She wanted to shout and clap her hands for joy but knew she needed to handle the moment carefully. "We can do that." Miranda smiled at him.

"Look at us," she said with a self-conscious laugh. "Here we are in our late twenties having trouble saying things to each other that kids half our age can say without a second thought."

"Yeah!" Rick actually smiled enough that the corners of his mouth broke. Aside from the scar, his face looked glorious wearing a smile. "I've missed out on a little," he said. "But I think the future's going to be better. I really do."

His words thrilled Miranda.

They talked.

Actually, Miranda talked. Rick mostly listened, but the balance was shifting. That, too, would take time. He showed her his grades. They celebrated. He asked for permission to attend the Tates' family barbecue. She wished she could go with him. Right now, she wanted to show him off to her parents and to Danny Komatsu.

When she dropped Rick in front of his apartment building, she leaned over and kissed him on the cheek. He was wearing cologne.

I'll remember that scent. And the way your cheek feels.

Rick climbed awkwardly out of the car and stood waving at the curb as she drove away.

Rick, you don't even know who you are. But you will. And I'll get what I want—in time. So long as nothing gets in the way.

Chapter 39

Miranda fumed. She stormed around her apartment, not exactly putting things back in place. She threw them; she slammed them; she kicked them into the general vicinity they normally occupied. Couch pillows. Towels. Books. Intimate apparel. Her running shoes. The only stuffed animal she owned—a six-foot-long green-and-pink snake with bulging black eyes and fangs of red felt.

She had no particular animosity toward the snake. It had been a door prize at a Halloween party. She kept it as a conversation piece but realized that she had fewer visitors to converse with as the years sped by. The snake's bizarre appearance had sometimes amused her when she had a day that made her feel freaky and out of place.

This evening, the poor snake was taking an undeserved beating.

"I hate you!" Miranda whispered coldly. She swung the hapless snake against the post of her kitchen door. "I hate you. Someday I'll find you. And when I do, I'm going to hurt you." *Whack*! The snake thudded against the side panel of her china cupboard; the dishes inside rattled dangerously. Then she turned and delivered a precisely aimed kick to one of the couch pillows that sent it sailing into the ceiling halfway across the room.

The day had started out so wonderfully. She rose early, still feeling the glow of love. She had cast away all caution as she and Rick really talked to each other for the first time. She knew what love felt like. She'd been there before. The sudden discovery of another person who fit all preferences and fantasies—or at least some of them. Another person who was attractive physically—and in so many other ways. Another person of substance. Another person who can be trusted, who's steady, who's alive and growing.

All day as she met with clients, staffed cases with other workers, and served the community in a thousand ways, her mind and heart kept bouncing back to Rick's haircut, to the smell of his cologne, the touch of his hand, the feel of his smooth cheek.

In the light of a new day, she had to remind herself repeatedly to move slowly. Rick was a work in progress. The events of each day were testing his mettle and working their magic on a man who had been, until just nine months earlier, homeless—a streetie. He needed time to prove himself—to himself.

As she unlocked her apartment door early in the evening, she could tell someone had been there. She felt it. At first, everything looked okay. Then as she walked through, looking carefully, she noticed things out of place. Her tablet, which she always left on either the breakfast bar or nightstand, was across the living room on a lamp table. There was a glass in the sink. Miranda always stuck her dishes into the dishwasher when she left home, a habit she'd learned from her mother. Her nightie was wadded up in the corner of her bedroom instead of lying across the foot of her bed, where she'd left it.

Miranda realized suddenly that someone had deliberately left signals of having been in the apartment, someone who knew her intimately, knew her habits. She felt waves of panic beginning to mount inside her.

Hi, Mom. Miranda. Did you visit my apartment today? A few things were out of place, and they made me think of you. Okay. I miss you and Dad. Love you. Bye. That was a conversation she could never have with her mom. Even the mention of a few things out of place would bring her mother running. Exhausting interrogation would follow. Her mom would immediately conclude the worst.

Miranda, princesa, I think we should call the police. Shouldn't we, Renny? Sweetheart, you're in danger. Let's get some of those people here who look for fingerprints. Oh, sweetie, I'm so sorry. I'm so worried for you.

That was definitely a conversation Miranda never wanted to have, so she dialed a different number.

"Ariana, this is Miranda from number eleven. Did you, by any chance, happen to be in my apartment today?"

"Oh, Miranda, I should have told you. I forgot," said the building manager. "The cable installation guy called just before I left for work and said he'd be by to replace your DVR at about 10 a.m. He said he'd talked to you and that you'd given permission to leave your door unlocked until he got here. He sounded really nice. He called you by name. Is anything wrong?"

"Nothing seems to be missing," Miranda replied, "but I didn't give anybody permission to go into my apartment, and I don't have a DVR."

Silence.

"Miranda, I'm so sorry. Like I said, he seemed really nice. Not weird or anything. He was from Comcast. Maybe we can call them and find out who he was."

"I don't think that would help, Ariana."

"I am so, so sorry. He called just as I was leaving to take Tiffie to day care. I barely had time to unlock your door. I couldn't wait till he got here. Ohhhhh! What do you want me to do?"

That was another conversation Miranda didn't want to have, but she had it. With Ariana's information in mind, she began looking more carefully through the apartment. The more she looked, the more she could tell that the intruder had been though *everything*. The more she recognized that, the more angry she became. Maddened by the certainty that somebody had searched everywhere, she became more and more violent. She found herself dumping out drawers, ripping off her bedding, leafing frantically through her financial papers. Every fiber of her privacy had been violated.

Her next impulse was to be angry at Ariana. Get her fired for being so careless. So gullible. So stupid.

But Ariana wasn't the criminal here. And a single mom with a two-year-old daughter didn't need any more worries.

So Miranda fumed. She raged. She cursed. She hurled insults and threats at her unseen villain. Then she did the only other thing she could.

She cried. She sobbed.

Finally she walked into the bathroom and looked at herself in the mirror. He eyes were puffy and red. Her skin looked blotchy. Her hair was a mess. She thought of her snake, went back into the living room, picked him up, carried him to the bathroom mirror, held his face up next to hers, and started to laugh.

Oh, Miranda. You must be in love. This just isn't you.

She picked up her phone and touched her mother's name on the favorites list. "Hi, Mom. Miranda. Would it be okay if I come over? I need to talk."

Chapter 40

SCHOOL STARTED AGAIN THE WEEK before Labor Day. Rick was nervous through the entire week, not about school but about the upcoming visit to the Tates' home.

On Labor Day, he arose early and worked a morning shift. Returning to the apartment, he showered, shaved, and dressed. He had plenty of time, so he gave careful attention to his hair.

The hair worried him. It would be a surprise to Linda and Dennis to see him looking even more like their son, Ryan. He hadn't gotten the haircut with them in mind, but he couldn't deny Ryan's influence on his decision. He decided that if the subject came up, he would lie and tell them the summer heat was unbearable with long hair. That should be something Dennis could accept.

The bus trip across town was easy. Rick knew the way.

As he approached the Tate home, he could hear voices and laughter coming from the back of the house. He felt himself tensing. His heart raced. His legs felt stiff. His movements were jerky. He wanted to walk away—but he couldn't.

Instead of ringing the doorbell, he walked to the east side of the house, where he could see a small garden gate standing partially open. He passed through and walked toward the back corner of the house. The foliage in the yard was lush, the lawn manicured. Before rounding the corner, he stopped and took several deep breaths.

While he still stood there, he heard a child's voice behind him.

"Who are you?"

Rick whirled about to face a boy. The lad's arms hung at his sides. His head cocked to one side, and he looked up with a frank expression, waiting for Rick's response.

Rick liked the boy immediately. His brown curly hair framed an innocent face with what must have been his mother's eyes, dark blue with a greenish cast.

"My name's Rick. What's yours?"

"Trevor Dennis Tate," the boy answered officiously.

Too bad about the Dennis.

"What happened to your face?" asked Trevor inspecting Rick carefully.

"I got cut," Rick answered.

"Oh," Trevor replied matter-of-factly. "I was shooting my gun and lost the bullet. Can you help me find it?"

Trevor was holding a plastic assault rifle that probably shot Nerf darts.

"Which direction did it go?" Rick asked him.

"I think it went in these bushes." Trevor pointed and headed back into a large shrub, parting the branches and kicking at the taller grass at its base.

"What color is it?" Rick asked.

"It's yellow, just like the gun."

They searched for a minute or two, and just as Rick spotted the missing bullet, he heard a woman's voice a few feet behind them.

"Trevor, what are you doing?"

"I lost one of my bullets. Rick's helping me find it."

Rick turned toward the woman, grasping the yellow bullet in his hand. "I think I found it," he said, holding it up.

The woman facing him was about his age. She was slender and wore dress pants and an ivory-colored blouse with a pleated front. Her hair was cut short and stylishly spiked. She wore a little makeup, just enough to give a glamorous accent to her overall appearance, which fitted together strikingly.

Seeing Rick fully for the first time, the woman yelped. She stepped backward, tripping over an exposed sprinkler head. Catching herself from falling at the last moment, she recovered her balance after a series of unladylike movements. Righting herself, she waved off Rick's offered hand as he stepped forward to steady her.

"I'm okay," she said, obviously still off-balance emotionally. She looked at him again, shaking her head, in disbelief and quickly turned her attention to the boy. "Trevor, get out of the shrubs," she commanded. "Stay in the yard where I can see you." Without further effort to get acquainted with Rick, she reversed her course and returned to the open yard, guiding Trevor's steps with a hand at the back of his head.

Rick slowly dropped his proffered hand.

He assumed that this must be Nicole, Ryan's wife. Maybe her cool reception was to be expected, but it wasn't very reassuring for Rick, who was now left to follow along behind.

Rounding the corner, he met Linda Tate. She had apparently come to see the cause of Nicole's cry. On seeing Rick, Linda's face clearly flashed a question mark then broke into a carefully managed smile. "Rick?" she asked.

Rick nodded, smiled as best he could, then let his gaze wander to the others gathered in the yard.

"Whew," Linda continued. "You still amaze me." She laughed. "I like your hair. It's wonderful to see you. We're so glad you came. Come and meet everyone."

Linda took Rick's elbow and moved him to the center of the gathering.

Nicole's aloof reaction to Rick had sparked a feeling of resentment in him. Despite a lifetime of rejection and enduring what might be viewed as social snobbery, Rick felt wrongly wounded for the first time in his adult life.

Always in the past, he'd had to confess that he was unworthy by birth and status and therefore accepted rejection as sad but justifiable. But this day, for the first time, his sense of social justice complained that her rejection of him was unfair.

Nicole could be excused for mourning the death of her husband. Feeling Ryan's absence in the presence of his look-alike brother could understandably rock her emotionally. It would be asking much of a woman to take one of life's greatest losses in stride without awkward moments. But that wasn't what Rick felt when Nicole looked at him. Her immediate reaction to him was to reject him as an inferior version of her husband, a lesser entity, a person not even meriting a civil greeting. She had simply turned her back as though he were an annoyance or, even more hurtfully, an object of no consequence.

Rick knew more about such treatment than most people did. He had endured it often. The difference on this day was that he no longer felt he deserved to be treated that way.

He had been continuously and successfully employed for many months. He had a semester of college behind him, one in which he showed that he had at least average intellectual abilities. He hadn't binged since New Year's Eve. He had his own apartment and his own possessions that he cared for meticulously. And above all, he had recently been kissed by Miranda Martinez, a woman of exceptional beauty, poise, intelligence, and professional achievement.

Rick Street was no longer a throwaway. At the moment he was smarting, wounded, and feeling a resentful edge. He was savoring his first taste of pride.

Linda Tate introduced Rick around the circle. Besides Trevor and his mother, Rick met Lizzie; her husband, Michael; her two daughters, Trina and Lucille; and her son, Rory. He met Mrs. Tate's mother, Elizabeth Hardy. Finally, Linda introduced two neighbor couples, Steve and Naomi Barton, and Russ and Suzie Anderson.

Perhaps the biggest surprise of the day was the way in which Dennis Tate's standoffishness toward Rick had moderated. Dennis actually engaged Rick in conversation, asking him about work, about school, about his plans. Maybe it was the holiday, maybe it was the festive setting, maybe it was the presence of other people. Maybe it was just a more generous effort on Dennis's part. Rick would find himself wondering, as he reflected on the events of the day, whether the change could be explained by something as simple as Rick's haircut.

Lizzie was particularly warm toward Rick. She talked to him about her relationship with Ryan, whom she seemed to idolize. Lizzie was round bodied, jovial, and seemed affectionate with both of her parents. She seemed especially close to Grandma Hardy.

Trevor clung to Rick throughout the day, peppering him with questions, talking about his boyish interests and the excitement of starting preschool. The two were only separated by Nicole's insistence that Trevor "stop bothering Mr. Street."

Of course, Trevor was no bother to Rick. Rick enjoyed his company. Trevor was the only person at the outing Rick could talk to without feeling he had to weigh his words.

Food, visiting, games, and a gradual quieting as the late afternoon sun sank lower over the Great Salt Lake seemed to bring the day to a natural end. The neighbors left early. The Bartons, who were parents to Ryan's boyhood friend Tubby told Rick that their son had been killed with Ryan in Afghanistan. They were a little teary-eyed as they took their leave.

The greatest delight of the day came from Grandma Hardy. A woman in her late seventies, Elizabeth Hardy looked much like her daughter. But unlike Linda, who had a natural reserve and strong sense of decorum,

Elizabeth's eyes betrayed a sort of mischievous mirth. She spent much of her day rankling Dennis. In one longish stretch while they ate, Elizabeth entertained the entire crowd with jokes, some of which made Rick laugh aloud and embarrassed the more proper women. Like Linda and Lizzie, Elizabeth showed no reserve about drawing Rick into the family. At one point, she proclaimed boldly that if Rick was her grandson's brother, then he was her grandchild too. Having made the declaration, she awaited Rick's response.

Rick had little idea what he should say. One glance at Nicole reminded him that not all shared this generous sentiment. Looking at Dennis prompted him to move cautiously. Still, Elizabeth, Linda, and Lizzie—the matriarchal line of the family—had all come out decidedly in his favor. He didn't want to disappoint them or take their acceptance too lightly. Having weighed the pros and cons quickly, Rick smiled at Elizabeth and nodded. "Okay, then Grandma Hardy it is," he said as casually as he could manage.

The elderly lady clapped her hands with glee then patted him playfully on the cheek. "I wish you'd been around when I was your age." She laughed, looking around at other family members.

Rick returned Ryan's journal to Linda. She sent him home with an additional box of Ryan's possessions. She only let him go when he had promised that he would contact them within a month.

Rick agreed. He wasn't likely to decline any future invitations. He felt he could avoid Nicole as necessary to enjoy occasional encounters with the rest of the family—even Dennis.

When the day was over and Rick waited for his bus back to the other side of town, he mentally tallied the day's social gains and losses, posting up the results on a sort of internal social scoreboard.

I'm not a throwaway anymore.

He barely noticed as a black-helmeted bullet-bike rider in black leathers slowed to check him out and then sped away.

Chapter 41

DEAR MRS. TATE,

I just want to thank you and Mr. Tate for inviting me to your family party on Labor Day. It was great to meet Grandma Hardy, Trevor, Nicole, Lizzie and Michael and their kids, Mr. and Mrs. Barton, and Mr. and Mrs. Anderson. Thank you for making me feel right at home. I will remember your kindness.

Thank you also for letting me take more of Ryan's keepsakes. I have been inspecting them all carefully. I can see that he was a special person. I know you loved him. I'm sure he loved you. When I have looked at all his things, I'll get them back to you.

Thanks very much for everything,
Rick Street

Chapter 42

PHOTO: FIVE YOUNG MEN IN an MEPS (military entrance processing station), standing in front of a flag, being sworn in by a soldier in uniform.

Caption: *The five amigos enlisting in the Utah National Guard two days after high school graduation, (L to R) Ryan Tate, Header Carmickle, Joey Frost, Austin Smart, Tim (Tub) Barton.*

Photo: Two Mormon missionaries in baptismal clothing standing in a meetinghouse foyer with a middle-age black woman and a younger couple.

Caption: *Elder Norton (left), Cynthia Clyde, Michael Greenwell (son-in-law) and Missey Greenwell, Elder Tate (right).*

Photo: 150 Mormon missionaries standing in front of a Latter-day Saint temple.

Caption: *Elders and sisters of the Toronto Ontario Mission, President and Sister Shoesmith (first row center).*

Photo: A group of young men in the lobby of a fraternity house.

Caption: *Pledges to Sigma Chi. Third row center, Ryan Tate.*

Photo: Ryan Tate and Nicole Underwood attending University of Utah Army ROTC Cadet Ball, he in uniform, she in a gown.

Caption: *Me and Nicole Underwood, the most beautiful lady at the ball.*

Photo: Ryan in coat and tie.

Caption: *Sophomore class yearbook picture.*

Photo: Dennis and Ryan dressed in camo, holding hunting rifles, squatting beside a downed five-point buck.

Caption: *Dad's deer on north slope of Mt. Nebo.*

Photo: Linda, Dennis, Ryan, Lizzie in wedding gown, and Michael in tux.

Caption: *Lizzie's wedding.*

Photo: University rugby team members roiled in dirt, blood, and grass stains, arms on teammates' shoulders, huge grins.

Caption: *Killer squad, Tub Barton (front row, right wing), Ryan (top row, right wing).*

Photo: Ryan in military uniform.

Caption: *Ryan Tate, Commandant of Cadets, University of Utah ROTC.*

Photo: Ryan and Nicole in caps and gowns, Linda and Dennis, another older couple.

Caption: *Graduation Day.*

Photos: Set of eight, showing Ryan during various military training activities.

Captions: *US Army Officer Basic Course, Ft. Benning, Georgia. Barracks inspection. Weapons qualification. Infiltration course. Night combat course. KP duty. Chemical weapons defense. First jump. Special Forces training, Ft. Bragg, N.C.*

Photo: Officer pinning bar on Ryan's shoulder.

Caption: *2nd Lt. Ryan Dennis Tate UANG.*

Photo: Officer pinning jump wings on Lieutenant Tate's chest.

Caption: *Airborne! Fort Benning.*

Photo: Officer placing green beret on Lieutenant Tate's head.

Caption: *De Oppresso Liber (Special Forces Motto). Special Forces qualification course at Fort Bragg.*

Photo: Sergeant Tim Barton and rank of Green Berets saluting Ryan.

Caption: *Band of Brothers.*

Photo: Ryan in dress uniform, Nicole in wedding gown passing beneath a saber arch in front of a military chapel.

Caption: *Lt. and Mrs. Tate.*

Certificate: *Birth of male baby, St. Mark's Hospital, Salt Lake City, Utah, 25 December. Mother, Jennifer Sopel, age 19, Draper, Utah. Father, unknown.*

Certificate: *Adoption of male child, Salt Lake City, Utah, 3 July. Adoptive parents, Dennis Troy Tate, age 27, Salt Lake City, and Linda Louise Hardy, age 25, Salt Lake City.*

Diploma: University of Utah, Bachelor of Science, Civil Engineering, Ryan Dennis Tate.

Commission: Utah National Guard, 2nd Lieutenant Ryan Dennis Tate.

Letter: Nicole to Ryan.

Text: *Ryan, my love.*

I am so proud of you. It is no surprise that you completed you officer basic course at the top of your class. I have never known you to be second best at anything. You are a credit to your country, to your parents and family, to your school, and lastly to me. I fill with pride whenever I think of us together. I know you are a man of duty and that we must be apart because of that.

If our love and our lives together continue to unfold as they have so far, it will be a great thrill to become your wife and the mother of your children. Your intelligence, your compassion, and your tireless drive will prepare you to be a force for good in the community. I want to be a part of that. I want to stand beside you and be with you always. I will try to make my own life reflect the same excellence you have shown.

I love you with all my heart, my darling Ryan. Please come see me as soon as you return home. I'll kiss you until you faint for lack of oxygen.

With never-ending love,

Nicole

Chapter 43

RICK DREAMED.

When he woke the next morning and tried to pull the fragments of his dream together, he remembered only that the dream introduced him to Jennifer Sopel, the mother named in Ryan's birth certificate. He remembered looking at the girl and thinking that she was also his mother—even though she was only nineteen—younger than his present age. He tried to treat her with respect. At first, she didn't recognize him. When he told her who he was, she seemed embarrassed and started making excuses for her decision to give him away. Rick tried to assure her that he had no hard feelings, but Jennifer couldn't be consoled.

Through the long day of work, school, and studying, Rick pondered the last words she'd spoken: "I had to do what was best for you."

Chapter 44

"Mrs. Tate, this is Rick Street."

"Yes, Rick. How wonderful to hear you. How is everything?"

"Um, things are going good. Thanks."

"I'm so glad you've called," continued Linda. "How can I help?"

"Mrs. Tate, you've already done more than I can tell you. I hope you got my note about Labor Day. And thanks for lending me the box of pictures and other stuff from Ryan. They're really helping me get to know him."

"Rick, you're most welcome. Please call me Linda, if you're comfortable with that."

A long pause followed.

"Okay," replied Rick quietly.

"Is there anything special you wanted to know?" Linda asked, realizing that a call like this wouldn't have been easy for Rick to make. Linda wanted to smooth the way, encouraging Rick to call often.

"Yes," Rick answered. "One of the things in the box was Ryan's birth certificate."

Linda could hear the sound of shuffling papers on the other end of the line as though Rick were searching for the document he wanted to talk about.

"The birth certificate shows Ryan's real mom as Jennifer Sopel. Do you know her?"

"I can understand why you'd like to know that," replied Linda. "That's very important to you, isn't it?"

"Yes," Rick answered.

Linda thought about how to best answer his question. "First, Rick, let me say that I think of myself as Ryan's *real* mother. We were as close as a mother and son could be."

"Sorry," Rick stuttered. "I didn't mean anything by that."

"I know you didn't, dear," Linda replied. "But as we talk about Jennifer, I just want to put her in the right perspective. I've never met Jennifer, but I have corresponded with her. In fact, we exchanged letters not too long ago. When you boys were born and placed for adoption, all adoptions were closed. That means that the birth mother and the adoptive parents didn't know each other or where to find one another. But during the 1980s and 1990s, advocates for open adoption managed to get the adoption laws changed in many states. Utah was slower to allow open adoptions than some states. But by the time you boys were teens, birth parents were able, in many cases, to find the children they had placed for adoption.

"When Ryan was about fourteen, we got a letter from Jennifer. She shared some information about her past life and told us that, since placing Ryan for adoption, she had married and borne other children. Those would be your half brothers and half sisters. She didn't tell us that Ryan was a twin, so we didn't know about you. She asked us to pass her information on to Ryan. She wanted us to ask Ryan if he'd like to meet her. It was a very nice letter. She left the matter in our hands, saying she would understand whatever we decided to do.

"You can imagine the anguish that Dennis and I experienced as a result of her request. Dennis, bless his heart, thought we should ignore it. I couldn't do that to another woman who probably loved her children as much as I loved mine.

"In the end, we let Ryan read her letter. We answered all his questions as best we could. He decided, on his own, not to meet her or correspond with her. He said, 'I'm glad she wrote to us, and I'm glad you let me read the letter. It makes me feel better to know that she cared about me. But I don't want to meet her or write to her. She did what she had to do. Now you're my parents. Lizzie is my sister. I love you. I don't need any other parents. Could you write back and tell her thanks for me?'

"We did as Ryan asked. But I told Jennifer that if she would keep us informed about changes in her address, I would write from time to time and let her know how Ryan was doing. I've tried to do that. She is always appreciative and interested. And based on that information, we had Ryan's birth certificate amended to show Jennifer as the birth mother."

Rick was obviously listening and thinking. When he didn't speak, Linda continued. "When we first met you this winter and had the first DNA test done, I wrote Jennifer a letter. I told her about you, not in any great detail—what a wonderful person you are and how hard you're working to set a positive pattern for your life. Maybe I shouldn't have done that without your permission, but you already know I'm an old busybody. My only excuse is that I like to see the people I love be happy. I loved Ryan. I love you. And indeed, I love Jennifer. If there's anything I can do to bring happiness, I'm going to do it. Even if people are sometimes mad at me for it."

Linda thought she could hear sniffles on the other end of the line, but when Rick answered, his voice was steady. "I've never been mad at you," Rick answered. "I give you permission to do anything you think will be good for me."

"Rick," replied Linda, becoming a little teary-eyed, "you are a sweet boy. I can't tell you how much it means to us that you have come into our lives."

"Can I ask you an honest question?" came Rick's reply.

"Of course, dear. Ask what you will."

Rick's question was slow in coming. He asked it in a manner that showed he was phrasing it carefully. "Is there anybody in the family who is sorry I've come along? Who wishes things had stayed the way they were?" Before Linda could speak, Rick continued. "You don't have to answer that if you think your answer will hurt any of us."

Linda was touched by Rick's generous spirit. She felt she could trust him with an honest answer. "Rick, just then it felt like you were reading my mind. I'm used to that because that's what your brother used to do to me." She laughed. "I'll be honest, trusting that you're mature enough to realize that not all relationships start out as well as they end. Dennis has been a little resentful, but I can feel him softening. Can you feel that?"

"Yes," replied Rick.

"He's kind of crusty," she told Rick. "But he has a tender heart. And the most wonderful quality my husband possesses is that once he discovers the good in others, he becomes extremely loyal to them. Believe me, being in Dennis's good graces is a marvelous place to be."

"I believe that," she heard Rick say. "Anybody else?"

Linda hesitated but felt she had no choice. Honesty was the best policy at the moment. "Yes," she replied with a sigh. "Nicole is struggling with this development in our lives. I understand, in part, why she resists your coming. Do you?"

"Yes," Rick replied simply.

Linda continued. "Nicole is a good woman—a good person. She was a devoted wife and is an excellent mother. In some ways, I think she's like Dennis. She doesn't accept easily or quickly, but once converted, shall we say, she's fiercely loyal and very generous."

"That's what I would have guessed," replied Rick. "What do you think I should do?"

Linda was thinking out loud as well as answering. "I think it will take time. I don't believe you should do anything differently. On the contrary, I think it's crucial that you be yourself, without pretense or apology. Nicole is very sensitive to genuineness. She tries to be genuine, and she judges others the same way."

"Okay," replied Rick.

"Did that answer your question?"

"Yes. Thank you."

"Any other questions?" Linda asked. She had been standing next to the kitchen counter for so long that her legs were becoming stiff.

"Hold on for a minute, dear. I'm changing to another phone so I can sit down."

When Linda came back on the line, Rick asked, "Do you know anything about our father?"

"I asked Jennifer about him in one of my letters," Linda answered. "I think I still have the letters. I'll dig them out and let you read them for yourself. But to answer the question for today, I recall that Jennifer was a university student from a good family. Your father was a truck driver. I don't recall how they met. They became a little too passionate in their affection. Jennifer didn't give me his name, but she hinted that he was a bright man with a good work ethic. As I recall, he was eager to start his own business. When your mother realized she was expecting, she notified him of the happy news, but he wasn't happy. He refused to accept responsibility and bowed out of the picture, leaving her to solve the problem of what would be best for you."

Rick was silent. When he spoke again, his voice was ragged. "How could she be sure that he was the father?"

"Because she had never been with another man. And, according to her account, wasn't again until she married her present husband."

"Do you still have her address?" Rick asked.

"Yes," replied Linda. "Do you want it?"

"I'll have to think about that," he replied. "One last question," Rick continued. "I'm sorry to take up so much of your time. Ryan's journal and the box of stuff you shared with me ends about the time he and Nicole got married. Did he keep a journal after that?"

"I'm certain he did," answered Linda. "It was a daily ritual with him." Linda laughed as she thought about Ryan's devotion to his journal. "I once asked him," she told Rick, "why he was so driven to record everything about his life. He thought about it the way he always approached meaty questions—the same way you do—and he said, 'I don't know. It's like I'm writing for somebody else. Maybe my future children. It's like somebody out there really cares what happens to me.' 'I care what happens to you,' I told him. 'I know, Mom,' he said. 'But you already know everything. There isn't anything I wouldn't tell you. I feel like there's somebody else who cares. Someone who will want to know.'"

"Did he tell you everything?" asked Rick.

"I think so," Linda replied.

"Did he tell you about his relationship with Nicole?"

The question startled Linda. But it seemed natural for Rick to ask. That's the kind of question brothers would take interest in.

"Ryan told me about that," she responded cautiously. "But that's not something I can tell you. Sorry."

"No, I'm sorry for asking," replied Rick. "I doubt Nicole will want to let me read Ryan's journal since they got married. That means there are about six years of his life I can't know much about."

"You're probably right," agreed Linda. "But in time, she too may soften. I'm trying to think of a way to help you with that."

Linda tried to think of other possibilities for peeking into Ryan's married years. "You're free to call or visit Lizzie. She and Ryan were very close. I'm sure she'll have some insights. And remember Ryan's unit served two deployments to the Middle East during the last five years of his life. The deployments would account for about half of those five years. You could talk to Ray Lindquist. He and Ryan were very close through both deployments. Ray was there when Ryan died. He'll be able to tell you a lot about Ryan during the years in Afghanistan. I'll give you his number."

Before thanking her and saying good-bye, Rick asked her to give his greetings to Trevor. This thoughtful remembrance of Trevor was a moment Linda had been hoping for throughout the conversation.

"I certainly will," she replied. "That poor little guy. He's such an angel. But I know he misses his father terribly. Little boys need their fathers. It was good of you to spend time with him on Labor Day. In a way, I wish Nicole could remarry. At the same time, I know a marriage would move her and Trevor further from our family toward the new husband's family. That would break my heart."

She paused to see if Rick would comment. He didn't.

"That's the problem with being a grandmother." She laughed. "You want everything to work out perfectly in the lives of these little ones. Sometimes it doesn't happen. But I'll tell Trevor hello for you. I know he'll be excited to hear from you.

"Good-bye, dear. I love you."

She had signed off with the same words she always left ringing in Ryan's ears.

Ryan would reply, "I love you too, Mom. Say hi to Dad."

In Rick's case, Linda's affectionate farewell led to a lengthy pause and an unintelligible grunt. Linda smiled.

She felt aglow as she later replayed the conversation with Rick in her mind.

Rick, you're a godsend. And Trevor needs a dad.

Chapter 45

"I FOUND A GRAY HAIR in my brush this morning."

Miranda sat in Danny Komatsu's office following her workout.

Danny's smile came and went so fast that Miranda only caught half of it between blinks.

"Got to happen sooner or later," he said, running his hand across the gray stubble on his own head.

Miranda stretched her legs out in front of her to ease the tension on the tendons in her right knee. The knee had stiffened, the aftereffects of an old injury causing some discomfort.

"Knee still bothering you?" Danny asked.

"It'll heal soon," she answered with typical optimism.

"Maybe," said Danny. His tone was thoughtful as he searched Miranda's face for answers to his unspoken questions.

"Come on," Miranda said with a laugh. "I'm only twenty-five. I have a long life ahead of me, despite my first gray hair."

"Long life. Yes," replied Danny. "May you have a long and *happy* life. While you're living it, be careful not to let the light go out."

"What are you talking about?" Miranda's voice was touched with impatience. She was feeling a little unsettled and didn't have much patience for a searching conversation, even with Danny.

"Just as I suspected. Something's troubling you," he said, flipping a pencil end over end with one hand.

Miranda smiled. "You think you know so much. Everything's fine. The knee will heal. Stop with the Oriental wisdom routine."

"So how's your love life?" Danny pressed forward undeterred.

"None of your business." Miranda was beginning to feel the pressure of interrogation and wondering what Danny was after. "Okay, it's fine. I'm doing fine. I'm in love," she finally said to satisfy Danny.

"That's good," said Danny. "But move slowly. You're so confused right now that it wouldn't be a good time to make any decisions about your future."

"Is that right?" Miranda's impatience was turning to annoyance. "And how do you know all this?"

"Gray hair," answered Danny.

"Right. As usual, you know everything, and I know nothing."

"I'm not trying to make you angry, little one, but I can see that's the only way you'll tell me what's happening inside you."

"What makes you think something's happening?"

Danny looked out the window at the deteriorating afternoon weather. "How do you know when it is about to snow?" he asked her.

Miranda's gaze followed Danny's. "The temperature drops, and the clouds move in."

"Precisely."

"Oh, please," laughed Miranda. "Okay, Mr. Know-It-All, why don't you tell me what's going on inside me."

Danny leaned back in his chair and looked up at the ceiling, humming.

"No, really, I mean it," said Miranda. "I'm ready. I'll listen."

Danny shook his head. "No," he said. "I'm a foolish old man. You have better things to do than listen to me."

"Oh, for heaven's sake." Miranda raised her voice. "Do you want me to beg you?"

"Okay," said Danny, a hint of victory showing on his face. "Since you've asked."

"Why do I put up with this?" she groaned.

"Miranda, dear girl." Danny's face and eyes showed gentleness that only a strong man dared reveal. "You have me worried. I hurt for you. You're stiffening. The play of competition is giving way to darker purposes. That's why you're getting injured. Where's my favorite girl these days?"

"My life isn't as simple as it used to be," Miranda replied.

"Ah, yes. I know. Love will do that." Danny flung his hands out as if resigning himself to inevitabilities.

Miranda dropped her gaze from the master and studied the fabric of her gi. With a sigh and a toss of her head, she said to the older man, "It's not love that's stealing my light."

"No, it isn't. Love adds light. Still troubled by your stalker?" he asked.

Miranda nodded silently.

"Let me tell you what's happening," Danny spoke softly. "Nothing's happening. That's what troubles you. The police can do little. You—and possibly other women—live your lives at this man's mercy. This shadow. This unseen and unseeable monster. He's convinced you that he can get to you anytime he wants. He hasn't chosen to become violent, but he's shown you that he could if he desired to.

"That sensation of living at the mercy of another is debilitating. It's a patently unfair arrangement in which one person intrudes violently into the world of another but remains beyond reach. Tension builds inside. The victim has trouble relaxing. Trouble sleeping. Trouble expressing emotions. Trouble loving. The tension shows in the body and threatens the soul.

"Eventually the victim develops vengeful feelings—a real hatred. It's the natural result of all the inconvenience, discomfort, and pain the stalker has caused." Danny paused, rubbing his face with both hands. The tension in Miranda's arms and shoulders began to ease.

"As the ancients have taught," Danny continued, "the problem for the victim is that good fruit and bad fruit can't spring from the same tree. No matter what psychologists may say, hate and love can't fill the same vessel. Unlike love, which fills us by degrees, hatred consumes us. If we allow hatred to take seat in the soul, it soon blunts and then drives out all other emotions. So even a person like you, skilled enough that you have no need to fear, is in peril. His wicked craft aims to undermine your natural love of people, eventually making you no longer fit company for others. It's insidious, this war he wages."

Another pause. Miranda was silent.

"What kind of evil aims to wear another down? To wear another out? To ruin another from within?" asked Danny. "One thing is certain, this obsession of his, if he's still out there, is intended to be a war of attrition. He's taking pleasure in wearing you down—you and any other women he's stalking. He's trying to break you down. Every sleepless night you have, every hateful thought you nurture toward him, every fearful glance over your shoulder is intended to change you, and not for the better. This is war. A war for the soul."

Miranda wiped tears on the short sleeve of her gi. Danny was spot on. She'd been doing her best to cope with the very feelings he was describing. "But why?" she asked. "Why would somebody do that?"

"Sadism," said Danny. "Some men are born to it; some are trained. One of the most effective forms of warfare is to set in motion factors that wear the enemy down—unrelenting worry, inescapable vigilance, daunting fear. Violent death is almost preferable to a miserable, inescapable grinding down of the spirits, undermining emotional and physical reserves, and ultimately crushing the hopes of an enemy."

"That's cheering," said Miranda with a shallow laugh. "I can't deny that what you say is true. I know you can see that happening in me. I'm powerless to do anything about it."

Miranda laughed again, just enough to dispel the notion that she had totally lost herself in this crisis of the soul. "I know you have some advice for me. I'm ready to hear it. I need it. I'm battling for my soul, as you say. And in some ways, I'm losing the battle. I'm constantly fighting off doubts. I'm confused about love. My invincible self-image is running for shelter." She laughed.

"Have you talked to your father about this?" asked Danny.

Miranda blanched. "Not really. I love Papa, but he's too busy with his private agenda."

"How so?"

"Do you know who Art Diaz is?" she asked.

"Arturo Diaz?" said Danny with a nod. "Sure. The rising star in the Latino community. Works for the governor, doesn't he?"

"He's a lawyer in the attorney general's office. On the side, he's pushing for lasting solutions to the immigration problem. He's stumping for support inside the Latino community. That brought him to Papa's doorstep.

"Papa introduced us. Now Papa's doing everything he can to fuel a romantic spark. After all, Art could solve a big problem in the family."

"And that would be?" asked Danny.

"A suitable marriage for a daughter who's prone to range too far from her cultural moorings and is in danger of becoming an elderly spinster."

Danny actually laughed—out loud. "Never happen," he said. "There's a line of suitors who would eat the crumbs you drop if you slowed down long enough to pay any attention to them."

"Aren't you sweet? Art can go all of them one better—a marriage within the church. My parents' lifelong goal." Miranda shrugged. "So they invite Art to dinner often. They show up at all his public engagements and lend open support to his immigration platform. And Art and Papa spend a lot of time together."

Danny nodded his understanding.

"At first," said Miranda, "I went along with the charade because it's so important to my parents. I understand their concern for me, and I'm way past the age of open rebellion against parental pressure. But if I'm honest, I have to admit that Art is an impressive man. He has a promising future. I can see how hitching my wagon to his could open the door to an exciting future. And it would sure make my parents happy."

"Then what's stopping you?" asked Danny, who had now propped his feet up on the corner of his desk.

Miranda flexed the sore knee a few times slowly. "It's not that simple."

"Never is," answered Danny.

"I . . ." Miranda hesitated, uncertain if she should go on.

Danny Komatsu waited.

"No, that's all," said Miranda.

Danny sat for a while in reflection. "So," he said when it was clear that Miranda would say no more, "this stalker is not merely an inconvenience and an annoyance. He's getting in the way of a blossoming romance?"

"Something like that," said Miranda softly. "So what advice do you have, Wise One? I'm open. Better speak while you've got the chance. I don't ask for advice very often."

"What advice?" asked Danny rhetorically, running his weathered hand across the stubble on his head once more. "First, I'd say that you should try to avoid letting this war with the stalker become personal. Likely you are just one of many women so troubled. Though you feel the impact personally, remind yourself that this is the community's problem, society's problem, not yours. Don't be afraid to talk about it with others. Evil grows in secret places—in dark places. It shrinks from the burning rays of the noonday sun. Tell your parents. Tell your lover. Tell your friends. This is their problem as much as it is yours."

Danny swiveled in his chair. He was no longer looking at Miranda but through the window to the outside world. "Second piece of advice," continued Danny leaning back in his chair, "try not to think about him. Try not to imagine how he looks. Try not to hear his voice in your head. Try not to imagine meeting him or fighting him. These fantasies steal your light and give the darkness a chance to grow inside you. You can't be rid of him for the time being. That isn't *your* task but society's.

"In the meantime, fill your life with light and love. Let your fantasies focus on the man you love. If that's Art Diaz, so be it. Though I have to say you don't talk about him like a woman in love." Danny paused again.

Miranda could feel his gaze searching her for additional clues. She chose to remain silent.

"If it's Art," continued Danny, "give yourself to him. Dream. Dream big—a family, children, a successful career, good things for the clients you serve. Doesn't some good book say that 'perfect love driveth out all fear?' Miranda, you can't afford to hate. You have too much to live for." Danny threw up his hands. "What am I talking about? What do I know about these things? Get yourself a therapist. She'll probably tell you the opposite."

Miranda rose from her chair, walked around Danny's desk, and kissed the master on his forehead. "Thank you, Danny," she said. "You're the only man I know who can turn one gray hair into a sermon."

Chapter 46

RICK AND MIRANDA SAT AT a table in the Red Iguana restaurant on North Temple Street. Rick was picking at the chips and salsa. Miranda was silent.

Though there were a couple of weeks in the late summer when Rick and Miranda had shared moments that bordered on romance, Miranda had pulled back. Rick was disappointed but not surprised.

He had become aware through Rudy Ruiz, one of the sales associates at Home Deport, that Miranda was seeing another man. Rudy was Latino and followed trends in the Latino community closely. Rudy had been there when Miranda visited the store for Rick's promotion party. When he read an article in the local Latino press that linked Miranda to Arturo Diaz, he recognized her and asked Rick about it. Rick didn't bring the matter up with Miranda, considering that to be her business. Still, he silently mourned the death of his hopes that one day his Herculean efforts could win her love.

"So, case manager," he said with a smile. "Any instructions for me?"

Miranda smiled wearily. "Rick, there's nothing I can tell you that you don't already know and do. You're perfect. Please keep going, for me." She leaned forward, her elbows on the table, her chin in her hands.

No, Miranda, you're perfect. I'll keep going, for you. Rick tried to conceal his emotions from her, knowing that she had another love in her life.

Miranda looked tired.

"Well, friend, you know how I feed on your approval," he said with a smile. "You look tired. Shall we make it short this evening?"

Miranda looked at him intently. He couldn't be sure what she was thinking, but her look was kind, endearing.

She looked down at the little flowers in the pottery vase that served as a centerpiece. Then she looked around the restaurant as if checking to see who was near. "I like it when you call me *friend*." She smiled softly. "You know I like you, Rick. I would kiss you if I could. But I can't do that here. Not in public."

Rick fidgeted. He swallowed and looked away but quickly forced himself to return her gaze. "I'm a little confused," he said. "I understand that you have a boyfriend or are engaged. A friend at work fills me in on it. Actually, I wish he wouldn't. I don't mean to intrude. I'm just happy to have you as a friend." He smiled. "And as my own private case manager."

It was Miranda's turn to look away. She said nothing, but her movements seemed uncharacteristically awkward. The delay in her reply seemed to confirm Rick's fears. She righted herself in her chair. She started to say something, but the waitress approached the table and placed two sizzling dishes in front of them.

As Rick looked up to say thanks, he noticed to his right, a couple of tables away, a man watching them. Rick turned his head to see a stranger, about his age, with long brown hair and a dark complexion. The man didn't look away immediately. For a few seconds, he fixed his gaze on Rick then turned back to the female companion sitting across from him. Rick also looked at the woman to see if he recognized her. He didn't.

By the time Rick looked back to Miranda, the waitress had started to the kitchen, passing between Rick and the mysterious stranger. Watching her go, he saw briefly that the stranger was once again looking at him.

This exchange of glances distracted Rick. He had definitely seen the man before but couldn't place him. The chance encounter changed Rick's mood, and the intimate moment developing between him and Miranda was lost.

She offered an explanation, but to Rick it seemed unduly thoughtful and somewhat evasive. Rick wasn't sure he understood and regretted putting her on the spot. Rick just chalked this shift in his beloved Miranda up to the mystery of womanhood.

So this is how a broken heart feels. I should have seen it coming.

Rick went to bed uneasy and arose the following day to resume his relentless routine of work, school, and study. The days merged into one. He didn't resent his life. It was a vast improvement on the past. Each day he measured and recorded his progress. His life was moving forward, inch by inch, but a light had gone out in his world.

Chapter 47

RICK AWOKE WITH A START. He sat bolt upright in bed and rubbed his temples. Several days had passed since his dinner with Miranda at the Red Iguana. He had continued to think about the dark stranger. He'd been unsuccessful in connecting a name or concrete memory to the somewhat familiar face. Until now.

Rick had dreamed. It was one of his dreams about the street, about street people, about life on the street. Like other dreams of its sort, this one was haunted by an evil presence from his past. That evil presence was a man Rick had known for only a few weeks prior to his arrest and entry into the Housing First program. The man was known in the Salt Lake street community as Slice. Unlike most street people, Slice was aggressive and cruel. Rick had seen him beat a couple of other streeties. Slice ruled by intimidation. And he always carried a weapon—a knife.

Rick wasn't sure whether the nickname came from the knife or from the frightful scar on Slice's face, which appeared to have been made by a knife. It started at the corner of his mouth and curved upward nearly to his eye. In a sense, it was similar to the scars on Rick's face except that it was far more prominent, probably resulting from a much deeper cut. Rick's were mostly superficial. Slice's seemed to go clear to the bone of his face. At their first meeting, Slice's scar had been an angry red color, suggesting that it was still young.

Rick hadn't seen the scar on the face of the man at the Red Iguana, but then, he'd seen the man mostly in profile. The scar could have been on the other side of his face. If Rick had seen the scar, he would have recognized Slice immediately. The stranger had the same dark complexion, the same haunting expression as Slice. But at the Red Iguana, the stranger wasn't in street attire. His hair, though long, was carefully combed. He was clean-shaven.

The more Rick thought about the pieces to this puzzle, the more he believed that the stranger was his nemesis of a year earlier.

For reasons he couldn't explain, bad blood had existed between Rick and Slice from the beginning. Rick could clearly remember Slice's reaction when they first met—like Slice was afraid of him. The guy had disappeared almost immediately. Gradually, after several encounters, Slice became more bold and eventually treated Rick with what could only be described as pure loathing. As was Rick's style, he avoided Slice whenever possible. He wasn't afraid of Slice, but life was too short to waste on unpleasant encounters.

On the night Rick was arrested in Pioneer Park, he'd been prepared to have it out with Slice. When SLCPD detectives cuffed Rick and led him away, Rick's final glance found Slice exultant, giving Rick the victory grin.

Rick had had the feeling that Slice was just passing through—not through town but through the culture. Slice was meaner than others on the street. He didn't abide the unwritten rules that allowed street people to coexist in relative peace, and he didn't care.

How could a man like Slice move in and out of the street community?

Why would anyone who didn't belong there *want* to move into the street community?

There could be only one answer. The street is a place where a man could hide if he didn't want to be found. Was it possible that Slice lived more than one life?

More than possible, wasn't it likely?

On only one occasion had Rick observed Slice acting humanely. One fall morning, an elderly bag lady had tipped her shopping cart off the cement curb along the street while attempting to pass by a line of people awaiting the arrival of the breakfast van from the shelter. The plastic bags containing all her belongings spilled into the street. She struggled alone to right the cart.

Several men moved to help her. Foremost among them was Slice. Reaching the distraught woman first, he quickly set the cart right then aided her in retrieving the scattered bags. This show of tenderness was so out of character for Slice that it mystified Rick. The scene contrasted dramatically with the generally uncaring manner Slice exhibited toward everyone else.

Rick's dream was also troubled by the presence of another recognizable person.

Miranda.

It wasn't possible in reality, but that's the way dreams sometimes were. In place of the stupid street girl Rick had followed into the park on that fateful winter night, Miranda was with Slice. She was in danger.

Rick was frightened for her, ready to fight for her. If need be, ready to die.

He awoke before the dream played out, but he lay awake the rest of the night, anxious about Miranda and wondering if he had actually seen Slice at the Red Iguana.

As for Slice's female companion in the restaurant, Rick had no further insight into her identity.

I worry for her too.

Chapter 48

THOUGH THE DAY OF RICK'S dream began uncomfortably, he looked forward to the third excursion out of his probation zone in nearly a year. Twice he'd traveled by bus to the home of Linda and Dennis Tate. This time, he would travel all the way out to the Utah Army National Guard headquarters in Draper to meet with Ryan's friend, Sergeant Ray Lindquist. Rick had made an appointment with Ray. Miranda arranged the permissions.

Early winter had arrived again. Fall semester had just ended and Rick was feeling the relief of a semester break. With no classes or studying to do, he was planning to work a morning shift then catch a bus for his scheduled afternoon meeting.

Rick was only a little over a month from completing the electronically monitored portion of his probation. For a year he had been wearing the ankle bracelet that continuously tracked his whereabouts. He had become so accustomed to wearing it that he wondered how he would feel without it. Yet he hungered to be free of it.

The anklet was a hateful thing. It felt like a tumor or some other malignant appendage to his foot. The only positive aspect of wearing it was that it motivated Rick to meet the demands of probation flawlessly. And miserable as the blasted thing was, it was a lesser imprisonment than spending the same amount of time in jail. For that, Rick was supremely grateful.

His shift completed and the bus ride behind him, Rick arrived at the National Guard headquarters on time. The building was set back from the street and bordered on three sides by a fenced-in vehicle and equipment area. The building was redbrick, single story, with a high roofline. It had the utilitarian look of a government facility, probably built during the Cold War.

A Guard member walked Rick across the tile and concrete floors to a small office on the perimeter of the open gymnasium-like interior of the building. There he faced a door with a nameplate that read, *Ray Lindquist, Operations Sergeant.*

Stepping aside, the soldier waved Rick into the office.

A graying, fortyish man rose from a chair behind the metal desk, his military bearing obvious. "Ray Lindquist." He started to extend a hand but froze.

Rick was becoming accustomed to the shock experienced by people who had known Ryan well but didn't know he had a twin.

"I'm not Ryan Tate," Rick said hastily. "But I would like to talk to you about him."

"Whoa!" said Lindquist with a pained laugh. "You could have fooled me." He offered Rick a seat and continued to study him as he reclaimed his own seat. "What can I do for you?"

"My name is Rick Street. I didn't mean to startle you. I get that a lot these days. It's a long story, but I'll make it short. I'm Ryan's twin."

Lindquist looked at Rick suspiciously, shaking his head in amazement. "I knew Lieutenant Tate well, maybe as well as anybody. He never mentioned a brother."

"Truth is," replied Rick, "he didn't know about me. And I didn't know about him until six months ago. We were identical twins. Our birth mom put us both up for adoption, but we were adopted separately.

"Ryan's mom, Linda Tate, discovered the link. She had a DNA test done. She gave me your name as somebody who could fill me in on Ryan's life for the last five or six years."

"Wow, that's amazing." Lindquist shook his head again. "Did you say it was Rick?"

"Right."

"Well, it's a pleasure to meet you, Rick," Lindquist said finally. "Ryan, your brother, was one of the best young officers I ever met. One of the best people. He wasn't only my commander on the National Guard side but a close personal friend. I'll tell you what I can. What do you want to know?"

"Did you know Ryan from the time he got married until his death?"

"Yes. In fact, I knew him before that. He and a bunch of other kids joined the Guard when they were in high school—or just out. Ryan was in ROTC during his university years. When he graduated, he went to officer basic course and did a stint on active duty. That's where he got airborne qualified and joined Special Forces. As I recall, he and Nicole got married while he was on active duty. I guess you know his wife, Nicole?"

"A little," replied Rick.

"Yeah, that's another story," Lindquist continued. "Anyway, when the LT came back from active duty, he transferred into Company C, 1st Battalion, 19th Special Forces Group. That was about five years ago now. A couple of his other buddies, Tim Barton and Joey Frost, moved over when he did. Frost went to the ODB, but Barton, unfortunately, came to us."

Rick interrupted Lindquist's explanation. "I'm sorry. I've never been in the military. I don't know what an ODB is."

Lindquist nodded. "An ODA is an Operational Detachment Alpha. In Special Forces they're called A-teams. Your brother commanded an A-team. An ODB is an Operational Detachment Bravo, a headquarters and support detachment. That's where Frost went.

"A-teams engage mostly in advisory operations like counterinsurgency, infiltration, search-and-destroy missions— that kind of stuff. They support and strengthen frontline fighters."

Rick nodded.

"Ryan was an acting ODA commander during our first deployment to Afghanistan. During the second, he was the ODA commander; he'd made the promotion list for captain. He was one of the best-rated officers in the battalion.

"Both deployments seconded us to the 3rd Special Forces Group of the active army. Our first tour was east of Kandahar. The second was in the mountains of Kunar Province along the Pakistani border. That's where he was killed."

Lindquist sat quietly. His narrative had clearly brought to his memory many images and experiences on which he was beginning to reflect as the two men visited.

"Were the deployments about a year long?" asked Rick.

"More like fifteen months," replied Lindquist. "We did fifteen, then came home for fifteen, then returned for fifteen. But we didn't complete the last tour."

"My brother wrote a letter to his mom that I had a chance to read," Rick told him. "In it he said he'd been wounded and other men in his unit killed. Did he die from that wound?"

"No," answered Lindquist. "Ryan recovered mostly from that wound. He insisted on returning to duty. He was killed later, in another action."

"Can you tell me about that?" Rick asked him.

Lindquist looked at Rick steadily for a long moment. He shook his head and laughed. "I can't believe this," he said. "Sitting here talking to you is like talking to a ghost. You look like him. You sound like him. Your eyes even dig like his did. It's amazing." He laughed again, shaking his head. "The only real difference is that Lieutenant Tate was a born leader. He had that command presence. He knew how to pull a team together and get the best out of every team member, and he did it in a way that soldiers love to follow. He inspired confidence and showed respect for his men. I only knew one man who wouldn't have followed him into fire or taken a bullet for him.

He sighed. "I'll tell you what I can about the LT's death. Much of it's classified. But first, there's something you should read."

Lindquist rose and moved stiffly to a steel filing cabinet five feet from his desk. He passed in front of a wall of photographs, certificates, and diplomas bearing his name. In one of those photos, Rick could see Ryan in field gear standing next to Lindquist. The pair was looking at the photographer. Neither was smiling. In the distant background, Rick could see a cluster of three men in Arab attire.

Returning with a book in hand, Lindquist handed it to Rick. The book showed all the signs of hard use. The leather was worn bare on the corners. The face and part of the spine of the book were stained by some liquid now turned black.

Was it blood? Oil?

"That was Lieutenant Tate's deployment journal," Lindquist explained. "He wrote in it almost daily. The beginning describes the first deployment. There's a break, then the second deployment. The LT wrote in it the morning before he was killed. I know because I watched him do it." Lindquist's voice was quiet and respectful. "I tried to give it to Nicole, but she didn't want it. Didn't want to read it. She didn't want anything to do with the Guard or the active army. I guess I can understand that, in a way. But she never approved of the unit or our mission. I think she wanted a different life for them. But her husband was the kind of man who had to fight for a worthy cause. That's where he found his meaning."

Lindquist scratched his head, acting as though he wanted to sit but remained standing. "So she doesn't want it, and it'll be years before their boy is ready to read it. You may as well have a shot at it."

Rick leafed through the soiled and dusty pages that were already yellowing, the ink fading in some spots. Those spots were barely readable.

By the time Trevor was old enough to read the journal, much of it would be lost to the ravages of time. "Thanks," replied Rick. "I'll read it all."

"When you finish it, give me a call. Maybe we can get together again. I'll tell you what I can about the last hours. Ryan Tate was a hero," Lindquist said with obvious emotion. "His nation owes him a debt of gratitude." Lindquist stared directly down into Rick's eyes. "You have a high mark to live up to," he said. "I envy you for being his brother."

"It sounds to me like you *were* his brother," Rick answered.

"We were friends, but he was my commander. There's always a distance there that can't be closed. It has to be that way. At any minute he could order me to my death. I don't think you could do that to your brother."

Rick took leave of Ray Lindquist with a promise to return. He carried Ryan's wartime journal inside his coat. In all, he now had access to journals that covered all of Ryan's life except about three years. *And anything from those years will be in Nicole's hands.*

Chapter 49

ODA 8052 IS STATIONED AT our small forward base near FJI City. It's a rat hole. Our billets down at TK were far better. FJI is in the valley. The river supports small local farms, mostly corn. Everybody here knows that the main cash crop is opium, but we turn our backs on that. Our mission is not to right the wrongs of Afghan society but to help stabilize levels of government until the Afghans can govern themselves . . .

The provincial governor of Kunar is Sayed Fazlullah Wahidi. The district governor is Jowzjan, a brother-in-law to Wahidi. What a pair they are . . .

Our current assignment is to stabilize the villages along the road east toward the border. Every day we convoy up into the villages and meet with the elders. We've worked with them on school construction, helped dig wells, hardened police stations, anything we can to preserve order and build goodwill. All the time, we're gathering intel . . .

Yesterday, we were attacked on the road up to Raptor Three. Intel was that the road had been mined. Engineers from the 101st swept the road, but the delays set us up for attack. We were pinned down for forty minutes under automatic weapons fire. Four RPG strikes. We lost two vehicles. Bandit and Patriot were both wounded. Patriot took a round in the chest that passed clear through him. When the firefight died down, we trucked him back to the crossroads, where a medevac chopper picked him up.

The strike was just a delaying tactic. We could have been hurt much worse. The opposition is gaining strength. They also have new weapons and more ammo. Satellite intel shows a buildup ten klicks up the stream. We think they're using that route to bring in personnel and weapons from Pkstn. We'll go back tonight and sweep the target with our Afghan sidekicks. They're security forces that belong to Jowzjan . . .

Our night raids are producing body count. Last night we tagged and bagged eleven known T-bans. We're coming under pressure to do less night work because of the innocent casualties, collateral damages. Last night's net included three boys, just kids. More of the night work will be done by Jowzjan's ASF units . . .

One of the KIA T-bans was carrying a video camera. We sent it back to ODB for an intel screen. It showed hardcores crossing the mountains from Pkstn, heavily armed. Bigger numbers than we've seen before. More weapons. These are Al Qaedas or Al Qaeda–backed . . .

Nasty, dirty work. Hard days at boiling temps. Cold nights. Constant pressure. Some cracks in our team. Lantern, my 18B, is steady on. I'd die without him, literally.

Some of the body count are hardcores. Others are local peasants. Farmers. Kids. They're dirt poor and need money, so the hardcores offer them a few Afghanis (currency) to shoot an RPG, plant a mine, whatever. The guys have no choice. They can't turn down the money. But when I lose a man, we don't ask why the other guy was shooting. We just go after him . . .

Trouble with Bandit, our 18Z. We get into the villages during the day. The team disperses with interpreters to make contacts and gather intel for night ops. Fraternization with Afghani women is strictly verboten, of course. The mullahs are always on the lookout for any infraction. An incident between a GI and an Afghani woman will have disastrous consequences. Bandit is always making eyes at them. I've reamed him out for it several times. This afternoon at Raptor Seven, word came back from an interpreter that Bandit and one of the village girls were actually touching. They may have been seen. Time for a showdown . . .

Armageddon. I'm back after thirty-six days. Relieved my acting ODA commander. Four KIA in my ODA. I was hit in the shoulder, just under my body armor. The bullet fragged, one piece passing near my heart, nicked an artery. But I'm out of the woods. Could have been reassigned, but I elected to return to duty. The shooting happened up near Raptor Seven on a night ops. Bad intel. We were set up. Our ASF sidekicks melted, left us with the heat.

Had a visit in the MASH from Osprey, our ODC commander, threatening to court martial me for the incident. Ospey is active army, doesn't have much use for NG units. Told me he received a complaint from Jowzjan about fraternization among my men. I denied. Told him I was on top of it. He told me we were jeopardizing his whole mission in the district and he wished he could send us all home. Nobody in my ODA would argue that, least of all me. It's times like these that I miss being home, miss home bitterly. Maybe I should have been a schoolteacher. We're here trying to save a country. Trying to make a better world. The politics make me sick.

Osprey is known among all of his ODAs as a climber. His real ambition is to get a full bird. It wouldn't surprise me if he threw people away to get it. Feeling among my ODA is that we were sacrificed to keep peace with Jowzjan. Osprey may have sold us out. Could have been an exchange of arms or drugs for arms, not sure where the treachery happened. We'll keep our eyes open. Next time we'll know better.

But one thing is certain. Osprey is my CO. I will follow command or die trying. No way I could go home on a medical and leave Lantern, Anchor, Frisbee, Fletch, and the others behind. Been a long deployment. Maybe 70 days to go. Not sure I can ever come back . . .

Four packs transferred over from 8012 to bring us to full strength. Lantern was also wounded in the Raptor Seven firefight. Bandit escaped. Don't know how. Bad blood between him and others in the ODA. The feeling is that his hanky-panky set us up. I've broken up three fights in the team between Bandit and other team members. We can't go on this way . . .

I keep Bandit in my sight 24/7. More rumors of fraternization. Lantern thinks he went too far, that Bandit has money on his head. If so, we're all dead men. I had a heart-to-heart with Lantern, who told me he thinks I sold out the ODA when I refused to discipline Bandit. Hard words between us. I pulled him up short then asked him to support me. I have my reasons with Bandit. Maybe I'm not cut out for command.

This thing is wearing me down. Real tired. Wound still hurting. Thinking about home . . .

Orders for a night ops with Jowzjan's ASF. Objective is a weapons cache belonging to T-bans of warlord Jamalludin Sherzai. Not a local op. Orders came down from ODC, some kind of deal with Jowzjan. Full packs. Full bore. 2200 hrs.

Ryan's journal ended.

Chapter 50

"MIRANDA, TAYLOR HERE. THOUGHT I'D let you know that we found your boy, Slice. Warner and Patton ran him down. He still shows up in the community over there. Claims to have a job. We told him we were getting close on the homeless woman murders and that he's on our short list, but he denied any involvement. He said he doubted we had any evidence, and he's right. Forensics are coming up short on finding our killer—or killers. Varying MOs. We gotta get to the bottom of this."

"How many women in all?" asked Miranda.

"Four—that we know of. Warner also told him we're looking at him on stalking charges, that he'd been fingered by a reliable witness. Warner didn't name you, but Slice might put two and two together. I'm thinking they probably shook him a little. Better be on the lookout. All we can do is shake the cage. See if anything jumps out."

"Thanks again," said Miranda. "I'll be in touch."

Chapter 51

OTHER THAN PULLING HIS SHIFTS at Home Depot, all that Rick really did through the holidays was read Ryan's journal. The pages were filled with military jargon. Through most of two deployments, the young officer had steadfastly held to the belief that his involvement in the war in Afghanistan was a patriotic duty. He and the men he led endured unceasing hardships.

Especially during the second deployment, Ryan's unit lost an increasing number of men, eight that Rick could count. These were all National Guard members. They were fathers and husbands, employees of businesses in the Salt Lake City area. They would be missed, as all casualties of war are.

Since discovering his twin, Rick had been curious to know all he could about Ryan. But in reading Ryan's combat journal, Rick began to empathize. He felt Ryan's discomfort. He shared some of the pain caused by Ryan's losses.

He felt anger mounting as he learned more of the supreme dilemma that put all of Ryan's men at risk. One soldier, code name Bandit, had apparently jeopardized the lives of his comrades because he continually chased Afghani women. According to the journal, this willful violation of military law also placed the women in mortal danger. Muslim women caught in sexual encounters with infidels could be murdered by their own family members for bringing shame on their homes. The journal didn't confirm that such had been the case, but it clearly left the possibility open.

Who was Bandit?

Why didn't Ryan stop him before things got out of hand?

Had a senior commander made a deal with a local district governor to abandon American troops in the face of fire?

These were matters that Rick would press to know from Ray Lindquist.

Who was Lantern? Rick suspected that the code names for team members corresponded to their surnames. *Would Lantern be Ray Lindquist?*

Who was Bandit?

What was clear beyond all else was Ryan's commitment to his men. Apparently that commitment exceeded even his longing to be at home with Nicole and Trevor. Also clear was the wear and tear of combat. It was especially apparent after Ryan's wound and the loss of four team members in one action. Putting two and two together, Rick concluded that the combat, the wound, and the losses were the same Ryan had written to his mother about in the letter that originally led Rick to the Tate's home almost a year before.

Combat had worn Ryan down.

Obviously, one draining factor was Bandit's remorseless hunger for female companionship.

Was it a weakness that Bandit just couldn't control? Or was it a weapon he used to destroy his commander and comrades?

Chapter 52

By Christmas, Rick realized that some changes in his now-comfortable routine were fast approaching. He had to decide whether to begin working full-time. With the end of his electronically monitored probation, he would be able to move around more freely. Because he was steadily employed and succeeding in school, Miranda had been approached by the policy makers in her agency asking if it was time for Rick to leave the Housing First program. Funding was tight, and if Rick stayed, someone more needy would have to remain on the street.

Rick nervously anticipated the changes but was not really frightened by them. He'd been reading Ryan's journal and was quick to realize that some of Ryan's unassailable confidence was beginning to wear off on him. As long as he could stay employed and continue schooling, Rick felt he could keep moving forward. If either of those anchors was ripped away, however, he could imagine himself tumbling back. It wasn't hard to imagine being back on the street. But it was frightening. Terrifying.

Rick hadn't experienced it for years, but he knew that to people in the privileged world, the holidays were an occasion for family parties, work parties, and whatever other parties could be arranged. He was already invited to a work Christmas party at the store. He also received a written invitation to the Tates' family Christmas party on Saturday, December 18. What he would really have liked, but was realistic enough not to expect, was an invitation to a Christmas party from Miranda.

He was sure that any invitation to a party with her family would be reserved for her boyfriend, Arturo Diaz. He further imagined that the couple would be seen at Christmas parties for state employees and within the Latino community.

None of that could be helped.

Rick counseled himself to be patient. *Rome wasn't built in a day. A homeless felon doesn't suddenly become a leading citizen.*

Miranda did talk to Rick about the coming weeks, but her mind didn't seem to be on holiday parties. She wanted to be sure that he calendared January 15 for a court appearance. "You'll need to take the time off work and skip class if necessary," she instructed him.

Rick had never, in two full semesters, missed a class. He hesitated at her suggestion, but she insisted. "Rick, this isn't optional. You have to go to court to complete phase one of your probation. I'll see what time we can get on the docket. You can't miss this."

Next, Miranda wanted to talk about Rick's apartment.

"Am I going to lose it?" Rick asked.

"Will you miss it?"

"I have only you to thank for it." He blushed. "Yes, I'll miss it. Only a loser like me could fall in love with a place without furniture," he said, looking around. "Really good things have happened to me here."

"I've been thinking about what we can do," said Miranda. "I have a friend. His name is Danny Komatsu. His wife is Heiko. Their kids are grown. I was talking to him about needing to find a place. They have an apartment in their basement where her mom used to live. Danny said they'd be happy to talk to you about renting it. And it's actually closer to the campus. Is that something you would consider?"

Rick watched Miranda as she spoke. His gaze said all that he felt toward her. He was like a man who had fallen in love with a car and was enamored by the lines, the wheels, the interior, and the trim but had no money or credit to actually make the purchase. Rick was in love with the product, but a purchase was completely beyond his means. "You never stop doing good for me, do you?" he asked. "That sounds like it might be good. I just keep owing you more and more."

"I told Danny and Heiko I'd talk to you about it. They said if you thought you'd be interested, you and I could come to dinner at their house Friday evening so they could meet you and discuss it. What do you think?"

Rick blushed again because he knew he was grinning like a goat and couldn't help himself.

Miranda saw his grin and started to laugh. "I'm sorry," she said. "It just makes me happy to see you smile."

"I'd like to meet them," Rick nodded. "Do you want me to meet you there?"

"Do you know where they live?" She laughed.

"No, but if you tell me, I can get myself there. I may seem totally helpless, but I do know how to get around."

"Don't be silly," she said. "I know you're not helpless. Anything but helpless."

*   *   *

Rick's first *Christmas in captivity*, as he called it, was charmed. The visit with the Komatsu's resulted in an agreement for Rick to move into their basement the first day of January. The Christmas social at the store was pleasant. Home Depot gave him a $250 bonus, which he added to his growing bank account.

He rode over to the Tates in corduroy pants and a cable-knit sweater that he purchased as his Christmas present to himself. He took with him a small Christmas gift he bought at Pier 1 Imports. He also bought a set of four children's books for the kids. His gifts were well received, as was he. Only Nicole remained distant.

After dinner, Rick spent much of the evening with the children, playing board games. Trevor was a bright player for his age, understanding not only the basic moves but the real aims behind the games. Trevor and Lucy, about the same age, were especially competitive. Rick watched them with delight. When the kids began to tire, they all joined the adults, who were listening to Christmas music and visiting quietly.

Rick sat against the wall on the carpet with his legs stretched out in front him. After a while, little Trevor wandered over and sat beside him. He gradually fell asleep, his head slumped against Rick's chest. Rick stroked the boy's thick hair thoughtlessly until he saw Nicole watching, a look of obvious consternation on her face. Rick dropped his hand.

When Christmas Eve came, Rick worked a double shift so that another sales associate could spend the time at home with his family. Then he returned to the apartment and spent the evening alone, just he and Jesus. He reread portions of Ryan's journal then wrote in his own. He was mightily tempted to walk to the liquor store and get himself a bottle to keep him company.

But that was moving backward.

He didn't want that anymore.

Instead, he walked over to St. Ignatius and attended the evening's Christmas mass. Father John was away. Another priest celebrated the mass.

It was still peaceful, and Rick had a rich, comfortable feeling. Possibly because of the season but also because his life was improving, Rick was thinking a lot about Jesus.

Jesus was a man who reached out to the homeless. He cared for blind people, the disabled, and the poor. He especially showed kindness to widows and orphans. That thought brought Nicole and Trevor Tate to mind, and eventually carried his mind to Jennifer Sopel.

I need to be more like Jesus, but I'm not sure how to do that.

Chapter 53

JANUARY 15, RICK'S LONG-AWAITED COURT date, didn't arrive before tragedy struck. Actually, the tragedy struck Miranda, but Rick felt it deeply.

On the second day into the New Year, Rudy Ruiz was waiting when Rick arrived at the store.

"Hear the news?" asked Rudy.

"Not really," answered Rick. "What's up?"

"Your girlfriend's boyfriend," Rudy paused then made the sign of slitting his own throat.

"What?" asked Rick.

Rudy repeated the gesture.

"What? You're jacking me around."

Rudy shook his head.

"He killed himself?"

"No! Somebody did it for him," Rudy replied.

Rick was shocked. "Where did you hear that?"

"The news."

"What did they say?"

"Art Diaz has been promoting pro-Latino legislation. He and your girl, Miranda, attended the New Year's Eve ball sponsored by the Hispanic Chamber of Commerce. He used it as an opportunity to make a statement about immigration, you know? There were a couple TV reporters. They put a little clip on the news. No big deal, really. But this morning, they reported that he had been killed—clearly a homicide. It's all over the Latino community. The police think it was related to the political debate, but they don't have suspects. No *persons of interest*," Rudy emphasized to ridicule the latest news terminology.

"How was he killed?" asked Rick. "Shot?"

"Noooo!" replied Rudy melodramatically. "Throat was cut."

"You're kidding me." Rick was appalled. To his own shame, his first emotional reaction was a twinge of relief that Art Diaz was gone from Miranda's life. Then he thought about Miranda. "That's horrible," he said.

"Look on the bright side," said Rudy. "That opens the door for you."

Rick shook his head. "Ruiz, you don't seem to be all torn up about it. I thought you were in favor of the reforms."

"I am," replied Rudy. "But at the same time, I don't like to see ambitious people use social issues to feed their careers. You know what I mean? A lot of people out there are getting the shaft. My problem with Diaz was that he always pushed himself to the front instead of pushing the needs of the people to the front."

"Maybe," Rick replied. "But there are lots of ways to solve social problems besides cutting a guy's throat."

"Don't you know it," agreed Rudy.

Chapter 54

"Taylor, Miranda."

"Hi, M."

"You heard about Art Diaz."

"Sure. Sorry."

"Thanks. We shook the cage and something jumped out."

"We're on it, M. Homicide already brought our boy in, but he had a bomb-proof alibi."

"You're kidding."

"Nope. But we're all over this thing. We'll find this guy. You be careful."

Chapter 55

AT THEIR LAST MEETING BEFORE year's end, Rick and Miranda had agreed that she would come for her weekly visit to his new place at Danny Komatsu's to check things out. On the Monday evening before her scheduled visit, Miranda left a message with the Komatsus for Rick: She wouldn't make their weekly appointment. Something had come up. She would try to reach him before their second appointment. If nothing worked out, then she would meet him at Matheson Courthouse, Courtroom C, at 9:45 a.m. on January 15.

Danny Komatsu shook his head in disbelief as he and Rick talked about Art's death in the living room of Rick's new apartment. The Komatsus could come down into the basement anytime they wanted just by descending the steps. Rick did have an outside entrance. He was beginning to wonder how well this cozy arrangement would work out. Rick needed privacy. He didn't mind living *near* somebody else, he just didn't want to live *with* somebody else.

"I feel bad for little Miranda," said Danny.

"Yeah, I'm sure she'll miss him," Rick answered.

"I don't think she was really sweet on him," said Danny, "but anytime a friend dies like that, it leaves a bad feeling for a long time."

"How did you and Heiko get to know Miranda?" Rick asked. "I know you told me already, but I can't remember."

"At my dojo. When Miranda was a little girl, she thought she'd be interested. Her parents brought her in. We got to know them and have kept in touch a little ever since."

"I see," Rick mumbled. "I wish I knew what to do to help her."

Danny considered Rick for a few moments. "Has Miranda ever said anything to you about being stalked?" asked Danny.

Rick shook his head. "Is somebody stalking her?" he asked.

"Well, if she hasn't said anything, then I probably shouldn't," said Danny.

She would have told me. Or would she?

"She mentioned it to me," Danny continued. "It was a while ago, so I don't know if it's still happening."

"Is that something to be worried about?"

"I don't know. But with this death being so close to her, it kind of makes you wonder."

Rick hadn't seen Diaz's death as being linked to Miranda in any way. The thought disquieted him.

"You ever had any self-defense training?" Danny asked.

Rick grinned. "I've been in a lot of fights, and I'm still here."

Danny laughed. "Actually, that's a pretty good sign. What about serious stuff? What if you or somebody you loved was threatened with serious injury?"

"I don't know."

"Could you take a gun or a knife away from somebody who wanted to use it on you?"

Rick whistled. "I don't know. What are you driving at?"

"Well," said Danny, "like I said, I'm a martial arts instructor. Some people think I'm an expert. I'm called a master. When I was young, I trained as a Navy Seal. Then for many years, I was a Marine Corps instructor. Seems like all my life I've been teaching people to defend themselves."

"I don't really have any enemies," replied Rick.

"I know you don't," Danny continued. "You seem pretty easy to get along with. What about people you love? Anybody you need to defend?"

Rick was embarrassed by the question about people he loved. Furthermore, he didn't know Danny well enough to talk about his personal life. But Danny was serious.

Rick decided to take the chance. "I guess if I'm truthful, I have to say there's one person I love—well, and a few in my new family."

"Can they all take care of themselves?"

"No," answered Rick simply. "I don't think they could."

"Can you take care of them?"

"I guess that depends."

"Depends on . . . ?"

"Who's trying to hurt them and how he's trying to do it."

"Do you want to learn how?" Danny asked unblinkingly.

Rick exhaled deeply. "I do. But I don't have much free time, and I don't have much money for lessons."

Danny laughed. "I'm not trying to sell you anything, Rick. I'm not talking about learning martial arts so you can compete. I'm just talking about a few techniques, a few moves, to be used only in dire emergencies. The way we used to train the Marines. Two or three lessons and a few weeks' practice could save your life or maybe help you save somebody else's."

Rick thought about this. "Why? What's this about?"

"I can't tell you everything," Danny answered. "But my offer is sincere. In fact, I'll make you a deal. If you'll learn my five deadly moves and practice them until you get really good, I'll cut your rent in half. How's that?"

"Wow, that sounds good," Rick answered. "But I have to be truthful. I've been in lots of fights, but I've never been what you would call a clean fighter. I fight to win. I don't want to kill anybody, but I want to make it so they can't fight anymore."

"Just what I had in mind." Danny Komatsu smiled.

Chapter 56

JANUARY 15 WAS THE DAY following the anniversary of Rick's conviction. He still hadn't seen or talked to Miranda since the Diaz murder. He was excited to get before the judge, but he was more excited to see Miranda. As he walked into the foyer of the courthouse, he searched for her. He could easily remember the first moment he saw her just a year earlier. As he stood looking around, he marveled at the changes in his world in that year. He knew he had Miranda to thank for most of them.

Miranda finally arrived a minute before ten in the company of the same public defender who had handled Rick's case a year before. Rick couldn't even remember the defender's name. The three entered the courtroom and waited at the defense table until Third District Court judge Alma Springer said, "The court will now consider the matter of State of Utah v. Richard Harrison Street."

Rick said nothing while his public defender and Miranda provided evidence of compliance with the court's previous order. Finally, Judge Springer turned to Rick. "It's nice to see you again, Mr. Street."

I doubt you can remember me. "It's nice to see you again, Your Honor. I've been anxious to come before you again."

"Anxious or eager?" she asked him.

Rick didn't quite understand the question.

Miranda answered for him. "Eager, Your Honor."

"Thank you, Ms. Martinez. I'm not sure why you're so eager to get here, Mr. Street. The good things you've been doing are just things you'll have to keep doing for the rest of your life." Judge Springer's facial expression was pleasant, as if she were actually trying to converse with him.

"You're right, Your Honor," replied Rick somewhat cautiously. "But hopefully I won't have to do it with an ankle bracelet."

Judge Springer laughed, as did Miranda. The public defender's face was blank.

"Mr. Street, I'm happy to hear you've heeded the direction of the court. It sounds like you're doing well. Accordingly, the court terminates electronic monitoring of your probation and orders you to return at the end of one more year on completion of your supervised probation. Do you have any questions?"

"No, Your Honor."

"Mr. Street, you're now free to go wherever you like as long as you're present for the required interviews with Ms. Martinez, your appointed probation counselor. You have done well so far. My advice to you is to keep with it. I remind you that if you violate the terms of your probation at any time in the next year, you'll still be going to jail. Are we clear?"

"We're clear, Your Honor."

Judge Springer brought her gavel down sharply on the block.

The public defender was gone before they could get out of the courtroom.

"Thanks for your help," Rick said once they were out in the hallway.

"We still have to go over to Corrections to get the anklet removed."

"I've missed you," said Rick. "Are you okay?"

Miranda shook her head. Her eyes were moist.

"I'm sorry about Mr. Diaz."

"So am I," said Miranda. "But I can't talk about it here." She glanced around them. "Let's go get you free of that thing."

Miranda wouldn't talk about the murder, but Rick couldn't think of anything else to talk about since that issue loomed enormously in Miranda's life.

"How are things going at your new place?" Miranda asked.

"Going great," replied Rick. "I'm hardly ever there. I never see Heiko. The only time I see Danny is during our martial arts lessons."

Miranda stiffened. "What lessons?" she asked.

"Danny is coaching me in some basic self-defense moves." He laughed. "He calls them the five deadly moves."

Rick could see the alarm in Miranda's eyes and the tightness of her face. "Why is he doing that?" she asked.

"I think it's because that's what Danny does," said Rick. "Like the old saying goes, 'When you have a hammer, everything looks like a nail.' When Danny wants to help somebody, I think he does it through the stuff he does best—martial arts. Besides," he shrugged, "he's cutting my rent in half just to motivate me."

He glanced at Miranda again and saw anger written on her face.

"He doesn't have to do that. I'm motivated anyway," Rick mumbled.

They pulled into the Komatsu driveway after traveling silently for most of the trip from the Corrections Department. Rick kept reaching down to this ankle, hardly able to believe he was now free of the dreaded anklet.

Miranda's distress was uncomfortable for him.

"Can we make an appointment for our next meeting?" he asked.

"Will your class schedule let us keep meeting on Tuesday evening?" she asked.

"Yes. Where?" he asked.

"I'm not sure," she answered. "I'll get word to you through the Komatsus."

Now that she was talking to him, some of the hardness in her voice seemed to melt away.

Rick looked at her carefully. "I've missed you," he said.

"You already said that," she snapped.

"I'm sorry. You're right." He waited, but she said nothing further. "Can I ask you a personal question?"

Miranda closed her eyes and shrugged.

"I don't mean to pry," said Rick. "And I don't want to offend you. But I kind of need to know."

Again, no response.

"Are you being stalked?" he asked.

Miranda's eyes snapped open. She turned on him.

"Why do you ask that?" she demanded.

"Danny hinted at it," he answered, realizing he was moving into dangerous territory. Still, he needed to know. He cared about her and wanted to help.

"I'll kill Danny." Her voice was icy.

"He didn't say much," Rick hurried to supply. "But it made me wonder. Can I help?"

"No, Rick. No! No! No! We can't even talk about this." She shook her head.

"Have you been down to Danny's dojo?" she asked.

"No," Rick replied.

"Where do you have your lessons?"

"Here, at my place."

"That's good," she said. "Please don't ever go to the dojo."

"All right," Rick answered. "I won't."

"Thank you, Rick." Miranda moaned. Silently, she slid her hand across the divider between the seats and grasped Rick's hand. She held it tightly for a few moments.

"Please, Rick. You have to trust me on this. It's true that someone is watching. I can't be affectionate with you in public. I shouldn't even see you. We have to limit our meetings to our scheduled appointments."

"I wish you'd tell me about it," he replied softly. "I can help you."

"No, you can't help me, Rick." The edge in her voice was obvious.

"I want to help you," he pressed.

She turned toward him. "If you really want to help me," she said, "please stay out of this. And stay safe."

Chapter 57

DANNY KOMATSU SAW HER COMING before she arrived. Filing student folders in the cabinet in his office, he saw Miranda flying toward the front door of the dojo. He had expected this visit. Turning his back fully toward the door, he braced himself for the onslaught. Of course, he wasn't afraid of Miranda's anger, and he knew he was doing the right thing, so he raised his eyebrows. A smile danced across his face, and he hummed a little tune.

"Danny Komatsu! What are you thinking?"

"Huh? Oh, hi, Miranda. It's early for a visit from you," he said, glancing up at the clock on the wall above her head.

"Don't act innocent with me." The scorn in her voice was withering.

Danny worked hard not to laugh. "Have a seat, and tell me what's on your mind."

He gestured toward the chair where Miranda usually sat. But Miranda was already moving, not toward him but in a circular path, like a lioness inspecting her prey. "Danny, I shared my concerns with you in confidence. Now you've spread them all over town. How could you do that to me?"

Ah, good strategy. Danny watched this magnificent woman circling her prey, gracefully, disarmingly, like a lethal predator, barely touching the earth as she feigned vulnerability just before the fatal charge.

Good. Appeal to my guilt. Turn my eye inward, away from the imminent danger awaiting me out there.

"All over town?" he asked, challenging her assumption. He would get to an apology in good time, but since she was on the offensive, he knew she would reveal her plan of attack before making her move.

"I told you I was in love with him," she hissed. "Instead of treating my confidence with respect, you decided to humiliate me. Even worse, you've started something that will place Rick in danger. There's no way he'll let this go. And that man out there, that stalker, is not some pathetic misfit. He's a killer. I didn't tell you before because I'm trying to protect the people close to me by keeping them from becoming involved, unlike you."

Keeping his face impassive, Danny nevertheless gloated.

Absorbing her aggression, he had learned two additional, vital pieces of information from the lioness. First, she *was* in love. She hadn't told him that earlier. Anger can mask memory and always makes one vulnerable. Miranda knew this. She was no beginner, no novice. Therefore, Danny could conclude that she had deliberately chosen this moment of apparent anger to reveal something she would otherwise have found awkward.

Second, her stalker was a killer. She also had not told him that earlier. She must have received some additional message from the stalker claiming or implying responsibility for the Arturo Diaz murder. If so, Miranda was already working with her police friends to draw the killer in. This concerned Danny but didn't frighten him. Of course, when the police have exhausted all their resources to *find* the killer, the only option left to them is to draw the killer in by making the prey appear easy to get at.

"If you won't tell me what's happening," he pretended not to know that Miranda was calling for help, "how can I know when I'm revealing something you want to keep hidden?"

"Don't try to pull that on me," she roared. "You know exactly what I'm thinking."

Miranda had turned her back and was walking to the opposite side of the office as she continued to talk. She was acting more like the prey than the hunter.

Danny realized she was telling him that she was being watched, even here at the dojo. This thing had gone further than he thought. "Then why are you angry with me, daughter?"

"Why am I angry? Haven't you been listening?" Miranda was standing behind her chair now, grasping the back, her long nails digging into the fine leather. Her gaze was unwavering. She had answered Danny's question with her own. The forward momentum of her aggression had slowed. She was trying to draw him out.

"I'm sorry if I have unknowingly revealed a secret you intended to reveal yourself and perhaps should have revealed earlier," he said carefully. "Perhaps this person you love is not as helpless as you fear."

"He's not helpless," Miranda replied more evenly, the roar in her voice beginning to abate, "but he's no match for this killer. He may be responsible for a string of deaths—some that the police are aware of and maybe others that haven't been discovered. He's very dangerous."

"Then wouldn't it be wise to prepare everyone who might be in danger?" Danny asked.

"That's my point," Miranda's voice rose again. "It might be *wise* to keep them out of danger in the first place."

"How can you do that?"

"By not involving them. By not training them in the *'five deadly moves.'*" Miranda's voice smoldered.

Danny was on the brink of smiling again. Of course Miranda knew there was no such thing as five deadly moves. But Rick didn't. Danny needed a simple explanation for the self-defense approach he was teaching Rick, and the "five deadly moves" had an exotic appeal.

"What kind of nonsense is that anyway?" she demanded.

"Please consider an important question," Danny said. "What if you're not the hunter's prey? What if the person you love is the prey?"

Miranda blanched. For a moment, she said nothing.

Ah! I have found the key. This stalker has told you that Diaz was killed because he was getting too close to you. You got a call. You got a note. Some message.

"Miranda, something here doesn't add up," Danny rose. He walked to the other side of the office and picked up a shuriken—a lethal-looking little curiosity sometimes called a ninja star. He kept it around as a discussion piece with potential students. "If the hunter is trying to isolate the prey, that suggests there may be more than one hunter or that the prey is really being used for bait to capture a larger prey. Predators who are hungry don't toy with the prey. They kill it. They eat it. If this hunter is toying with the prey, then possibly he's after someone else."

"I don't follow you." Miranda shook her head.

"Well . . ." Danny sighed. "Of course, I'm no match for you and the fine heads at the police department. You're far ahead in thinking and experience. But suppose that the hunter in this case is after someone like Rick. He's toying with you to draw Rick into battle on his own terms. If that were true, wouldn't it make sense to help Rick prepare? If this hunter is as dangerous as you think?"

"What are you talking about?" Miranda's tone was incredulous. "I'm the one being stalked," she said. "What does this have to do with Rick?"

"You said you're in love and that you're afraid for the one you love."

"I didn't say that was Rick Street."

"You deny it, then?"

"Danny, please," said Miranda, her storm giving way to a measure of calm—her demands beginning to sound more like appeals. "I'm just asking you to keep Rick out of this. He's just a renter. A student. A guy who's trying to work off his probation. I'm not sure where you come up with all this hunter and prey stuff. Please, as a favor to me, stop teaching Rick. He can't learn enough to make any difference. You're endangering him."

"You might be surprised to know," said Danny, "that your former homeless street dweller is quite capable. If I hadn't seen so many gifted athletes in the past, I might be tempted to claim that he's among the most gifted I've ever seen."

Miranda was silent. Danny remained silent.

"Does that mean you approve of Rick?" Miranda asked.

"More than approve."

"Approve of him as a person?"

"As a *man*," said Danny. Danny knew that Miranda understood the distinction.

Again, she remained silent.

"What do you think of Rick?" Danny asked.

"Ummm." Miranda finally sat.

"You *do* think of Rick, don't you?"

"Of course I think of him. He's my client."

"Just a client?" asked Danny.

"No," said Miranda, "not *just* a client."

"There's more then?"

"You never give up, do you?"

"Just trying to understand," said Danny.

Miranda nodded as Danny sat silently. She studied her nails, first up close then at a distance. She glanced across at Danny. Her face softened. "I like Rick," she said. "I really like him, Danny."

"I like him too," answered Danny. "What is it you like about him?"

"Oh, dear," she said, scanning the pictures on the wall behind Danny. He watched her carefully, this little girl, his prize student, now grown to splendid womanhood. He held his breath, hoping for one of those rare moments when Miranda allowed herself to be vulnerable—opened herself to another's view.

"I like Rick because I think . . . I feel . . . I *hope* he likes me."

"Everybody likes you, little one."

"Oh, wow!" she answered. "How little you know about men."

"I think I know a little about men," Danny replied, trying to sound a little defensive.

"I mean young men. You know, today's young men. The guys my age."

"They don't like you?"

"Some," said Miranda. "Sort of. I've dated guys who like my style. I think some of them like my looks, maybe my body. Some are like Art Diaz, who liked anybody that could be a political asset, a trophy wife. Then there are those guys who give me the impression that they'd like any woman who's willing to support them all their lives—the dependent ones."

"You don't want one of those," Danny agreed.

"Rick is different," said Miranda. "Maybe it's the way he grew up. Maybe he hasn't had many women to choose from. But honestly, I just get the feeling when he looks at me—when he touches me—that he really likes me, the real me, the person I am—when you take away all those other things. I think he really likes me, and it melts my heart."

Miranda sighed. "When he's near, I feel electricity. When there's danger, I'm afraid for him. When he leaves, I want him to stay. He's attentive. He treats me like you'd treat a treasure—something precious. He's interested—interesting. Helps me like myself better. And it doesn't hurt that he's a hunk."

"With all that, why haven't you gotten together?" asked Danny.

"We are together," she replied. "Kind of."

"Why don't you marry him?"

"It's not that easy. He's still trying to prove himself. I buy that. Then he discovered he has a family he didn't know about. It all takes time. Besides, he hasn't asked me."

"But if he asked, you'd say yes." It was a statement, not a question.

"We'll see. Anyway, I don't want him getting killed because he thinks he can defend himself with 'five deadly moves' or any other nonsense."

"No, we don't want that," Danny replied with a suitable shake of his head.

"You don't listen to me much, do you?"

"Hear every word."

Miranda repeated her request. "Please, as a favor to me."

"Of course, Miranda. Whatever you say," Danny replied.

"Do you know what?" She locked her stare on him. "I love you, but you're impossible." She turned and stormed from the office, deliberately slamming the door behind her. All the pictures and memorabilia on the office wall clattered with the impact.

Finally, Danny Komatsu smiled. *Miranda, you're magnificent. That Renny should have such a daughter! That any man should have such a daughter! But you must trust me. I teach Rick because I'm afraid for you.*

Rick must face this hunter. You're great in a show, but you're no match for a true killer. You weren't made to fight through spraying blood and crunching bones. Even if you survived, the emotional damage would never heal. Rick is already hardened. He's streetwise. He's street tough. He was made for this battle. It won't be easy, but his wounds will heal. It's for you that I'm teaching him.

Chapter 58

RAY LINDQUIST PARKED IN HIS assigned spot on the east side of the National Guard headquarters. He was returning from a lunch meeting with two members of his unit, men with whom he'd served twice during deployments to Afghanistan. The three were the only survivors of twelve who trained together for the first deployment. The others were all gone, eight killed in action, one missing in action. The weather was cold, even for February.

His two o'clock was Rick Street. The two first met the previous December. After visiting for half an hour with Street, Ray could see that Rick wasn't truly identical to Ryan Tate. Had they been standing side by side, Ray was sure he could tell them apart. Tate's teeth were straighter; Street had a couple of scars on his face. But aside from that, the match was astonishingly close.

In their initial visit, Ray loaned, or rather gave, Street Ryan's combat journal. Since then, Ray had done a little checking on the self-proclaimed twin.

He called Ryan's parents. Dennis confirmed that the look-alike was indeed an identical twin. Dennis also told Ray that Street was formerly homeless, now a student, and had a criminal record. Ray had made a mental note to be extremely cautious in sharing any information with Street that was in the least classified. In retrospect, Ray probably wouldn't have given Street the journal if he'd known about the criminal conviction. *What's done is done.*

Ray could also have called Nicole Tate for confirmation. The widow was a bright and attractive woman, but it was clear she resented Ryan's commitment to the service. Of course, since the worst had happened, she wanted nothing to do with the military or with any members of Ryan's unit.

She had declined to accept Ryan's journal and had grudgingly consented to military honors at his funeral. To Ray, her resentment and standoffishness detracted from her husband's heroic service. As a consequence, Ray also resented Nicole.

Ray was a civilian employee of the Utah National Guard as well as a member of the Guard. His grade was E-8, meaning that he was a master sergeant, a senior noncommissioned officer. As such, he had seen many officers come and go, both young officers and their seniors. In Ray's judgment, Ryan Tate was the best junior officer he'd ever met.

Ryan had been selfless. Totally devoted to the service, he'd always placed the mission and his men before himself. He was eager for command but never gave the impression that he served to magnify his own ego or his career. His tragic and unnecessary death was, in Ray's judgment, a black mark against the honor of the American military.

So he would share with Rick Street whatever he could about Ryan, but he would be cautious.

Street arrived on time. At their first meeting, Street seemed more reticent, less sure of himself. Only two months had passed since that meeting. The Street who showed up for this second meeting was different— more confident. Ray certainly wouldn't have guessed that Street was a convicted criminal.

"I've read the journal over and over," Street told him. "Thanks for letting me borrow it." Street reached the book toward Ray.

"The journal isn't military property. It belonged to your brother," Ray told him. "If I turn it in to our ODB, they'll probably burn it just to be on the safe side. You've read it. You're next of kin. It's yours if you want it."

"Thanks," Street replied. "Yeah, I'd like that." Tapping the journal with his fingers, he laid it in his lap. "When you gave me the journal to read, you said you'd fill in some of the blanks. Can you do that now?"

Ray nodded, pausing to think about how he could give Street what he was asking for without compromising security. "I understand you're asking for your own information," Ray began. "If you intend to make any of this information public or are planning to take any legal action on Ryan's death, I have to refer you to the official record. This is just between us, right?"

"Right," answered Street.

"The final operation that resulted in Ryan's death, and in the deaths of six other team members, is being formally reviewed by the DOD. I have no idea how long that will take. The request was made by the families of the team members who were killed. If you're cooperating with them in that request or plan to do so in the future, please tell me now. In that case, it's better if I don't say anything more."

"I'm not cooperating in any review," said Street. "I don't know any family members of other soldiers. I'm not interested in challenging the military. My only interest is getting to know Ryan better. I'm interested in how, and why, he was killed. According to Ryan's journal, your ODA was scheduled to participate in a night operation with Jowzjan's ASF. Can you tell me what ASF is?"

"Stands for Afghan Security Force," replied Ray, "sort of comparable to our National Guard."

"Okay," said Rick. "The operation was ordered by your ODC, which I understand to be the battalion commander, code name Osprey, who was active army. Did something go wrong, or did Ryan's death result from the normal dangers of operations like that?"

Ray was momentarily stunned by Street's solid grasp of the situation. He had obviously studied the journal carefully and had done some impressive reading between the lines.

"Those operations, especially night ops, are always dangerous," Ray answered cautiously. "Even with night-vision gear, it's hard to read your surroundings. Lots of mistakes are made at night."

"Were any mistakes made that night?"

"I can't really answer that," Ray replied. "Mistakes are not uncommon." He paused then took a chance on Street. "Just between us, right?"

"Absolutely," relied Street. "Just between us."

"Truth is that Tate, his code name was Tiger, suspected the op as being bogus from the beginning. I'm not saying it was. I'm just saying that the LT talked to me about it, you know, made a few guesses, voiced his hunch. One of our guys had gotten into trouble."

"Bandit," Street supplied a name.

Ray nodded. "Yeah, Bandit. He couldn't stay away from the women. In Afghanistan, that's death. I mean literally, *death*. A GI gets caught with an Afghani girl, it's curtains for him, curtains for her. The GI goes missing. He's listed AWOL or MIA. His body is found later in a wadi or not at all. The girl is stoned or beaten or her throat is cut by her own people. It's *death*. Every GI knows that.

"But an ODA, an A-team, has a very sensitive balance. It's just twelve warriors alone in a hostile world. We were a long way, both geographically and psychologically, from any friendlies. We had to hang together, to use the old phrase. It all rested on the shoulders of the commander. Tiger knew that. He knew how to do that. When there was a rift in the team, he took it on personally. Whatever had to be done, that's what he did.

"When we first heard about Bandit and a local girl, it came through an interpreter. The interpreter warned us that Bandit had been seen. Word spread like wildfire in the villages. The elders who had previously warmed to us suddenly turned cold. Tiger had to go out and mend fences. He gave them his personal assurance that the offender would be punished and that it would never happen again—word was that it was just a little touching, and I don't know what happened to the girl.

"There was a lot of heat on the team. Everybody's life was on the line, and we all knew it. In the absence of a strong leader, the team would have disciplined its own. Bandit probably would have had an 'accident.' Might never have walked again. For sure, he would never have procreated. But Tiger was in charge, always in charge. It was up to him to accomplish the mission and bring every man back alive. So Tiger and Bandit went out behind the woodshed, if you know what I mean. Bandit was tough, but Tiger was tougher. When they came back in, harmony was restored.

"But the local governor still got his pound of flesh. We got into a firefight. Our local sidekicks melted. We were left to take the heat. Four members of our ODA were killed. The one guy who should have been killed wasn't. Tiger was wounded. Things went on for four months, an uneasy truce inside the ODA, treachery outside. But then we got word through the interpreter of Bandit's second infraction . . . The second time around, the girl involved was the daughter of a relative of Jowzjan's. Worst thing that could have happened.

"We'd already had four deaths on the team. Tiger had been wounded and away from the ODA for six weeks, eight weeks, something like that. When he returned, he was weakened physically. He should have gone back to the States, but that wasn't him. He would have stayed if he saw with one eye and walked on one toe.

"Word was that Bandit had gone all the way with the girl. The district was in an uproar. There we were surrounded by enemies who had always been our enemies and by enemies who should have been our friends. From that time on, we didn't have any friends. There were only twelve of us, and we were a long way from home.

"Unity in the team tanked. Some of the guys wanted to kill Bandit and hang his head up where everybody could see it. We could have blamed it on the hardcores. It would have saved our bacon."

Lindquist was speaking very quietly, not that he was afraid of being overheard but because as he related this story to Street, he was back there again, struggling with resentment and with fear. He shuddered. He was so glad to be home. He never wanted to go back. Just talking to Street, he could taste venom in his mouth.

"I can't blame it on everybody else. I volunteered to pull the trigger and do the cutting. There was never any love lost between me and Bandit anyway. Nobody liked him. Nobody trusted him. I still fight with myself over Tiger's decision.

"'I don't want to hear any talk of turning one of our guys over,' Tiger told us. 'We're in this together, to the end. I mean that. To the end!' He looked every member of the team in the eyes, including Bandit, and said, 'No matter what you do. No matter what happens to us, we're a team. We came together. We go home together. We never leave a man behind. Never have, never will. No matter what the cost. Are we all clear on that?' I admit, when Tiger talked to us, it put my fears to rest. His confidence was unshakable, and we had confidence in him. Tiger and Bandit went out behind the woodshed again, but this time Tiger couldn't make it stick. He'd been wounded badly. I thought then and still think that Bandit was beyond saving. He was bad to the bone. You know what I mean?"

Street's response was a slow nod of his head.

"Still, life got back to normal for a few days," Ray continued. "I tried to convince Tiger to turn Bandit over to ODC. Throw the stinkin' guy to the wolves. Every neck was on the block. Bandit had his chance to reform, to show us that he put the team first—all of us were doing that—but Tiger couldn't be moved. I still don't know why. It's like he owed something to Bandit. I asked him how he was going to feel if backing Bandit cost him the life of another member of our team. He wouldn't answer, didn't want to think that was possible.

"When the final op order came down, we were acting in support of the ASF. The objective was to flush out known T-bans in a village code-named Raptor Two. We made the rendezvous at 2200 hrs. Tiger met with their commander, the village police, and our interpreter. Our interpreter's code name was Hairpin. He was skinny as a wire and usually squatted when we were waiting or at rest so that he almost bent double. Anyway, after the rendezvous Hairpin told me to watch my back. 'Why?' I asked him. 'Because that's where you'll find the ASF.' I knew then that we were being set up and the ASF would melt.

"I told Tiger. He just nodded. He'd already figured it out. He got on the phone and called ODC. I wasn't there, so I can't be sure, but I think an investigation will show that he talked to Osprey, our CO. I'm betting he asked Osprey to rescind our orders. It happened all the time. If the ground commander smelled something fishy, orders were rescinded to avoid any mass casualties. No individual operation was worth losing an ODA over. But Osprey turned him down. I think Osprey already knew. I think he had made a deal to pacify Jowzjan. All because of our friend Bandit.

"We were supposed to split up, two men with each ASF squad. At the last minute, Tiger changed the game plan. 'Can't divide up that small tonight,' he told the ASF commander. 'We can only work in teams of four.'

"Before we split, Tiger met with me and Windmill, who were the other team leaders. 'If anything smells wrong tonight, get together. Converge on Lantern's position. Forget the ASF. Hold out until we can get to you. We may be on our own this time.' Tiger took Bandit with him. Of course, he'd seen it coming. We'd all seen it coming. We started on one side of the little walled square near the center of the village. All the houses were deserted. Then somebody gave a signal. I mean somebody who wanted us dead. We didn't have a chance.

"When the shooting started, we broke into the closest house and barricaded the door. I sent two men to the roof to cover us from above. They got into a firefight and never came back. Bullets were flying everywhere. We had night vision, so we were taking down the enemy. But judging from the fire patterns, I'm certain that the entire ASF turned on us. I have no doubt they were ordered to exterminate us. Three minutes into the fight, we heard a call from outside. We gave the challenge, got the password, and opened. Tiger, Woodcock, and Runner came in. Runner was badly wounded. So there were five of us, one wounded.

"Tiger set a guard on the stairs. We assigned fields of fire. Orders were to take all the small arms rounds we could. Let them use up their ammo. They usually didn't have a lot. Our mission was to pick off any RPG's. They could destroy us. Beyond that, we had to hold out, until morning if necessary. Tiger had radioed for relief, but neither he nor we believed it would come in time.

"Our attackers poured it on. First they threw all their small arms stuff at us. We were sparse in return fire. Tried to make every round count. They no doubt held off on the big stuff to spare the house if they could.

"I asked Tiger if Bandit had bought the farm. 'No, when the shooting started, and we moved to converge, Bandit ran,' Tiger told me. 'His chances aren't good but probably as good as ours.' We held out for forty-five minutes against fifty guys. In the end, I guess they thought the house was wasted by small arms fire and they might as well finish us off. There's no doubt they were being paid. ASF's don't fight for patriotism. They fight for money.

"One RPG round landed on the far right just under the window and blew that end of the front wall down. That took out Woodcock. Before they came in through the hole, Tiger said to me, 'Ray, if you get back to the house, dig around in my stuff and find my journal. Take it with you, will you?' I said, 'Take it yourself.' Tiger laughed. I still hear that laugh sometimes. He moved to the hole in the wall, told me to keep covering the door. It was only a few minutes after that.

"He went out just the way you would want your brother or best friend to go out. He was a man to the end. Best man I ever met. Best junior commander.

"I took three rounds, one in the neck, one in the knee, one in the thigh. Lost a lot of blood. When the shooting stopped on our end, they came in. Poked everybody to make sure we were all dead. They could see that I was still alive. One of them put a rifle muzzle to my head. I must have fainted; I was losing a lot of blood. I guess they figured they might as well save a bullet.

"Help arrived in the form of a rifle company from the 101st, but by the time they got there, the shooting was over; the ASF were gone. Nobody knew anything."

Rick hadn't moved and hardly blinked while Ray related his story. Ray had to stand and move around. He asked Street if he needed a drink of water. Street declined. Ray walked out of the office and along the wall to the water cooler. When he returned, Street was still in the same position.

Ray sat down and fingered the scar on this neck as he often did. "Your brother was a good man. A fine leader. An able warrior."

Street cleared his throat. "You got the journal." It was a statement, not a question. He had the journal in his hands.

"I got the journal. It was in his personal gear. They sent me home with the body. That was an honorary thing. Actually, I was on a stretcher. But we arrived home at the same time. I had his gear packed up with mine. As I said before, I offered the journal to Nicole. She didn't want it. She was in no mood to talk. I've never had a visit like this with her. I guess that's understandable."

Rick nodded his agreement. "Are you the only one who came home?" he asked.

"No, three of us. Three of twelve." Ray Lindquist closed his eyes and relaxed. He had told the story. That's all he could do.

"What happened to Bandit?" Street asked.

"No idea," answered Ray.

"Is it possible that he made it out?"

"I don't see how. It would have taken a miracle for him to get out of that village alive. He's officially listed as MIA. So if he survived, the army doesn't know about it."

"No way he could have gotten back to the States?" Street asked.

Ray thought about this. "He'd have to get out of the country then halfway around the world without being discovered. I don't think there's any way he could have gotten back."

"You don't happen to have a picture of Bandit, do you?" Street asked.

"Why do you ask?"

"Like I say, this is all new to me. I'm just trying to put the pieces together." After another pause he continued, "I'm interested in the code names. Tate was Tiger, his 18Z was Lantern, and so forth. Seems to me the code names might correspond to the surnames of the team members."

"That's a good guess," replied Ray.

"So if Lantern stood for somebody like Lindquist, then I'm imagining that Bandit corresponded to a surname starting with *B*. Could I be right?"

"The code names and identities of our team members are classified," Ray replied.

Street pulled a manila envelope out of his coat. From the envelope he extracted an eight-by-ten-inch black-and-white photo of five teens standing in front of a younger Ray Lindquist swearing them into the National Guard.

"Recognize any of those boys?" Street asked.

Ray looked at Street with a deeper respect for his intellect. "Of course I recognize them," he answered.

"Would Bandit happen to be in that group?" asked Street.

Ray smiled despite himself. "That would be classified," he answered, handing the photo back to Street.

Chapter 59

Dear Mrs. Jennifer Franklin,

My name is Richard Harrison Street. I have just turned twenty-nine, born on Christmas Day. Mrs. Linda Tate of Salt Lake City gave me your name and address.

Mrs. Tate has shown me a birth certificate for her son Ryan Tate, born on the same day as I was, that shows you as the natural mother under your maiden name, Jennifer Sopel.

The story of my coming to know about you is too long to tell in a letter. I think Mrs. Tate has told you that Ryan and I were identical twin brothers. That would make you my mother.

I don't write to make you feel bad in any way. I hope you're happy and that your life has been good. Mine hasn't been good until lately. But I'm still young, and I think the future is going to be good.

I just have a few questions. If you don't want to answer them, I'll understand.

Question one: Why did you put us up for adoption separately instead of together?

Question two: Do you know which one of us was born first?

Question three: Do you know who adopted me?

Mrs. Tate has told me what she knows about our father. That's enough for me, unless you can tell me his name.

It would be nice to hear from you.

Sincerely,

Rick Street

Chapter 60

DEAR RICK:

I was surprised and thrilled to receive your letter. Thank you for writing. I knew from the last letter I received from Linda Tate that you had finally been found after all these years. I can't tell you what a relief that is to me.

I found Ryan about fifteen years ago. It was so good to know that he was in a wonderful family and doing so well. I also tried to find you. For at least five years, I tried in every way I knew to locate you, but I never could.

You asked me some questions in your letter. You wanted to know why I placed you and your twin for adoption separately. There isn't really a good answer for that.

Please remember that I was only nineteen years old. My parents were kind people. They still live in Salt Lake City. They had a large family of their own. After prayerful consideration, they decided they couldn't raise twin boys in addition to their eight children.

I was the oldest. They urged me to place you for adoption. Our church, the Mormon Church, had an adoption agency. We could have placed you through that and maybe you would have been adopted together, though at the time it seemed unlikely.

But my parents knew of a young couple that were never able to have children and wanted to adopt. So my parents took me to an attorney who arranged that adoption. The attorney also made arrangements for a second family to adopt you. That's how you came to go in separate directions.

I can't tell you whether you were the first or second to be born. The second baby had a dark brown circle about the diameter of a pencil on his chest just to the left of his sternum. The delivering doctor pointed this out to me. It wasn't a hereditary birthmark but a pigment patch that developed for some reason. If you have that mark on your chest, you're the younger boy. If not, you're the firstborn.

Even though I couldn't find you in the 1990s while I was searching, I did find the couple that originally planned to adopt you. Their names were Burt and Karen Nelson. They were a young couple adopting because they were unable to have children. Six months after beginning the process, Karen conceived. They decided they couldn't raise two children the same age, so they terminated the adoption process.

The state placed you in a foster home while attempting to arrange another adoption. I found eleven families who had you in their homes during your first eight years, including the couple who adopted you and gave you the name Street. Then I lost your trail. I'm sorry to report that when I found the Nelsons, they had divorced, and Karen was raising her children alone.

I have grieved for your loss since the day I handed you over to the attorney, and for Ryan only slightly less. Linda wrote me about Ryan's death in Afghanistan. I made a terrible mistake in getting pregnant out of wedlock. And I bungled the adoption. Not a very good report card for a mother, is it?

I'm so pleased to hear that good things are happening to you. If there's any consolation in this, I want you to know that I have prayed for you every day of your life. I still do. Every day! I ask our Heavenly Father to bless you, protect you, and watch over you. I know He loves you.

I have carried with me a burden of guilt that, at times, I can hardly bear. Please forgive me!

My very best wishes to you,
Jennifer Sopel Franklin

Chapter 61

DEAR JENNIFER,

Thank you for your letter. I have read it many times. When I read, I try to imagine your voice.

I have very tender feelings for that nineteen-year-old girl. I'll make you a deal. I'll forgive her if you will. I've been nineteen. It wasn't my best time. But it was better than some others.

I especially thank you for your prayers. I have a picture of Jesus in my living room. I visit with him every day. I consider him a friend. I never thought before that God was watching over me. Now I can see that he is.

Try to be happy when you think of me, and I'll try to make you proud.

Rick

Chapter 62

WHEN RICK MOVED TO THE Komatsu basement, he decided against full-time employment. The crew at Home Deport kept him on as before. He stepped up his efforts in school. By the time spring came to the Wasatch Range, Rick was closing in on the end of another semester.

Miranda had mentioned once or twice her continuing desire to go to law school. Rick's experience with attorneys hadn't been especially good, so he merely tried to act interested when she mentioned the possibility.

He didn't ask Miranda further about the stalker. He didn't dare to. But he thought about it. The more he pondered Ryan's journals and the account provided by Ray Lindquist, the more the picture came into focus and the more driven he was to learn what Danny had to teach. He did so quietly, without further discussion of either the tragedy in Afghanistan or the worrisome presence of a stalker.

Danny was an able teacher. They worked on balance, anticipation, using the opponent's momentum, feints, kicks, jabs, chops, holds, and recovery. Danny's approach was no-nonsense. It didn't matter to Danny how things looked. All that mattered was the outcome.

As semester end approached, the weather warmed and daylight savings time left several hours of pleasant evening to be enjoyed. Meeting in his apartment one week, he asked Miranda if their next appointment could be held across town at Liberty Park.

"We could just walk around the park," Rick entreated. "I promise not to put the moves on you."

Miranda laughed. Her dark eyes caught the gleam of the setting sun passing through the windows high on the basement wall. Rick had left the apartment radio playing low in the background. An evening romantic music program was underway. Miranda looked so lovely that Rick chose to just watch her for a second.

"The park sounds wonderful," said Miranda. "I would love to go walking. Just give me a little more time."

"Still missing Arturo?" Rick asked, knowing he was straying into forbidden territory.

"No, it's not that," Miranda answered wearily. "I mean, yes, I'm missing him, of course, but that's not the reason for wanting to wait a little longer."

"You're still worried," he said softly.

"Still a little worried."

"I understand. I'll wait."

Miranda must have been listening to the music. She turned and looked at the radio. "Rick, will you dance with me?" she asked.

"Whoa." Rick laughed. "I offended you, and you're trying to get even by embarrassing me."

"No, really. Let's dance."

Rick laughed again, shaking his head. "I don't know how to dance at all," he said. "I'm sorry. I promise I'll learn."

Miranda stood and reached her hand out to him. "I'll show you."

"No, Miranda. Really. I want to. I really do. I'm such a dork at it. I always have been."

"Please." She reached down, taking his hand and tugging him up. "It's like anything else, you just have to learn. It's not hard."

"Easy for you to say," he answered.

With Miranda holding his hand, Rick no longer cared if the dancing turned out to be a disaster. The thrill of putting his hand on the small of her back was to die for. He felt the fire of nervous energy throughout his system.

Miranda moved in close to him. He could feel her breathing, smell her hair, feel the electricity in her skin. He knew he would make a fool of himself, but he had wanted to hold her so many times that he decided to enjoy the moment for as long as it lasted.

"What do I do?"

Miranda laid her head on this shoulder. "Just move to the music," she answered. "Let your feet follow the rhythm."

Rick tried, but it didn't go well. He began to feel the palm of his hand sweating. "Sorry."

"Don't be sorry, Rick. Just hold me."

Rick looked down into her eyes. She was so beautiful and felt so good in his arms. He let loose her hand and put his arms around her. She reached her arms around his neck, her face upturned, her lips only slightly parted.

Rick kissed her, tasting her lips, feasting all his senses, embracing her, loving her until he thought the air would explode from his lungs.

Gasping for air, he said as casually as he could, "So that's what dancing's all about."

"I think that's it," she replied. She kissed him again.

Rick Street was transported to a new place. A place he had never been before. A place he never wanted to leave.

Chapter 63

AT SEMESTER'S END, RICK BUMPED into Father John in the student center. The priest insisted on buying Rick a hotdog and a soft drink.

"I find that more mature students like you come to education with sharper focus and stronger drive," the priest told him. "You were already a good student when you took my class. Sounds like you've improved since then. Where do you go from here?"

"If I can keep it all together," Rick replied, "I'll wrap things up at school this December. I'll have an associate degree. That probably means nothing to most students. To me, it'll be like standing on the summit of Everest or reaching the moon. This is a big deal to me."

"That is so wonderful." Father John laughed in delight, swinging around on his stool so that the countertop behind served as a seat back. "Rick, I can't tell you how much I admire you."

"Thanks, Father. I feel the same way about you."

Father John laughed again and gave his shoulder a brotherly tap.

"This fall, I plan to apply for admission to the university. That's where my friend will be, the one who's also my case manager." Rick shrugged. "She got her degree in sociology. I think I'll follow her. Couldn't have a better example."

"Right. That's what you should do." Father John nodded. "I'd really like to meet her. Any chance of that?"

Rick shrugged again. "I don't know. She's the boss. I could suggest it."

"You do that," Father John said more seriously. "Sounds to me like she could be more than a professional acquaintance."

"I don't know," Rick replied. "Like I said, she's the boss."

"But you like her, right?"

Rick grinned. "Yeah, Father. I like her."

"Then I've got to meet her. Any friend of yours is a friend of mine." The priest looked at Rick with a playful expression that soon turned serious. "You're not getting any younger," he said. "Any chance she might be the one?"

"Could be," Rick smiled. "I owe her everything. But I can't think seriously about that yet."

"Why not?" asked Father John. "School's important, but it's not *that* important. Neither is Home Depot."

"Yeah," replied Rick with a laugh. "There's not much to my life, is there?"

"There's a lot to your life," said Father John. "And there will be more as time goes on."

"Truth is," said Rick, "I'm still a felon. I'm still on probation until next January. Then I'll be a free man."

"You'll still have a felony conviction on your record, won't you?"

Rick looked at the priest with a suddenly intense expression. "No," he said more forcefully than he intended to. "Unless I mess up, the judge will terminate my probation and expunge both the arrest and conviction from my record. I'll be clean. Then I can . . . offer a woman a life with an honorable man."

"Rick," Father John began with a hint of lecture in his voice, "there are many men who've made mistakes. Some of them very bad mistakes. They've been convicted just like you. But they've also changed. They've overcome. They're not fortunate enough to have their records cleared, but they're still honorable men."

"I understand, Father. No offense intended toward them. But that isn't me. I want to hear that judge say, 'Mr. Street, you've met all the conditions of your probation. You're no longer a convict. You never need to tell anyone again that you are a convicted felon. Go. Live a happy life. Try to forget you were ever in my court.'" Rick searched the priest's eyes as if seeking absolution.

"You're a good man, Rick. It's an honor to be your friend. I've been thinking as we sit here. Do you realize that a year ago you couldn't carry on a conversation like this? You're no better now than you were then, but you're a more capable man now. You've learned some important lessons."

"I've had some great teachers," replied Rick. "Like you."

"You just proved my point." The priest smiled his approval.

Chapter 64

NORTHERN UTAH HAD ENDURED A second heavy winter in a row. The snowpack in the Wasatch Mountains east of Salt Lake City hardly seemed diminished as Memorial Day weekend approached. The streams were swollen and rushing, some thundering. The weekend was unseasonably warm.

Nicole Tate and her six-year-old son, Trevor, dressed for warm weather, loaded the picnic basket, and buckled into Nicole's Toyota Camry, the one Ryan bought for her new before he left on his second and final deployment to Afghanistan. Nicole hadn't put many miles on the car. It was now three years old but in top shape.

Each time she and Trevor got in, she in front, he in his booster seat in the back, she thought about Ryan. She remembered how insistent Ryan was that she have a new car when he left. A car that was totally reliable. He didn't want her to worry about transportation or to find herself stranded or at the mercy of strangers. That was so typical of Ryan. He was not only her friend and lover, he was her protector.

As they had each Memorial Day since her marriage to Ryan, the Tate family was gathering to celebrate the holiday at a grassy picnic area on the river's edge in Provo Canyon. The picnics were always enjoyable, and little Trevor was beside himself with excitement. As they made the drive south from Salt Lake City, he jabbered without pause until he began to tire and finally slumped into a nap. Nicole smiled as she glimpsed him through the rearview mirror.

Trevor was her angel. He was active but never out of control. He knew how to mind. From his earliest days, he was kind. Fun-loving. Curious. Loved to read. Always wanting to draw or color. He seemed a very masculine boy. In all, she felt that his exposure to Ryan, though only for three years or so, had produced the imprint of noble manhood. Of course, like all children, he could be a little poop when he wanted to, self-willed and stubborn, but those moments usually passed quickly and bothered her little.

Of course, being a widow was not easy. The entire responsibility for the home and their lives rested upon her often-weary shoulders. Thankfully, Ryan had left her financially secure.

Bless him for that.

Ryan's entire family came to the picnic except for Grandma Hardy, who asked to be excused because she was feeling under the weather. Lizzie and Michael came late because Lucy had been sick to her stomach. Lucy, the livelier of Lizzie's girls, still looked like she wasn't feeling well. She mostly lay on a blanket and tried to be happy in honor of the holiday.

Nicole was secretly relieved, not because she wanted to see the girl suffer but because without Lucy's rousing influence, Trevor was also more subdued. When they first arrived at the picnic area, Dennis, Linda, and Rick—who had come at the Tates' invitation and had ridden with them—were arranging the tables and setting out the food. Dennis and Rick fired up the charcoal cooker and were readying the meat for cooking.

Trevor went directly to Rick as he did each time they were together. Once again, Nicole marveled that this fast friendship could survive months of separation without any apparent cooling. Trevor generally held back from adults until he knew them well enough to become comfortable. Rick was clearly an exception.

She had to confess that her son and her husband's brother had some kind of chemistry. Secretly, Nicole enjoyed the banter between the two. Trevor seemed more mature when he was around Rick, and Rick seemed to function at about Trevor's level.

I hope he's harmless.

She could see that Rick was always vigilant, as though he knew that she didn't approve. He respectfully reminded Trevor to listen to his mother.

Nicole was especially wary of the river. The water roared down the canyon. There were no fishermen either in the water or on the bank, which was unusual for that area. The waters were somewhat muddy and far too surly for fishing.

Children of other picnickers were at the water's edge, doing what most children seem unable to resist—throwing stones into the moving water. On several occasions, Nicole called to Trevor, commanding him to stand back from the rocks that had been placed along the grassy edge of the picnic area to retard erosion. Older children were standing on the rocks because they afforded good footing. The rushing waters lapped at their feet. Nicole began to wonder where the parents of these other children were.

Feeling a little alarmed, she rose and walked toward the riverbank, intending to bring Trevor back to the table where the others were playing board games.

Like the other children, Trevor was reaching down to the riverbank for rocks and then throwing them as hard as he could. He watched the older children and obviously wanted to give a good account of himself by throwing far.

On one of these throws, he didn't release the rock early enough and actually threw it into the rocks right in front of him. One or two other children who saw his error laughed at him.

Immediately, Trevor turned pink. He looked around to see if any in his own family had seen this mortal blunder. Seeing his mom coming toward him and likely feeling his embarrassment, he quickly stepped forward onto the rocks to pick up the misaimed stone and correct his error. The footing in front of him was uneven and in his eagerness to retrieve the stone, Trevor stumbled forward into the rushing water.

Nicole felt a sudden shock.

Catching her breath, she watched for a second or two to see Trevor's head break the surface of the water where he had fallen. Other children around him began to yell and point. When Trevor's head emerged from the surface of the water, he wasn't anywhere near the point of his fall. He had already moved ten or fifteen feet out into the current and down river.

"Trevor!" Nicole screamed his name.

She willed her feet to move. She rushed toward the shore, scattering the other children, some of whom were looking behind them for help while others ran for a downed branch or something to throw to the boy.

Nicole ran along the bank, screaming Trevor's name. In seconds, she felt more than heard the heavy steps of Dennis Tate passing her as he sped along the grass to the head of the river trail a few yards distant.

In the next instant, a dark form flashed before Nicole's eyes. In bounding strides, Rick Street cleared the riverbank, vaulting as far into the current of the river as his flight would carry him. Trevor's tiny head was many yards ahead, bobbing like a ball in the turbulent waves.

Nicole was choking with emotion.

Trevor's head was out of sight. She didn't know whether he was underwater or had already been swept around the corner of the streambed. Rick was swimming forward, head and arms in and out of the current, moving much faster than Nicole and Dennis, who were now fighting undergrowth and the uneven surface of the river trail.

She couldn't keep pace with Dennis. "Hurry, Dennis. Hurry!" was all she could think to say.

The river was to Nicole's left. At times, the path skirted the water and then ducked into the trees. She had to go where the path led if she was to have any hope of finding a spot where they could reach something that Trevor could hold on to.

Seconds were flying by, and Nicole soon realized that minutes were passing.

How many minutes could a little boy survive in the water? Two? Three? Certainly not more than four or five.

And what if he inhaled water? Nicole couldn't think about that.

Nicole knew how to run. She ran short distance events in high school. But too many years had flown. By the time about two minutes had passed, she had to stop and catch her breath. Dennis was nowhere in sight. She hoped she hadn't passed him anywhere along the bank but didn't think she had.

Hands on her knees, heaving for breath, panic began to grip her. She had to keep moving. Praying silently, she started again, moving at a more moderate pace. At one point, she climbed up the bank onto the shoulder of the highway that ran along the river.

From there she thought she could see Dennis's hat moving along the edge of the river. She ran down the slope again and continued.

Too much time is passing. She had no idea how far she had come, but she knew this wasn't good. *Oh, please, Heavenly Father. Please. Don't take my baby from me. Please!*

Nicole stopped to catch her breath once more. In her mind's eye, she saw the embarrassment on Trevor's face, his earnest effort to save his dignity by picking up that miserable stone and throwing it again. She wanted to cry. She couldn't. She had to keep going.

When Nicole thought her lungs would burst, the path neared the river's edge, passing through a stand of head-high willows on both sides. She couldn't see the water, but she suddenly heard Dennis's voice on the other side of the willows, just out of sight. She halted and pushed her way between the bushes. She saw Dennis first, yelling into his cell phone. Behind him, a crook in the river had created a sandy shoal. On the bank she could see the water-soaked form of Rick Street bent over the still form of her little boy.

"Trevor!" Nicole screamed and started for the pair. She hadn't moved more than a step when she felt Dennis's powerful arm circle her waist, restraining her. She fought to free herself.

"Nicole. Nicole. Please. Stay with me. Leave Rick some room. He's doing everything humanly possible. You don't want to see Trevor like this."

"Let me go," she screamed, trying to hit Dennis in the face. She twisted, trying to break his grasp. "Let me go. *Let me go!*"

"Please, Nicole." Dennis was unmoving, and she was powerless to break free. "Nicole, this is not your time. Your time will come. Please help us."

Michael broke through the willows out of breath and behind him two other men that Nicole didn't recognize.

Nicole stopped struggling, and when she stopped, the barrier of her tears ruptured. "Oh, Dennis," she sobbed, "I can't lose him. Oh, my baby."

She had never felt especially close to Dennis. She'd been scared of him when she dated Ryan as a teen. His gruffness kept her on edge. But on this day, when she stopped struggling, Dennis held her gently to him. She let him hold her. She needed to be held. She put her head on his chest and sobbed.

Nicole sobbed for her baby.

She sobbed for her fears.

She sobbed for her lost love and for a life that was fortunate but not at all what she'd dreamed.

She sobbed without restraint, letting her hot tears spill on the chest of her late husband's father, who, with all his failings, was kind enough to receive them.

"He's going to be okay, Nicole. It's going to work out. Rick is doing everything possible, and help is on the way."

Through her tears, Nicole turned to look to the spot where Rick still knelt over Trevor. He was doing CPR, rhythmically compressing the boy's chest and then breathing into his mouth, watching for the vital chest rise.

Others were arriving. Linda's arms enclosed Nicole, still in Dennis's embrace. All stood at a distance except for two unfamiliar men, who knelt in the sand helping Rick. No one spoke. The only sound was the rushing river and the occasional swish of passing traffic on the highway above.

Rick sat back on his heels. He looked at one of the men near him and shook his head. His arms dropped to his sides, and his chin went down on his chest. Nicole's heart stopped.

Then, as if on impulse, Rick stood. He reached down and picked Trevor up in his arms. Letting the boys head drop down, Rick held him by his knees so that he was fully upside down. Water poured from Trevor's clothing and possibly from his stomach and airway. Rick bounced him and struck him on the back several times. More debris rushed from Trevor's mouth. Laying the boy gently on the sand again, Rick knelt once more and resumed his resuscitation.

Rick's body blocked Nicole's view of Trevor. In her continued sorrow and fear, she wept and let Linda and Dennis console her.

She then noticed two of the men kneeling by Rick nodding and talking to one another. One of them turned to the bystanders and gave a hopeful nod, a thumbs up. A muted excitement rippled through the little gathering.

Then on a shift of the canyon breeze, Nicole heard a siren down the canyon. Her hopes began to revive.

"Can you see any movement?" she asked Linda.

"No, dear. And I can't hear what they're saying."

"He's alive," called one of the men at Rick's side. "He just took a breath. At least, part of one."

A cheer went up from the onlookers. People began breathing again. Nicole could hear bits of several conversations.

Rick stood again. His head was down, his shoulders slumped, his fatigue apparent. This time, he rolled Trevor over and hoisted the boy by his waistband onto his hands and knees. Trevor's little head moved up and down as mighty coughs racked his tiny frame between violent breaths. With each cough, he expelled water and heaved the contents of his stomach.

Nicole now felt a rush of excitement. Still anxious to see if Trevor would be well, she nevertheless could hear herself calling to anyone and no one. "He's alive. He's alive. Oh, thank you. Thank you!"

An ambulance approached but seemed forever in arriving. The lights flashed above them on the highway's edge at the top of an embankment. As soon as it pulled to a halt, the crew unloaded a stretcher and started down the slope toward the river. The guide who had stood on the road to flag down the ambulance was flashing his uplifted thumb.

"Let's climb up to the ambulance," Dennis suggested.

Nicole followed. Looking back repeatedly, her eyes were drawn to Rick Street. Each time she looked, she saw Ryan.

They are so alike.

She helped Linda to the top, where they waited until Trevor, piled high with blankets and wearing an oxygen mask, was at last rushed past her into the ambulance. She gave her car keys to Dennis with her thanks and a huge kiss on the cheek.

Dennis blushed a dozen shades of red.

Nicole climbed into the ambulance with her baby.

Chapter 65

Rick Street didn't think too much about his role in saving Trevor's life. What he had done was his natural reaction to the crisis at hand. The event made the evening news, and Rick became the victim of a few days of unsought celebrity at work and at Primary Children's Medical Center, where Trevor was being treated.

Springtime drownings were not uncommon along Utah's Wasatch Front. Numerous snowmelt-swollen streams plunged past mountain recreation areas. Residents, tired of winter weather and eager for a summer retreat, flocked to those areas around Memorial Day, the season's first opportunity. Those friendly streams that children loved to wade in, to throw stones into, to float sticks and cups in later in the summer could be murderous during runoff.

The Tate family's near tragedy occasioned the usual Monday morning quarterbacking among media people and rescue workers.

"It's better to reach or throw than to go," ran the conventional advice about rescuing potential drowning victims.

Rick remained aloof from the discussion. The tiny boy had been in the water alone struggling to keep his head above the raging current—struggling for his life. Chances of rescue from the shore were uncertain. What Trevor needed was someone to lift him above the surface and, if possible, to drag him to shore. Of course, a second person in the river was also in danger of drowning. That's the way raging rivers are. But somebody had to take the risk. Rick had chosen himself for that role. He hadn't drowned. Trevor hadn't drowned. It worked out about as well as it could.

What else is there to talk about?

Rick shied away from media interviews. He stuck to his course. With Trevor safe and recovering, his mind returned immediately to the mystery that consumed him.

Could a soldier who fled from his comrades in Afghanistan return to the States without being detected? Could he go MIA and not be sought by the military? Wouldn't that be the perfect time?

What would he need to pull it off? Money? A change of appearance? Some ability with Arabic?

And why would he want to do it? Maybe because he had caused the death of his commander and comrades? Maybe because he was trying to save his own skin? Maybe because he had unfinished business at home?

And how could he remain invisible once home? He couldn't announce himself, couldn't have a coming-home party. In fact, he couldn't make contact with family, friends, or his employer. Doing so would immediately signal the authorities that he was not MIA but AWOL—a deserter.

He'd need a place to hide out. A place where people are lost and willingly forgotten. A place where fingerprints weren't taken, IDs weren't checked, drug tests weren't performed, and tax returns weren't filed.

The street.

That's where people go to disappear.

Rick knew this much. If Tim Barton was Bandit, he was in trouble. He'd caused the deaths of at least a half dozen of his comrades. Ray Lindquist and two other soldiers had survived the massacre and could testify against Barton. If Barton had been killed, his body mutilated or hidden, that was the end of the matter. Then he was MIA as officially reported. His case might be solved later if the body were discovered.

If Barton wasn't killed and didn't come home from the deployment with his unit, he must still be in Afghanistan or one of the neighboring nations, or he must have successfully made his way back to the States. Rick could only imagine the ways a person could accomplish that. But it didn't seem impossible to Rick.

Rick knew little about international travel, but of one thing he was certain, false papers were available to anyone with money.

Rick reached the conclusion that Barton could be dead—if so, good riddance. Or he could be alive. If he were alive, he could be back in Salt Lake City living on the street or mingling with street people.

This mystery intrigued Rick. He couldn't stop thinking about it.

Back in school for the summer semester, he'd chosen an entry-level course in Criminal Justice to fill one of his elective credits. The class fueled his preoccupation with the mystery. He wasn't sure why he should be interested in what had happened, except that every time he saw Nicole and Trevor, his internal sense of rage became aroused. They had been wronged. Their lives had, in some measure, been blighted by an injustice that occurred halfway around the world when their husband and father had been wrongfully taken from them.

Rick had also been injured by this wicked act. His twin, whom he'd never known and could now know only through secondhand accounts, had been taken from him. Linda and Dennis had been wronged. So had Lizzie. Jennifer Sopel was wronged. He didn't even want to think about the wrongs and heartbreak endured by Barton's unfortunate parents.

Is Tub Barton alive? Is he hiding in the street community?

I have to know.

Chapter 66

RICK VISITED THE HOSPITAL EACH day Trevor was there. On the first day, he approached Trevor's room, passing hand-painted murals on the walls and a waiting area supplied with toys.

He moved with a little difficulty.

His swim the day before had left him with three broken ribs, the result of a collision with one of the submerged boulders in the rushing stream. A gash in his thigh had been sewn, and several deep abrasions were bandaged by the doctor to prevent infection. There were not many spots on his body that hadn't been bruised.

Rick had tried to wave away medical attention when he returned from the river with the Tates. He didn't have much by way of medical insurance and didn't want to deplete his growing savings account by fixing things that would heal on their own anyway.

Dennis had insisted he would cover any costs, saying he would consider it the height of ingratitude for the family to neglect Rick's injuries when he had just saved the life of a grandchild. That kind of talk made Rick uncomfortable. He acquiesced just to move the focus away from himself.

Trevor was in a room with another child. A curtain had been drawn down the center of the room as a temporary partition. Nicole sat alone with Trevor, who was awake but had been medicated. The boy didn't show his normal level of alertness.

Rick knocked quietly on the door with one knuckle. Nicole smiled somewhat deliberately and stood, signaling Rick to enter. Trevor's gaze followed Rick into the room, but there was little sign of recognition. The child obviously felt sick and miserable.

"How's he doing?" Rick asked, standing at the foot of the bed. Nicole approached Rick, the first time she had ever been welcoming in any degree.

"He's not feeling well. They've sedated him. He just woke up." She then turned to Trevor. "Sweetie, do you want to say hi to Rick?"

Trevor just looked at her and then back at Rick.

"Is he going to be okay?" Rick asked.

"They worked on him in the ER in Provo last night, trying to get his core temperature back up to normal. The water was so cold. The doctor there told me that in children this young, the body sometimes shuts down circulation to the hands and feet and shunts it to the brain and vital organs. They think that may have helped prevent any brain damage, but it increases the risk of nerve damage in the extremities."

Nicole was pale. She looked drawn. She had obviously been with Trevor all night. She wasn't wearing any makeup, and her hair had been brushed hurriedly. Rick could tell she was aware of and uncomfortable with her appearance. She kept smoothing the back of her hair with a hand and often touched her face with her hands.

He considered her without letting his gaze alight on her in any way that would increase her discomfort. Even in this roughest of states, Nicole was still a beautiful woman. And she was obviously a woman who loved her child more than herself.

"I had never thought about what happens when a child almost drowns," said Nicole. She took care to explain what she had learned to Rick, maybe because it was constantly on her mind or maybe because it was something impersonal she could focus on with a man she felt indebted to but didn't really like.

But this was no time to sort out relationship issues.

"The ER doc told me that the lungs are lined with a fluid called surfactant," Nicole explained. "It's a coating that bathes and maintains the inside of the lungs. When that gets washed away by water in the lungs, the victim can suffer pulmonary edema, a buildup of fluid in the lung tissues. That's what has happened to Trev. He's suffering from ARDS, acute respiratory distress syndrome. If you listen closely, you can hear how badly he's wheezing. They want him to stay that way for a day or two." Nicole laughed self-consciously. "I sound like a medical encyclopedia, don't I?"

"You're doing great," Rick replied. "Trevor's a lucky boy to have a mom who loves him so much."

Nicole seemed to be working to keep her emotions in check, but she started to weep. She reached beside her on the tray table for a tissue.

Rick felt for her. His normal impulse was to put an arm around her, providing emotional support, but he didn't dare do that with Nicole.

Without looking at Rick, Nicole moved closer to him until they were touching. Rick took that as a signal that he might risk putting his arm around her shoulder. When he did so, she leaned into him, laying her head against him. Rick reached around cautiously with his other arm until his embrace encircled her. The movement made the ribs on the right side of his body scream. For a second, he felt faint. But he successfully stifled a yelp.

A few moments later, Nicole dropped her hands from her face and put them around Rick's waist, embracing him—hard. Rick's eyes practically rolled back into his head. Beads of sweat broke out on his forehead. The room started to swim in his vision.

"Rick," Nicole cried, "I'm so sorry. I am so sorry! I have treated you terribly. Please forgive me. I'm just a stupid, silly girl. I let my own fears blind me to the good in other people. Thank you. Thank you for saving my baby."

Nicole turned her face up and loosened her embrace slightly.

Rick felt his ribs move in his chest, grinding against one another. The doctor had left the ribs unbandaged, saying that there was little he could do for ribs and encouraging Rick to be as gentle with them as he could. He warned Rick that he would feel movement until the bone ends started to knit. Rick had hardly noticed the ribs while doing CPR on the riverbank the day before. He could tell he was injured but was pumped with adrenalin. Now he was beginning to understand what the doctor's warning meant.

Rick wanted to say something that would comfort Nicole. He couldn't think of anything that would sound good. "You haven't treated me badly," he attempted. "I understand that a mom watching out for her child can be protective around strangers. Especially when those strangers are criminal and homeless people. Not a good combination for inspiring confidence," he added.

Nicole cried harder and tightened her grip around Rick's chest again.

Ow! That was the wrong thing to say.

"Oh, dear. I'm losing it." Nicole sniffled. But she didn't move away from Rick. That made him a bit uncomfortable, but he didn't feel it was his place to initiate any moves with Nicole at this point, either together or apart.

Nicole put her hands on his chest and looked up into his eyes. Rick now realized that Nicole was not a bashful, self-doubting woman. And he could see how she might be irresistible. After all, she was beautiful, able, intelligent, and without doubt, a really good person.

Who wouldn't want such a partner?

"I know this isn't fair to you," Nicole said to him.

Rick swallowed hard. Having survived a pain-induced fainting spell, he was about to succumb to an intimacy-induced fainting spell.

"When I saw you leap into the river without a thought for your own safety to save Trevor's life, I was seeing his father. You did . . ." Her voice caught in her throat, followed by a sob. "You did exactly what Ryan would have done. It's not a matter of measuring up to Ryan. You were as much like Ryan as Ryan could be. I knew at that moment, when I saw you on the riverbank, that no matter what road you took to get where you are, you're as good a man as your brother." Nicole broke into sobbing once more.

Rick held her silently until she began to calm.

"That's the highest praise I could give to any man," she whispered.

Rick nodded, drawing Nicole into his embrace—actually into half of his embrace. His right side wasn't up to embracing at the moment. "I understand," he said softly. "I'm sorry Ryan's gone, Nicole, for your sake and for Trevor's. I wish I could have known him."

Their visit was soon interrupted by medical attention to Trevor, but the rest of the visit was more comfortable for Rick. A wall had been breached, a barrier removed. Though he'd known Nicole for less than a year, and not well, they increasingly visited as though their friendship was from old times. He admired Nicole for her willingness to put aside the prejudices that had troubled her so deeply, to treat a man she had originally considered a homeless criminal as though he were a friend.

Chapter 67

"RICK, CAN YOU AFFORD TO get a cell phone?" asked Miranda. "I heard the news last night, and I was so worried about you. I tried to call the house, but the Komatsus are away. You didn't answer. I almost drove over last night to find out if you were okay. It would really help me if I could reach you anytime."

"I've never had one," Rick replied with a grin. "But you're right. I'll get one for you."

Rick told Miranda about the visit he'd just had with Nicole Tate. "She's been wicked cold toward me. Then suddenly, she really warms up. I know she's been through the wringer emotionally, but I was pretty amazed that she could flip positions so completely," he said. "That takes a lot of emotional strength."

Instead of marveling with him, Miranda stiffened. Rick wasn't so naïve in his understanding of women or romance that he couldn't see a little jealousy showing through Miranda's reactions. It pleased him, but he was also surprised. After all, Miranda had openly dated Arturo Diaz. Rick didn't think he'd shown any jealousy at that relationship.

When he told Miranda he planned to visit the hospital the next day, she stiffened more.

"Please be careful," Miranda said.

"Be careful?" asked Rick. "It's a hospital. The worst thing that could happen would be slipping on a bar of soap. And then help wouldn't be very far away."

Miranda nodded. "Please be careful."

Chapter 68

THE NEXT AFTERNOON, RICK FOUND both Linda and Lizzie in Trevor's hospital room. They hugged him warmly. His ribs couldn't take much more affection.

He reached his hand out to Nicole, who stood beside the boy's bed. Instead of shaking it, she put it to her cheek and said hello.

Trevor was sitting up in bed, still appearing lethargic and with a tube in his wrist.

"Hi, Rick," he said weakly. "Look what Grandma brought me."

Grandma turned out to be Grandma Underwood, Nicole's mother, who had visited earlier in the day. Grandma Underwood had given Trevor an action figure. Despite Trevor's nasty cough, the superhero performed some pretty amazing feats.

"Pretty cool," said Rick. "You look like you're feeling a little better."

"His pediatrician is satisfied with his progress," said Nicole. "She was afraid of nerve damage, but the tests are encouraging, and there's no real indication of ischemia. He has some numbness in his feet, but she thinks that may be the result of bumping and bruising and should heal in a week or so. Otherwise, it's just scrapes and bruises. He's lucky there weren't any broken bones. Thanks to you, he's going to get well and whole."

"He's a tough little guy, aren't you, tiger?" Rick's use of *tiger* related unintentionally to Ryan's code name in Afghanistan. Rick looked around at the women to see if any of them recognized this connection. The conversation continued without interruption, meaning that no one else, including Nicole, knew much about what had happened in Afghanistan. In all likelihood, Rick alone knew the true story of Ryan's death.

After standing against a wall listening to the women visit for a while, Rick noticed Nicole looking at him. He smiled in return. Nicole stood and stretched.

"Linda," she said, "could you stay with Trev for a while if Rick and I go for a walk? I really need to stretch my legs."

"Sure, dear," replied Linda. "You two go ahead."

"Do you mind?" Nicole asked as she passed Rick on her way to the door.

The west entrance to Primary Children's Medical Center opened to a parking area and the Trax light-rail station. Nicole led Rick to the sidewalk heading south until they crossed the memorial suspension bridge constructed for the 2002 Salt Lake City Winter Olympics. This put them on the University of Utah campus, where they could stroll along grassy, tree-lined walks and parks. It was late afternoon, but there were still several hours of daylight ahead.

Nicole talked almost constantly. She wasn't at all reluctant to speak of personal matters that involved the family, her relationship with Ryan, or her hopes for Trevor. Rick was getting to know her better by the minute.

He discovered that Nicole had a refreshing sense of humor. She was lively and enthusiastic. But she also confessed her terrible loneliness since Ryan's death.

"It's tough being lonely, isn't it?" Rick said, trying to acknowledge her feelings.

Nicole looked at him intently and finally stopped walking. They stood under a tree that shaded them from the hot rays of the late-afternoon sun. Nicole moved near to Rick but didn't touch him. Her arms were folded across her chest.

"Ryan was a strong man," she said. "I mean physically strong. He didn't have an ounce of fat on him. He protected us. I always felt safe when Ryan was home. He was also strong in character," she said, looking off down the campus. "He was constant. He could be trusted completely. I think he was the kind of man every woman wants." She sighed. "The only rough edge was that he tended to be tough when I wanted tender."

They resumed their walk. Nicole kept talking. "He wasn't always that way. When we were high school sweethearts, Ryan was a star athlete, a top student, the guy every girl wanted—with a great personality and a killer body—but he was also full of fun. He pulled April Fool's pranks on his mom; he wrestled with Lizzie on the front room floor; he had a whacky nickname for everybody in school, including himself. He once carried me piggyback onto the stage at a school assembly. He joked with the teachers. He loved goofy movies."

Nicole turned to Rick and looked at him earnestly. "Is this more than you want to know, Rick? Shall I stop?"

"Not at all," he answered. "Thanks for sharing. This is exactly what I want to hear."

"You'll have to take the bad with the good." She looked into his eyes questioningly.

"Keep going," said Rick.

"I want to tell you something very personal," said Nicole. "Ryan knew, but I couldn't tell anyone else."

She paused. "Could we sit down over there?" she asked.

The pair crossed to an adjacent sidewalk with a shaded bench.

"I don't expect you to do anything about this, Rick. I don't want you to try. I just need to tell somebody. I can't carry it alone. It wears on me, grinds me down." She sighed again. "I'm being watched by somebody. Always. I don't know who. I don't know why. I don't encourage attention from men. I can never relax. I'm afraid—for me, for Trevor. I lock my doors. I pull the curtains. Half the nights I can't sleep because I'm listening for an intruder."

Nicole looked off into the distance. Her face showed her weariness.

Rick felt suddenly alert. Miranda's stalker came immediately to mind. "You *feel* you're being watched, or you *know* you are?"

"I know I am."

"How?"

Nicole moaned. "Sometimes I get notes. They're on my car or in the mailbox. Once even in a milk bottle. Sometimes it's a phone call. One night last week, I was getting ready for bed"—she shuddered—"I heard a scratching on my bedroom window screen. I thought maybe it was a cat or a tree branch."

"And?" asked Rick.

"Well, there's no tree outside the window. There's no sill where a cat could sit. I heard it three times. I finally got up the nerve to open the blind. I saw a man—at least his shadow—moving away in the dark. I was scared to death. I went in and sat with Trevor until I fell asleep at the foot of his bed."

Nicole's smile pleaded for understanding. "It wasn't a good night for me."

"No. Of course it wasn't," said Rick. "I'm sorry. How long has this been going on?"

"Forever," Nicole said with a nervous laugh. "Since I was in high school. I knew who it was in those days."

"Can you tell me?" asked Rick.

"His name was Tim Barton," replied Nicole. "He was our age. I think you met his parents at Dennis and Linda's last Labor Day get-together."

"I did," answered Rick. "I know who you're talking about."

"When I started dating Ryan in high school, I told him about it. He talked to Tim. I think they actually fought. I thought it was so cool to have boys fighting over me. When Ryan served his mission in Canada, I worked in Connecticut as a nanny to the family of an FBI senior executive. I felt really safe. Through all our years at the university, it wasn't that bad—because of Ryan. But it was always there. Then Ryan went away to military school. It got worse—much worse. I can't even tell you how bad." Nicole's face was blank. Her eyes stared into the distance. She talked absently, like Rick wasn't even there.

"Nicole, are you okay?" he asked her.

She nodded numbly. "If a woman in a living hell can be okay, then I'm okay."

"I'm so sorry." Rick reached over and took her hand. "Keep talking. Tell me about it. What's happened since?"

Nicole was obviously deciding how much she wanted to say. "When Ryan went to Afghanistan on his first deployment, I was free for fifteen months. I missed Ryan terribly, but I was free of Tim because he was in Ryan's outfit. When they came home, it started again. I stayed with Ryan every minute I could. Then they went back to Afghanistan. It stopped again."

She let out a mirthless laugh. "You'd think after all these years I'd have gotten used to it and not paid any attention. But that's impossible. After Ryan was killed . . ." Nicole stopped and shook her head, unable to continue.

"Let me guess," Rick said. "It started again."

Nicole put her hands to her face.

"You were surprised," said Rick, "because you were told that Tim Barton had been killed in Afghanistan. You thought you were rid of him forever, so when it started again, you thought somebody else must be watching you."

Nicole barely nodded in confirmation.

"I'm guessing it wasn't too long after it started again that I came on the scene. It was so hard to believe that Ryan had a twin that you wondered if I was the person watching you, maybe someone who had just made himself look like Ryan."

Nicole was silent. Her eyes dropped to the grass. "It's true," she said. "You're right."

They sat silently.

Nicole was first to speak. "But when you jumped into that river to save a helpless little boy, I knew it wasn't you," she said. "A man who stalks a woman, who preys on her fears, isn't a man at all. He's a coward."

She looked at Rick. "And you're not a coward, Rick. I'm sorry I misjudged you."

"Don't blame yourself." Rick squeezed her hand. "I understand. I think any woman could do the same. We've got to get you some help with this."

"No!" Nicole cried. "Rick, please promise me that you won't tell anyone."

"Why, Nicole? How can you live like this?"

"I'll do anything to protect Trevor," she said, her eyes tearing. "No matter what happens, I don't want Trevor labeled. I don't want his life smudged by this. You've got to promise me. I'm only telling you because I need somebody to know. Somebody I can trust. And I feel like I can trust you."

Rick slid close to Nicole and put an arm around her shoulder, still holding her hand. "You *can* trust me. I'm going to find a way to stop this."

"Rick, promise me you won't make this public in any way. Please, promise me."

"I promise," said Rick.

Chapter 69

RICK AND NICOLE CONTINUED TO walk. She was less talkative, probably lost in reflections on her past.

They reached the Huntsman Center, having already walked quite a distance. They decided to slip into the air-conditioned building and find a secluded place to sit where they could talk for a few more minutes.

"Rick, I've dumped all my problems on you," said Nicole. "I hope you don't hate me."

"You know I don't hate you," he answered.

"I want to tell you more," she said. "The whole story . . . or most of it. We might not get another chance like this, and I need the support, the relief. Is that okay?"

"Of course," said Rick.

"It's not very pretty."

Rick paused. "You be the judge," he said. "Don't hesitate on my account."

"Something happened," Nicole began cautiously, "while Ryan was away doing military training. Before we were married. I'll tell you. I want to. But I have to do it my way. Please don't ask any questions."

"Okay."

"I told you I never liked Tim Barton. The truth is I loathed him. I never trusted him. He wasn't a good person." She was speaking barely above a whisper.

"When we graduated from the U and Ryan left for months at a time, Tim came back into my life. I tried to keep away from him. He was unbelievably persistent. Maddeningly! Finally, trying to appease him, I agreed to a date. It was just a walk downtown to see the Christmas lights."

Nicole's eyes clouded over, and tears began running down her cheeks. She fished a tissue out of her pocket. She couldn't go on. She wept silently and tried to manage the flow of tears. Then she sobbed uncontrollably.

Rick tugged her to him.

In time, she looked up with a sad smile and leaned her head against his neck.

They sat silently. Rick said nothing, asked nothing.

Gradually, Nicole gained control of her emotions. "The night ended in horror," she whispered.

Rick sat quietly, holding his brother's widow as tenderly as he knew how while she related her tearful account—and his anger raged. He had a million questions that he couldn't ask.

When Nicole could stand again, she wanted to resume the walk. "I'm sorry I told you that," she said. "I know there's nothing to be done. It's just that I can't carry the burden alone. Someone has to know. Ryan helped me. He propped me up. And he protected me—protected us. I loved him so much. I miss him more than I can say. Oh, dear. What's the matter with me?" she said, fanning her face with her hand. She looked at Rick, who walked along with his hands in his pockets and his head down. "I'm sorry, Rick. Really I am. You can talk." She laughed finally.

"I don't have anything to say except I'm sorry that happened to you," said Rick. "I only have questions."

"Don't ask me anything about that night," Nicole pled.

"Please go on with the story," said Rick.

"Soon after that night," said Nicole, "Ryan returned on leave from his school. I was utterly shaken. I pressed him to move forward with our marriage plans. I needed him. I needed his support, his protection. He saw how things were, and he agreed. We married a week later in a military wedding. It wasn't the way either of us wanted to get married, but that made it possible for me to go back to Fort Benning with him for the rest of his training. After that, we were never separated except during his two deployments. But the army took that away from me—took *him* away from me and from Trevor. We need him so badly."

The sun was beginning to move toward the horizon. They walked for longer stretches in silence.

"I'm glad I wore my walking shoes." Nicole laughed.

"Looks like we've about made our way back," said Rick.

"I have needed this," said Nicole. "Thank you for listening."

"I'm the one who should say thanks," Rick replied.

They were near the medical center. They sat for a last time.

"I don't want our visit to end," said Nicole.

"I'll be near in the future," said Rick. "Anything else you'd like to tell me?"

"Well, as time passed and Ryan shouldered more responsibilities, the fun gradually faded from our lives," said Nicole softly. "In a measure, the romance did too. Sometimes I felt like I was replaced by another idol in Ryan's life. Not that he was ever unkind to me—that's unthinkable—but as his devotion to the military intensified, his devotion to me seemed to gradually transform from joy to duty. It hurt me. I confessed it to myself but tried to hide it from everybody else.

"It got worse after Ryan's first deployment. I guess it couldn't be helped. Ryan's duty was important to him. He realized what was happening to us, just as I did. I know he tried to reverse the trend. But the more he tried, the more his efforts seemed like just another duty. I asked myself what I could do—where it would lead. I grieved the wilting of my dreams, the death of my prince, long before he was torn from my life."

Rick nodded his understanding. "What kind of father was he?" Rick asked.

"There couldn't be a better father. Trevor worshipped him. No chore, no sacrifice for Trevor was too great for his dad. Ryan would have died for Trevor—in an instant, without hesitation."

She smiled sadly. "He'd have died for me too. The difference was that I didn't want him to die for me. I wanted him to live for me. What hurt me most—and angered me most—was the realization that Ryan chose to sacrifice himself rather than choosing to save himself for me."

Chapter 70

RICK'S RIBS HEALED SLOWLY. As soon as he could, he began working out again with Danny Komatsu. Danny exhibited more intensity as time passed. Five weeks after Trevor's near drowning, Danny introduced what he called naked-knife practice. In these exercises, Danny wielded a real knife, unsheathed and extremely sharp.

During the first few sessions, Rick focused his emotional energies almost solely on the effort to cope with his long-held fear of knives. On several occasions, the wicked blades cut him as he tried to disarm Danny. The cuts were mostly superficial, but dressing and redressing his wounds kept Rick constantly aware of the danger. Gradually, he was able to turn his attention away from his fears to solving the problem of how to take the knife away.

"You're getting good at this, Rick," Danny told him one summer evening as they battled in Danny's secluded backyard. "I don't think anybody's born a fighter. Those who fight well have learned the art. You've learned much. You fight with purpose, like you're preparing to face a real attacker. Is that so?"

"I don't know him," replied Rick, "but I know a lot about him."

"I see," said Danny. "You've taken the knife very seriously. Is the knife your adversary's weapon of choice?"

"I think so," replied Rick. "I've seen him use it before."

"Did he use it well?"

"I don't know," answered Rick. "His opponent was unarmed and helpless."

"Hmmm," Danny thought about this for a moment. "Then I think you'll have an advantage. The best weapon one can bring to a fight is a pure soul. It sounds like your opponent will come unarmed in that respect."

"I think he will." Rick nodded.

"Is he trained?" asked Danny.

"Former military. Green Beret."

"That tells me much. Is he a warrior?"

"He's been to Afghanistan twice," Rick answered. "But he ran and left his comrades in a fight to the death."

"Did you have a special interest in any of those who were killed?"

"A brother," said Rick solemnly.

"I'm beginning to see the picture." Danny nodded. "I'm sure you know already that revenge is a poor ally in combat. Emotion exacts a price. If two men come to combat, one with an empty soul, the other filled with righteous indignation, I would bet the outcome on the lesser man because the greater man carries too much baggage."

Rick was listening carefully, first because he had come to trust Danny's judgment, and secondly because he had discovered the same to be true through his own sad experience. He knew that the best man doesn't always win, but the best-prepared man usually does.

Danny wanted to talk more about Rick's adversary. "I'm surprised that you're envisioning combat with this ex-soldier instead of the man who has made Miranda's life miserable. I thought we were preparing you to meet him." Danny's voice had grown gruff. His visage assumed that thunderous quality for which he was widely known. "Perhaps Miranda isn't as important to you as you are to her," said Danny without looking at Rick.

Rick weighed this information. "She's important to me, all right. But I'm sometimes confused by what's important to Miranda," replied Rick. "Sometimes I think she likes me. Other times I can feel her pushing me away."

"And you think she pushes you away because she doesn't like you?"

"Is there another explanation?" asked Rick.

"Perhaps because she's trying to protect you, to keep you from wandering into harm's way."

"Protect me?" asked Rick. "From who?"

"Dunno. My thinking has been to slow down Miranda's adversary. Sounds like you've got somebody else in mind. Getting a little confusing."

"Yeah. Sorry." Rick scratched the short hair on the back of his neck. "But not so confusing if they're the same guy."

Chapter 71

MIRANDA SAT IN THE OFFICE of Lieutenant Taylor once again. Taylor was showing signs of fatigue. The job was aging him. The two detective teams who had been working with Miranda's case were also present, Detective Warner sitting, the other three standing in various poses around the office.

"Your perp's note didn't produce," said Warner. "The phrasing is similar, but the handwriting isn't the same. No prints on either note. There was a spot on the note that our lab has identified as saliva. Possibly the writer drooled a little or was talking and spit a small drop. We can possibly get some DNA, but at this point we have nothing to match it against."

"Was there any match with DNA from Art's murder?" asked Miranda.

"Nothing yet," replied the lieutenant, rubbing his tired eyes. "The prosecutors say the note could establish a link between the Diaz murder and your stalker, if we had the stalker's DNA. We know that the street murders had similar MOs, but each was committed with a different weapon. We've got to have a viable suspect before we can link all the killings. If this is a serial killer, the guy's been very thorough. But as I said before, he'll make a mistake somewhere; then we'll get him."

"I've been thinking," said Miranda. "Suppose our killer gets a different person to write each of his notes."

"We've thought of that," replied Taylor. "All of the handwriting samples look to be female. And they're flawless—no cross-outs, no misspellings, no other mistakes. We think he writes the notes out in advance and gets women to copy what he puts in front of them."

"How many notes do you have?" asked Miranda.

"Handwriting from at least eight different people."

"That's a lot of witnesses or accomplices," said Detective Patton, Warner's partner. "No guy can keep that many women happy. Sooner or later, somebody will sour and come forward."

"If they're still alive," muttered Warner.

"Have you interviewed all the women who were in the batch you took from that suspect last winter?" Miranda asked.

"We have," replied Warner.

"What do they have in common?" she asked.

"We haven't discovered a pattern yet," Warner replied. "First of all, they're scattered over three Western states. Two of them are missing without a trace. Interestingly, three deny having been approached by a stalker. Either they were just being developed as targets, or they're afraid to admit they were stalked. Women will do that. If they don't perceive the risk of violence to be high, many will just hope that it passes."

"Can I see the names again?" asked Miranda.

Taylor handed her a list. She read them slowly, trying to find a connection she might have with any. About four down from the top, she spied the name Nicole Tate. She had seen Nicole's name on the list when the materials were first discovered, but that was before Rick and Nicole had grown close. Now the name jumped off the page at her.

"I see one connection," Miranda told Taylor, holding up the list and pointing at Nicole's name. "There is a connection between me and Nicole Tate."

All of the detectives in the room were alert to this new piece of information.

"What's the connection?" asked Taylor.

"We're connected through a pair of brothers."

"You're dating a guy named Tate?" asked Warner.

"Not dating," replied Miranda. "And not Tate. My client, Rick Street."

"Your client, named Street, is a brother to another guy named Tate?" asked one of the junior partners.

"Long story," replied Miranda. "What did Nicole Tate say when you interviewed her?"

"She denied. No stalking activity. She was surprised by it."

"I don't know many stalkers," replied Miranda, "really just my own, but it seems strange that one of these guys would take all the time to watch a woman and do some detective work on her and then not make contact. The contact is what it's all about, right?"

"Maybe we'd better have another conversation with Mrs. Tate," said Lieutenant Taylor. "Warner, Patton, talk to her again. Ask her if the connection between the brothers or to Miranda rings any chimes."

Chapter 72

RICK AND MIRANDA WALKED SLOWLY from the library building at the college to her car in visitor parking. It was a hot Tuesday evening early in August. Rick was in the last week of another semester.

"If I'm going to go to law school, it has to be now," said Miranda. "I qualified for admission four years ago but decided to put it off for a while to get some real-world experience. I've done that. If I wait any longer, I'll have to retake the LSAT and go through the whole admissions process again. It's now or never."

"So you've made up your mind?" asked Rick.

"I have. I've already given notice to the state."

"What does that mean for us?" he asked.

"You've got less than five months to go on your probation. My boss recommended to the court that we leave things as they stand. The judge agreed. So I'll supervise your probation to the end."

"Won't that be tough while you're going to school?"

"Are you tired of me?" Miranda asked. "Want us to ask the judge to assign another probation officer?"

"Not a chance." Rick smiled.

"Can I ask you a question about Nicole Tate?"

"You can ask," answered Rick, "but I'm not sure I have many answers."

"Has she ever said anything to you about being stalked?"

Rick stopped and turned to Miranda. "Why do you ask?"

"Answering a question with a question is the oldest evasive move in the book," Miranda teased. "I take that to mean she's mentioned it to you."

"I didn't say that," Rick replied.

"Can you deny it?"

"Truth is there are a few things she confided to me that I can't talk about."

"Sounds like a fairly intimate relationship," said Miranda with a little heat in her voice.

"Nothing like that," replied Rick. "But I think you'd understand if a woman is reluctant to talk about being stalked. You won't talk to me about a similar situation in your life."

"Rick, I didn't ask for details. I'm just asking if she's having that kind of trouble."

Rick nodded. He didn't want to let Nicole's revelation become a point of contention between him and Miranda. "I'm sorry. I'd tell you if I could."

Miranda calmed somewhat. "I understand," she said. She looked Rick in the eye. "Don't tell me. Just answer this question. Can you think of any possible connection between my stalker and a person who might stalk Nicole, if she were being stalked?"

Rick pointed to an outdoor bench in the quadrangle surrounded by buildings. "Can we sit for a minute?" Once they sat, he continued, "I'll do everything I can to answer if you tell me about your stalker."

At first, Miranda shook her head. "I don't want to talk about it," she said forcefully. "It makes me furious. It's such a cowardly, hateful thing to do. It makes me feel dirty. Violated."

"I'm really sorry, Miranda. I would stop this thing if I knew how."

"I don't want you to do anything, Rick. It's not your fight. It's mine. You have enough on your plate at the moment."

"Miranda, I owe you everything good that's happened in my life for the past two years. There's nothing I wouldn't do for you."

Miranda put her hand on Rick's knee as they sat together. "I know that, Rick. I'm sure you would make the same offer to Nicole."

"Maybe." Rick shrugged. "But I'm not comparing my feelings for her with my feelings for you."

"There isn't anything you can do for me," continued Miranda. "We don't know who's stalking me or why. We certainly don't know where to find him. Is that the way it is with Nicole?"

"There are a lot of similarities," said Rick.

"So she is being stalked. What's the connection?"

"I'm working on that," mumbled Rick. "There may be a way to find our man."

"And that would be?"

"Well," he said, "you probably don't know much about the events that led to my arrest. It was a police sting. The cops were tailing a suspect who was alone in the park with a helpless street girl. I think the guy she was with, the suspect, really was a killer—is a killer. I got in the way. I didn't know they were there. I was trying to protect her. I know if I hadn't stopped him, or the police hadn't, that girl would've been dead meat.

Miranda cringed visably.

"Sorry," he said. "That was crude. My point is the way to find the stalker is to lure him out."

"What's the draw?" asked Miranda.

"I think there's a connection between you and Nicole, but I think the stalker is really after Nicole."

"So what does that have to do with me?"

"On one level, I don't think the stalker can help himself," said Rick. "He's addicted to watching women. And you're certainly worth watching."

"I don't know whether to take that as a compliment," answered Miranda.

"It was meant as one, but I know the attention of a guy like that isn't very flattering. On another level, keeping you worried is helping the stalker get what he wants from Nicole."

"How?"

"You're holding the attention of the one person who can get in his way, the person he has to get out of his way."

"And who would that be?"

"That would be me."

"You?"

"Hard to believe, huh? Who'd be interested in a street rat?"

"That's not what I meant, Rick. But I don't understand why the stalker would be after you."

"I don't have all the pieces yet, but I have to ask myself why this thing has dragged out so long. And why kill your friend, Arturo, if the stalker hasn't really threatened you?"

"Did I say he hasn't threatened me?"

"No, you didn't say that. I guess I was basing the guess on similarities."

"Similarities with Nicole's situation?"

"I really can't say."

Rick stood to stretch away the discomfort from the hard bench. "I could be completely off base here. It isn't easy to follow a path laid out by a monster with a twisted mind."

Chapter 73

RICK WALKED INTO THE VESTIBULE of St. Ignatius and waved a greeting to the secretary in the office. "Would Father John be in?" he asked.

"He's gone to make a quick visit. He said he'd be back by three," she replied.

Rick checked the clock on the wall. "Is it okay if I wait?"

"Sure; you can sit in here if you'd like," she replied.

"I think I'll sit in the sanctuary, if that's okay."

"Of course. I'll tell Father John you're here as soon as he comes in."

The priest joined Rick on the back pew of the sanctuary when he returned. They sat visiting quietly, talking of things that suited the hallowed spot.

"Father, have you ever been in love?"

Father John laughed quietly. "Rick, you're not supposed to ask a priest that question."

"I need some seasoned advice," Rick replied. "I think I have a decision to make. It's still a few months away, but I want to be ready when the time comes."

"Sounds reasonable," said Father John. "Tell me about it."

"I've told you about my dilemma before. Miranda is my former case manager, turned friend, turned sweetheart. She's everything a guy could want. I can tell I love her because I can't stop thinking about her.

"Then there's my brother's widow. Her name is Nicole, Nicole Tate. She's gorgeous. She has a six-year-old boy. We've gotten to be very close. I mean me and the boy, Trevor. Nicole is a fantastic woman, no doubt about that. She's alone. She's often afraid. Her son, Trevor, needs a dad. So what you have here, basically, is a loser who could become the husband of one or the other. Either would be a dream."

"Are you sure that either one of them wants you?" asked Father John with a smile.

Rick laughed. "No. That's the right question to ask. I'm not sure. I'm guessing that Miranda sort of likes me. We've kissed. I haven't tried to kiss Nicole. That doesn't feel right, you know, to kiss your brother's widow. But Nicole is very nice, and in my wildest dreams, I get the feeling that she thinks I wouldn't be a total waste as a husband. She's really committed to Trevor. I know she wants him to have a father."

"But she didn't say you were the guy?" asked Father John.

"Well, she hasn't asked me to marry her, if that's what you mean." Rick was smiling despite himself.

"Have you talked with either woman about the other?" the priest asked.

"They know about each other," replied Rick. "But I haven't gone any further than that."

"Good! Don't," said the priest flatly. "You know, Rick, lots of people think priests don't know anything about love because they've never been married or had romantic relationships of their own. While that's mostly true, or should be true, you have to remember that priests hear the confessions of and give counsel to many married people. We hear things you wouldn't believe. In that sense, we have a much broader understanding of romance and marriage than most people."

Father John lowered his voice. "I did have a romantic relationship before I entered the priesthood. A friend turned sweetheart. She was a glorious girl. I wouldn't call her gorgeous. But she was wonderful. I'm sure she would have become a marvelous wife and mother. Like you, I had to make a choice—not between two women but between two passions. One was the desire to be a husband to a fine woman and father to my own little flock. The other was to be a vicar of Christ and tend a much larger flock. I made the mistake of discussing my dilemma with Carla. That was her name. I thought my reasoned contemplation would impress her, that she would admire me for making an intelligent comparison and reaching a thoughtful conclusion. I was wrong. When I told her of my love for her, I could see the light of love shining in her eyes. Then when I told her of my devotion to Christ and His church and the possibility that God wanted me to sacrifice worldly desires to accept a higher ordination, tears doused that light in her eyes. I tried to convince her that I hadn't truly made a decision yet and asked her to give me some time. She wanted nothing to do with it. She wished me well. I never saw her again in a romantic setting.

"You see, in a woman's mind—or heart—failing to decide *for* her is the same as deciding *against* her. What she wants is a clear, unmistakable choice in which the desire to be with her reigns above all other considerations. Nothing else will suffice. That's not really selfishness. Carla loved God, and she loved His church. She was happy for me that I could become a keeper of his flock and a dispenser of the holy sacraments. But from the instant she really understood that another passion could rival her, she knew that the essential ingredients for a lifetime of happy marriage weren't there. Bam! She was gone.

"So, Rick, if I can offer you any advice worth taking, it's this. Don't discuss your thinking with either of these women. Don't discuss it with anyone they know. If there's a decision to make, you must decide, *alone*. If you try to include either of the women in your deliberation, you'll lose her. Even if she's desperate and accepts your proposal anyway, you'll lose part of her—the most delicate and precious part.

"As for the question of motive, just an additional thought there. The only good reason to marry is for love. I can assure you, as one who has seen many fail, that marriages of convenience, marriages of duty, marriages of obligation, and marriages of charity don't last in the long run.

"Our life's circumstances change so dramatically with time. What makes sense today may make no sense in a few years. Nicole has a helpless son. He needs a dad. There's a special bond between you. But in ten short years, and I emphasize *short* because the years will soon begin to race past you, he will be a teen who may not think he needs a dad. Another ten short years later, he won't need you as a dad, just as a friend. And you can still be his friend, even if you aren't married to his mom. I don't doubt that there are other considerations you're aware of and I'm not. That's as it should be. This is your decision to make, not mine. But if you're asking advice, mine is short and simple: marry for love. If you want to know which direction to go, ask your heart."

Chapter 74

As they had the year before, the Tates invited Rick to their Labor Day barbecue. This time he accepted readily. He welcomed the opportunity to spend a day with Trevor, and he wanted more time with Nicole.

The Labor Day festivities were much like the prior year's, but he was far more comfortable. For one thing, Nicole welcomed him warmly. For another, Dennis had made the switch predicted by his wife, Linda. He no longer seemed suspicious of Rick. On the contrary, he took an active interest in Rick.

This time, Rick took more interest in the neighbors, particularly Steve and Naomi Barton, parents of Tub Barton. Rick visited with the Bartons, asking about their son. Steve was mostly quiet. Naomi talked freely of Tim's boyhood.

"Tim was a very quiet child," Naomi said. "Not very active. He was the youngest of our four children.

"He was very chubby. He weighed almost twenty-five pounds by the time he was six months old. That's when he got the nickname 'Tub' from his dad." She laughed, patting Steve on the cheek. "Tim was slow to walk, almost twenty months by the time he really walked. We thought he just loved to crawl. Later we realized that he had a chronic inner-ear infection that caused equilibrium problems. There was no lasting damage, but it got him off to a slow start.

"Since Steve worked at the post office and things were tight for us, we lived with Steve's mom. I worked most of those years, and Grandma Barton watched the kids for us. When Tim was in grade school, we discovered that both he and his older sister, Hannah, had reading disabilities. That was a hard time for them. The poor little guy was overweight anyway, which meant he became the brunt of ridicule from his classmates."

At this point in her narrative, Naomi glanced over at Linda as if she were looking for Linda's agreement. Linda smiled and nodded reassuringly. Naomi continued. "The reading disability on top of his weight problem was a terrible struggle for him. Naturally, he didn't understand why the other kids called him Fatso and told him he was stupid. He used to tell me about his days at school when I came home from work. It broke my heart."

Naomi, herself a woman of rounding figure, sat on a lawn chair with her legs crossed in front of her. Lost in the reflections that the narrative awakened within her, she gazed absentmindedly at a pretty butterfly flitting among Linda's four-o'clocks. She fell silent.

Steve took up the narrative, watching his wife from the corner of his eye. "My mom passed away from an accidental fall when the kids were in elementary school. We couldn't have stayed here"—he gestured around him with his outstretched hands as if indicating the neighborhood—"except that Mom left us the house."

Naomi added, "Tim loved his grandma so much. She really raised him during those years. He took her death as hard as a child can."

Rick continued to nod his understanding.

"The poor little guy blamed himself for her accident. We tried and tried to help him understand it wasn't his fault. Things like that just happen sometimes. Otherwise, Tim's boyhood was pretty normal. He suffered from a lot of nightmares. Kids do. He'd wake up screaming sometimes, just soaked with sweat. That went on for . . ." Naomi couldn't seem to remember the details.

Steve provided them. "The dreams went on until he was in his teens, then they gradually died away. We thought of taking him to a therapist but really couldn't afford to."

At about that point, Steve seemed to feel they were neglecting their hosts with this lengthy narrative, and he rushed to conclude it quickly. "Those are just the things kids go through. Tim graduated from the U, became a Green Beret, and ultimately gave his life for his country. A guy can't do much more than that, can he?" Steve asked with a forced laugh.

"No, he can't," agreed Rick.

At one or two points in the conversation, Naomi Barton mentioned how discouraging some of Tub's teen years had been. But the overall impression Rick carried away was that all's well that ends well. Tub had died with honor. Any prior difficulties could be forgotten. Rick nodded and congratulated them on their excellent work as parents.

During the discussion, members of the Tate family listened in. They were silent. Rick could see the clouds on Nicole's brow. She occasionally shook her head, but only when Tub's parents couldn't see her reaction.

For his part, Rick was careful not to fuel any fires. He simply listened respectfully. No good purpose would be served by relating what he now accepted as the truth about Tub Barton's sordid life and crimes.

The only dim spot in the day's festivities was Trevor's illness. Though he'd recovered from the near drowning three months earlier, his little constitution seemed shaken by it. Nicole reported him as more fearful. He had occasional nightmares about water and drowning. He clung to her more closely. She was worried that these symptoms might signal some lasting emotional problems or that they might interfere with a good start to the coming school year.

After visiting for a while, Nicole decided to take Trevor home and put him to bed. The boy was disappointed to be leaving early.

Rick gave him a big hug. "You get better fast, okay? You don't want to miss any school. Maybe we could go to the park and feed the ducks sometime, if it's okay with your mom. I'll call you, all right? Love you, big guy. Be sure to mind your mom."

Chapter 75

AFTER NICOLE AND TREVOR LEFT, the neighbors bade farewell and followed suit. Michael napped in a chaise lounge, and Lizzie and the kids played croquette with Dennis. Rick was in the kitchen helping Linda clean up.

"Well, another successful party for the world's best hostess," Rick said to Linda.

Linda looked at him with a smile. "Rick, you're becoming a regular flatterer," she said. "You'll be sweeping the women off their feet."

"Not likely," Rick replied, replacing the plastic wrap on a partially empty bowl of potato salad.

"You can't fool me. I know you're a chick magnet," she laughed, "or whatever hot guys are called these days. When I was young, they were called killers."

"I can do without being called that!" Rick laughed.

"Have any plans for the future?" Linda asked a little more seriously.

"You know," answered Rick, "stay in school until I finish. Keep working to pay the bills. Try to stay out of trouble."

"You just don't seem like the kind of person to get into trouble." Linda laid her hand on his arm. "In truth, you never did. At least, not since I've known you."

"Thanks," said Rick. "I'll try not to disappoint you."

"Any plans for marriage?" Linda was asking this in a casual tone, looking away from Rick at the work she was doing.

"Don't you think it's a little early for me to be making any plans like that?" Rick asked. "I don't have much to offer a woman."

"That's not true. Rick, you're a good man, through and through. I think most of the women close to you know that."

"Anyone you would recommend?"

Linda laughed. "Just the obvious one. You already know we'd love to see you and Nicole together."

"Doesn't that seem a little strange?" he asked. "A man married to his brother's widow. How do you think Ryan would feel about that?"

"I think Ryan would be ecstatic. In fact, I think that's what he planned from the beginning."

"Ryan didn't even know about me," Rick objected.

"It's hard to say what he knew," replied Linda, shrugging. "Sometimes we know things we can't fully explain." She exhaled slowly, gazing out into the yard where other members of the family were occupied.

"Rick, I want to tell you something extremely confidential. I only do it because it may make some of your future decisions easier." She paused as if deciding where to begin. "Ryan and Nicole dated a lot during their high school years," she said. "I think Nicole really loved him, but for Ryan, the relationship was mostly a friendship. He talked to me about it a lot during his senior year. The kids had talked about getting married some day, but Ryan wanted to make a career of the military. He knew that it takes a special kind of woman to survive a life in the service. Often, those are women whose fathers were career soldiers. They know how to enjoy the benefits of service life without being worn down by the hardships. At least, that was Ryan's thinking.

"After his mission and graduation from the university, Ryan went off to military schools until he was finally commissioned. He told Nicole what he planned to do. She was hurt, and I think she held out hopes that he would change his mind once he saw what service life was really like.

"He did change his mind. He changed it when he came home on leave. He told me Nicole was expecting a baby. Ryan didn't tell me who the father was but assured me it wasn't him. Of course, he'd been away from home for a year, so that seemed obvious. He was worried about Nicole because she had decided to keep the baby.

"According to Ryan, Nicole had been forced and was afraid of the father. This led to a period of hurried soul searching on Ryan's part. In the end, he thought he had found a way to solve Nicole's problem. He decided to marry her and raise Trevor as his own. Ryan was a good husband to her and a good father to Trevor. Nicole has told me that in the way women share those sorts of things. Ryan was true to his commitment, and I believe he carried through to the end of his days."

Rick listened without blinking. Finally, he nodded his understanding. "I really admire him for that," he said softly. "Not every man could do that. Not every man *would* do that."

"You're certainly right there," Linda agreed. "But there's another piece to the story. No one knows this but me—not even Dennis. You should know it. I trust you to treat it with the almost sacred confidence it deserves."

"You can trust me," said Rick.

"During the year Ryan was away, he went to church on Sundays whenever he could. He was in training at Fort Bragg, North Carolina. He met a girl there. Her father was a commander of one of the Special Forces units. She was a Latter-day Saint, as was Ryan. He fell in love. I mean, he really fell for this girl. Her name was Sarah. He proposed to Sarah the evening before he came home on leave." Linda stood looking at Rick. Her kind eyes were reading his face. "Do you see how this story is going to turn out?" she asked.

"I do," replied Rick. "I see it all. Ryan came home, discovered Nicole's peril, and realized that he was the man to save her and her unborn baby. He made his decision, asked Nicole to marry him, and then had to tell the girl he loved that he was no longer free to marry. Unless I'm mistaken, Nicole never even knew about the other girl. He did what had to be done because he was a man of honor."

Linda watched Rick, her eyes tearing up.

"Thanks for sharing that," said Rick softly. "It answered a lot of questions."

"Will it help with your decisions?" Linda asked.

"What do you think I should do?" asked Rick.

"Oh, dear. I wouldn't attempt to answer that. I didn't try to influence Ryan's decision." Linda was now washing out a pitcher from which she had served punch. "I admired Ryan for his choice. And I say without any hesitation whatever that I love Nicole like a daughter. Trevor is my angel, my grandson. I think Ryan did the right thing. Still . . ." Linda choked a little on her emotion. "Sorry," she said tapping her chest. "I think I've said too much already."

"I don't mean to push you," replied Rick gently. "But I need you to finish that sentence. Still, *what*?"

Linda smiled sadly. "I was going to say, 'What about that other girl? Sarah?' Her heart must have been broken. When Ryan told her what he had to do, she begged him to reconsider. He tried to console her but couldn't. Sometimes I think duty leaves as many casualties as survivors."

"You're wonderful, Linda," said Rick. "Thanks so much for all you've done for me. Will you still invite me to family parties if I choose someone other than Nicole?" he asked this as playfully as he could manage.

"Rick, you're part of this family. You always will be. I'm sorry we didn't know you boys were twins from the beginning. We'd have adopted you both."

You don't know how badly I wish that had happened.

With a moment's reflection, Rick thought of Ryan's impossible dilemma and the inevitable heartache it brought. He thought of Ryan's misfortune in growing up a few yards from Tub Barton and the tragedies that nearness had spun and was still spinning. He thought of Ryan's early death. He thought of a brokenhearted girl somewhere, who was an undeserving victim of Ryan's overwhelming sense of duty. He recognized that neither Ryan's life nor Nicole's had turned out to be a party. *Maybe I wasn't the only one with problems.*

"One more question," said Rick. "I don't remember reading about Sarah or about that choice in his journals. Any thoughts about that?"

"I asked him about it," replied Linda. "He said, 'Mom, I'm in uncharted territory here. I don't have much to go on. I think I'd better wait and see how this turns out. Then I can write about it.'"

Rick put his arm around Linda. "You're the best. Ryan was lucky to have you as a mom. I'm lucky to have you as a friend." *Question is, am I bright enough to do what's best for all of us?*

Chapter 76

A WEEK AFTER THE TATES' Labor Day gathering, Rick took the bus over to Salt Lake's central transportation hub and walked the few blocks to the Rescue Mission. He was back in the swing of school, things seemed reasonably settled, and he hadn't been to the Mission for almost two years. A lifetime ago. He'd cleared the trip with Miranda. Surprisingly, she encouraged the trip but added her usual cautions.

He dressed for the occasion. His clothes were clean but the most worn of his meager wardrobe. He wanted to be inconspicuous. But even before he reached his destination, he knew there was no going back. Two years had changed him. He had more to live for now. He'd tasted accomplishment and wanted more. Still, he never wanted to forget his roots: who he was and where he came from.

It was familiar ground for Rick. The journey brought a flood of memories. He passed a few street people as he walked. There weren't many that time of day. Most were out doing what street people did—surviving, relating, working day jobs, experiencing life. They would come together in greater numbers at mealtime. Faces looked familiar. That was good enough. Though he hadn't told Miranda, he was coming to see only one person in particular—Slice.

Rick didn't want contact with Slice. Certainly no confrontation that might jeopardize his parole. But he wanted to see the guy. Look for recognition. Get any sense of what he might do to end the unwanted suffering that both Nicole and Miranda endured at the hands of this dangerous and twisted man. Rick was now certain that Slice moved through the homeless community to elude authorities, that he stalked and menaced the two women central to Rick's existence, and that he was the likely killer of an unknown number of other victims.

If he could just see Slice, Rick felt he'd know what to do next.

Rick reached the Mission and climbed the stairs. Two men sitting on the stairs nodded and scooted out of his way without giving any sign of recognition.

Once inside the familiar precincts, Rick recognized Kenny, who had come up through the ranks. Kenny was a resident program supervisor during Rick's last stay at the Mission. As Rick approached, Kenny was giving orders to two handymen. Kenny saw Rick coming and turned to him, a flicker of recognition crossing his face.

"How's it goin'?" he asked.

"Just wanted to check the place out," answered Rick.

"You needing a place?" asked Kenny, inspecting Rick. "You been here before, right?"

"Yeah," replied Rick. "I was with you for a while. Couple of years ago. Name's Rick Street."

Sudden recognition burst upon Kenny.

"Yeah, Street. Sure. Didn't recognize you. Got your hair cut."

"That's right," laughed Rick.

Kenny looked Rick over.

"Word on the street is that you got your own place now. School. A woman. A real job. Made good. That so?"

Rick felt himself blushing a little.

"Workin' on it," he said with a laugh.

"Good," said Kenny. "What can I do for you?"

"Thinkin' of bringin' a couple a friends down to the devotional and maybe join some of the volunteers to help serve the meal one of these nights," said Rick.

"Really made the big change, huh?" Kenny shook his head. "Gone all the way from homeless to volunteer?"

"Just wanna say hi to a few friends," Rick answered. "Maybe help out a little. Feel like I owe. Think I could get away with that?"

"S'pose so," said Kenny. "You know the drill. Be happy to see you whenever you get here. Might wanna come on a night when we don't get too many volunteer groups."

"Sure. I'll call," Rick said.

"While I'm thinkin' of it, ever see that dude around we used to call Slice?"

Kenny was silent, looking hard at Rick. "He a friend of yours?"

"Nope," said Rick. "Got me arrested. Got me kicked out of the program. Just wondered if he's ever around."

"Look, Street," said Kenny. "Great to see you again, but we don't want no trouble here. If you got a grudge, gotta take it someplace else."

"No grudge," said Rick. "No trouble from me."

Kenny nodded. "See him off and on. Not a regular like he was back then. Guess I can't help." Kenny lowered his voice. "But, I'm sayin', if you don't gotta see him, be glad. He can be a bad dude. Real mean."

"Yeah," Rick said, "Don't I know it. Just wonderin'. No big deal."

Kenny nodded.

"Mind if I walk through the hall?" Rick asked. "For old time's sake?"

"No. Knock yourself out," replied Kenny. "You heard that the Mission is workin' on gettin' a new place? Maybe out near the industrial park."

"That's a ways out of the district, isn't it?" asked Rick.

"Things are spreadin' out," Kenny replied. "The Road Home's got Palmer Court down on Tenth South and Main. That's a ways. It's a new day."

"Yeah, you're right," replied Rick.

It's a new day.

Rick left the Mission without seeing Slice, still unsure what to do. But one thing was sure: word would get around. There are no secrets on the street. He'd asked the question. If Slice was around, he'd know Rick had been looking for him.

Chapter 77

RICK REPORTED BACK TO MIRANDA after his visit to the Mission.

"How'd you feel about going down to the Mission with me for one of our Tuesday meetings?" Rick asked her. "I could show you around. Maybe that would help explain how I got the way I am." He smiled. "Good training for a future attorney."

Again, Rick was a bit surprised when Miranda readily agreed to go. Two more weeks passed before things came together for them to make the visit.

Rick didn't know quite what to expect from Miranda when the evening finally came. He could still remember how smoking hot she had looked when she came to his promotion party at Home Depot so many months ago. If she showed up to the Mission looking like that, he was sure there'd be a riot.

When Miranda picked him up at Danny's, she was dressed way down, about like he was.

Never question Miranda's judgment. She's always spot on.

A good crowd gathered at the Mission's evening devotional. As Rick and Miranda entered the hall, he scanned the crowd for Slice. No sign of him. At least, Rick didn't see anybody looking the way he remembered Slice. It seemed to Rick that Miranda might be doing the same.

They sat near the back. As usual, the devotional started with a welcome by the devotion leader, an older man currently in the rehab program. A small group of program people—including Reverend Marsh—sat in front facing the crowd. One of them was Kenny. The devotion leader recognized Kenny for some announcements.

"We wanna welcome our volunteers who've been helpin' to get the meal together and serve it."

Kenny named several, who then received a round of applause.

"We wanna recognize Rick Street, who's come back because he heard the food is real good," said Kenny.

There was a round of snickers.

"He's got his woman with him," Kenny nodded to Miranda. "We welcome you."

Rick held his breath, half expecting Miranda to take exception to being introduced as "his woman." But Miranda nodded pleasantly, and Kenny went on.

"Street was one of us a coupla years ago. Now he's got his own place and a steady job. He's beat his drinkin' ways. He just got a diploma from the community college. Street has set a real good example for us all. We're gonna spotlight him in one of our upcoming issues of the *Rescuer*. Let's give him a hand."

The room rang with applause. Rick looked steadily at the back of the seat in front of him and accepted slaps on the back from others sitting close. Miranda watched him with a smile.

"Stand up," she said. "Give 'em a wave."

Rick got awkwardly to his feet, waved a couple of times, and sat back down. Seeing the target of their applause, everyone clapped the louder.

Rick and Miranda joined in the devotional, singing revival hymns and listening to testimonials from several participants who had reformed their lives. When the last testimonial ended, the devotion leader stood, looking at Rick.

"Street?" he asked.

Rick shook his head to decline the invitation.

The crowd was dismissed down the stairs to the dining hall, servers and women first.

Other than being put on the spot, the entire event was a treat for Rick. He saw Scotty and Soapy, his two temporary roommates. He got lots of high-fives from men he'd known and from others he hadn't.

One girl came through the food line twice with her male escort. She was young, round-faced, wearing thick glasses. She was clean and dressed her best. She reminded Rick of the girl he had followed into the park the night of his arrest.

"What's your name?" Rick asked her.

"Happy," she said shyly. She was missing teeth, so she guarded against letting any smiles escape.

"What a great name," Rick replied with genuine delight.

He turned to Miranda, who was standing next to him holding out a large metal serving spoon laden with cut green beans. He was struck again by how beautiful Miranda was in any setting. For a second, he wondered how she would have looked if she were a homeless woman.

She'd probably still be beautiful.

"Isn't that a great name?" Rick asked Miranda.

"A pretty name for a pretty girl," Miranda replied, bringing a bigger smile to Rick's face.

"What's your last name?" he asked.

Happy blushed.

"Trails," she said.

"Happy Trails? You're kidding me. What a great name!" Rick was beaming. "It is so great to meet you, Happy Trails."

The meal served, the cleaning done, and a few acquaintances renewed, Rick sat with Miranda at a dining table, the plastic table cover still wet from being wiped down.

"Well, what do you think of my family home?" he spread his hands to take in the entire surroundings.

"Pretty nice," replied Miranda with a smile. "You're really happy this evening, aren't you?"

"I am. Visiting here reminds me that my life wasn't all bad," he reminisced. "Not saying I wanna go back, mind you. But it wasn't all bad. I met a lot of people I liked."

Miranda just listened.

"You know, it was an evening like this, but after the holidays, when I got into trouble and first met you. I thought it was the end of the world. Turns out that it was just the beginning."

"I *do* know," replied Miranda, leaning so close that Rick could feel her sweet breath on his face.

"Oh, really?" he asked moving even closer to her. "And how do you know?"

"I was here too," she answered.

"What do you mean?" asked Rick.

"I was here that night. I was just a stupid, pathetic street girl. I left with a guy who invited me to go for a walk up in the park. It got pretty steamy," Miranda said coyly. "Then we were interrupted by a crazy man with a two-by-four. Ruined the whole mood."

Miranda smiled defiantly at Rick.

Rick's mouth was open in astonishment. "I . . . what?"

"That's right," replied Miranda. "I've been on the street myself."

Rick took some time to process this.

"Noooo," he said.

"Yes."

"Huh?"

"Yep."

"No way." He laughed, shaking his head. "You are such an amazing woman."

He laughed again in astonishment.

"It was you. I remember you. The eyes . . ." he went on. "I followed those eyes into the night. I couldn't help myself. I didn't stand a chance, did I?"

"Nope." Miranda smiled and brushed the back of her fingers lightly across his cheek.

"Thanks for showing me your family home, Mr. Street. And thanks for coming to my rescue in the park. Only kidding about you interrupting the mood. As I'm sure you know, I couldn't stand the guy I was with."

"Slice?" asked Rick.

"Slice," answered Miranda.

"I think he may have engineered, or at least contributed to, my brother's death. He's listed by the military as MIA. But I think he may still be alive and back here, on the street. If he is, he's definitely AWOL from the military. I didn't see him here tonight."

Miranda seemed to be processing this information.

"Think he's stalking Nicole?"

"Can't say," said Rick. "I'm wondering if he's stalking anybody else."

"Can't say," said Miranda.

Chapter 78

"Taylor, Miranda again. Bet you wish I'd go away. We need to talk. Can I come see you? I think I've put the pieces together."

Chapter 79

TOWARD THE END OF SEPTEMBER, Rick arranged a visit to Liberty Park for Trevor's sake. He cleared the visit with Miranda, who voiced her concern about exposing the mother and son to a possible confrontation with the stalker. Rick felt he could protect them and that they needed a chance to break out of their prison of fear and relax.

Nicole offered to pick Rick up at his apartment, but he declined. So Nicole and Trevor were already waiting when Rick arrived on foot at their agreed meeting place on the south end of Liberty Park. The eighty-acre park had been continuously maintained by the city for more than a hundred years. Liberty Park offered numerous playgrounds, picnic areas, tennis and volleyball courts, a suitably sized lake, two museums, and the renowned Tracy Aviary. The centenary trees soared high overhead.

The park was crowded with typical city dwellers reveling in the coolish days of fall. The perimeter path teemed with walkers, skaters, boarders, and moms jogging behind strollers. In every playground, parents pushed their kids in swings and waited at the foot of slides for their toddlers—"Come on, bud. Dad'll catch you."

Young men in flip-flops and cutoffs tossed Frisbees to their dogs. Here and there, families picnicked on blankets.

During the cooling hours between six and nine, the grand old park was in its glory. Like most urban parks, the magic would start to disappear with the coming of nightfall. Though fairly well-lit and heavily patrolled, Liberty Park couldn't escape the plight suffered by its relatives in other cities. Americans had seen too many movies and TV shows to trust their parks after dark. In less than an hour every evening, the city park transformed from fairyland to haunted forest, from garden to graveyard.

It had been an ideal day for walking in the park, the kind of day that rewarded visitors for the effort to get there. Nicole suggested they meet early to enjoy the lingering hours of daylight.

Trevor asked several times to feed the ducks and geese. Nicole had brought a bag of dried bread crusts. Trevor stood a healthy distance from the water's edge and flung the pieces with all his might out onto the water. Soon a gaggle of squawking, flapping dole-takers had gathered. The boy laughed and clapped at the birds' antics.

Rick and Nicole sat on a sculpted metal bench beneath a tree only a few feet distant. Nicole talked about Trevor's readiness for school. It wasn't news to Rick that Trevor was bright. The boy had benefited immensely from the constant personal attention of a devoted mom. He knew the alphabet and all the corresponding phonic sounds and could read grade-level stories. He could count to a hundred and count backward from twenty. Trevor knew the basic shapes and could identify the primary colors. He was definitely ready and doing well early in the school year. Nicole spoke of him with understandable pride and confidence.

After feeding the ducks, the trio walked slowly north along the paved footpath. Trevor detoured to see all the sights, dragging Rick after him.

The evening cooled as expected. Twilight brought out the rich colors of foliage and graced the man-made objects. Given their speed, it was obvious to Rick that he, Nicole, and Trevor wouldn't have time to make the full loop. Instead, they decided to cut across the grass and start their return.

*   *   *

The evening seemed to Nicole an ideal time to explore possibilities for a future with Rick. Talk within the Tate family often included hints that everyone hoped the pair would get together. Trevor seemed to worship Rick—couldn't get enough of the man who was coming to feel like his father. Nicole's preference was always to discuss relationships openly. She didn't like to be left wondering what others were thinking and feeling.

She had tried to discuss the topic with Rick twice before, feeling it out, trying to sense where his emotions lay. Both times, she quickly recognized Rick's tentative response. He was always polite, always kind, always encouraging, but she needed to know if he *felt* anything for her.

Nicole took Rick's arm and studied his face as they stood watching Trevor kick a stone along the edge of the pathway. Rick's appearance wasn't as crisp as his brother's had been—Rick was softer—but that's where the differences ended. He seemed in every way the measure of the man Ryan had been, and Nicole could tell she was falling in love with him as she had been in love with Ryan.

"Rick," she began, "you know that I like you. I hope you like me."

She paused for a moment, not really expecting Rick to reply.

"I don't think I need to apologize for chasing a good man when I see one," she said boldly with a laugh in her voice. "I've never been especially timid, and I can assure you there aren't that many good men out there waiting to take on a ready-made family.

"I know you're coming to a crossroads in your life." She spoke softly. "In a few months, you'll wrap up your obligation to the court. You'll be a free man. I'm sure you'll be making some decisions about where to go with your life. A more timid woman would fold her hands in her lap and wait to see what happens. That's just not me. I hope you understand, Rick.

"Time's flying by. I've adjusted to Ryan's death as well as I can. Trev is in school. I hope my troubles with Tim Barton will end soon. I *pray* they'll end soon. And I think one way to end them is for me to marry again. Tim wouldn't dare bother us if Ryan were still here. The same would be true if I married another strong man. I ache to be rid of this—this plague. This nightmare!

"If marriage under the right conditions is possible, that's what I want to do. If not, I need to start thinking about getting a job. We're okay financially, but in addition to being Trevor's mom, I feel like I need to start growing again as a person." Nicole paused, looking at Rick again. "Does that make sense?" she asked.

"Sure. It makes sense," Rick replied. "Nicole, I promise that you're safe. I won't let anything happen to you or Trev."

"Thank you, Rick. You don't know how comforting that is." Then after a thoughtful pause, she continued, "Unfortunately, you can't be with us all the time. And the worst times are when nobody else is around."

"I'll find a way to make it stop," Rick said decisively.

Trevor wandered back toward them. "I'm thirsty. Can we find a water fountain?" Trevor asked.

Rick glanced around. Spotting a fountain by the tennis courts, he pointed it out to Trevor. "Go get yourself a drink. We'll watch you and be over in a minute."

Trevor walked away, detouring to scatter a flock of seagulls pecking at earthworms in the lawn.

"I've been dragging my feet, haven't I?" said Rick, turning back to Nicole. "That's not fair to you."

"I know you're waiting for your court date," Nicole answered. "I should leave you that much room before adding more to your plate. But I can't. I guess that's me."

She squeezed Rick's arm and leaned into him. "I hope I don't scare you to death," she said with a smile. "Just answer me this. Does it feel like there's anything between us that could grow into a lasting relationship? Is there any chance for us? If I get my hopes up, am I going to be disappointed?"

Rick didn't look away from her. That was one thing about Rick that positively thrilled Nicole. When she first met him little more than a year earlier, his eyes had been furtive. They would run at first chance. In this short time, a single year, Rick had mastered those emotions—at least as far as she could tell from his eyes. He definitely showed more confidence in himself.

He gazed steadily into her eyes. When he spoke, his voice was soft but not frightened. "You're right to ask. You shouldn't have to ask. I've had every chance to be forthright and clear. You deserve that. Trevor deserves it. The truth is I've struggled with my feelings. I could explain that struggle, and I think you'd be flattered by it. At least, I hope so. But you're not asking about *my* struggle. You're asking about *your* future."

Rick took a deep breath. "I honestly don't see us together in a marriage. That sounds terrible, and I'm sorry. Truly. I can think of a million reasons I should be trying to get you to marry me. But I can't think of any reasons why you would want to. The jury is still out on whether I can eventually make something of myself, even with enough time. Would I be good for Trevor? I hope so. Would I be a good provider? It looks promising, but I'm unproven. Would I be good for *you*? There's the question."

Nicole's spirits plunged. She could see where this was going. She increased the energy in her face to keep a smile showing, but she could also feel resentment rising inside her. It was inescapable.

Rick continued, "I'm betting deep down in your soul you aren't madly in love with me. Not yet, anyway. And who knows if that can happen?"

"I do like you, Rick, and you know I'm attracted to you." Nicole fished in her pocket for a tissue to dab the corners of her eyes. "I've been hoping you would accept my not-too-subtle invitation to date and see what the future might hold." She loosed her grasp on his arm. "I can't say it doesn't hurt to feel my offer being rejected, even for the best reasons."

She smiled, though she didn't feel like it. "That's one of the problems with being the way I am. On the outside, I'm this strong woman. On the inside, I'm just a frightened little girl who wants everybody to love her and can't understand why hearts have to be broken."

"Nicole, I'm sorry." Rick's pain was painted on his face. "You're a wonderful, beautiful, capable woman and a super mom. I'm here for you and for Trev. I'll always be close by. And I swear that I'll help you solve the problem with Tim. I just don't want to make any promises I can't carry through. You know?"

Nicole didn't want to punish Rick for his honesty. She couldn't be angry with him. He had risked his life to save Trevor. He had made such a positive difference in their lives. Still, she almost felt faint under the wave of rejection that swept through her.

There were moments in Nicole's past when she felt rejection, subtle but undeniable. Despite his constant assurances of love, she had felt rejection from Ryan—her idol, the man of men. Just the thought of those disappointing moments saddened her. She didn't understand how she had lost Ryan's love. She wanted to blame it on Tim Barton, but she wasn't sure that was completely fair.

If she was honest, Nicole had to admit that she felt like striking out in this painful moment. But she knew it wasn't fair to blame Rick. She really couldn't fix the blame anywhere.

"I understand," she answered Rick. "Thanks for being honest." She tried to smile for both of their sakes.

She took Rick's arm again as they collected Trevor and started back toward the car. Her heart was a little heavier. Her steps a little less buoyant. She pulled Trevor close. Nicole was sorry she'd brought the matter up. She wished she could have back the contentment and charm that began the evening.

Chapter 80

Lamps in the park slowly brightened. Rick and Nicole strolled silently along, pausing to watch Trevor gaze through the bars of the iron fence of the aviary. When he returned to the adults, he asked how far they had to walk until reaching the car. Rick offered him a piggyback ride to help rest his legs. Trevor happily accepted.

As they resumed their leisurely pace, a motorcycle pulled into a parking spot a dozen yards away. Rick, in the midst of his musings about the future, had little reason to notice or care about the bullet bike except he remembered seeing the helmeted rider circling the park earlier—more than once.

The evening had grown a bit too dark to see faces clearly, but this rider's build and longish hair sparked Rick's recognition. Now parked, the rider clearly watched Rick and Nicole as they walked along. Having secured the bike, he took up a course parallel to but behind the couple and the tiring boy.

Sensing danger, Rick's pulse quickened. He could feel adrenalin pumping into his system. He hoped he was being needlessly concerned. Still, he picked up the pace a little, bouncing Trevor on his shoulders. His goal was to get mother and son to the safety of their car before any confrontation could develop. Nicole, unaware of danger, lagged behind, strolling thoughtfully along.

Don't hurry her. She deserves space to think about things.

At the same time, Rick's natural instincts screamed at him to hurry.

The main path passed along the east side of the aviary among trees and shrubs. It followed the lake's edge to the park's south entrance, where Nicole's car waited. The motorcycle rider followed a path on the west side of the aviary. The paths rejoined farther south, but each was shielded for a distance from view of the other.

Rick and Nicole were only a hundred yards from the car, but much of the path ahead was shadowed by trees and dense bushes. Rounding a curve, the path passed through the deep shadows.

Rick saw immediately before them the form of the motorcycle rider.

Nicole spied him at about the same moment with a start. "Oh," she said, "Sorry. You frightened me."

"Hi, Nicole," said the rider in low voice. "I've missed you."

Nicole cried out and reached for Trevor. The boy appeared equally frightened. Rick could feel Trevor's shudder as the boy slid into his mother's arms.

"Oh no," she cried. "Please, not now. Please, leave us alone."

"No chance," said Tim Barton. "I've missed you both. I need to see my boy."

"No, please," cried Nicole. "No!"

Nicole was pressing Trevor against her shoulder, trying to keep him from looking at the intruder.

"Nicole, take Trevor and run," Rick ordered in a steady voice.

Barton was advancing on them.

"Shut up, fishbait, you stupid street bum. What do you know? It's time for me to take care of you so I can spend more time with my little family."

"Nicole, go. *Now!*" Rick emphasized.

Nicole didn't move. "This isn't your fight, Rick," she said with resignation. "It's mine. This is my life."

Barton was now ten feet away.

"Nicole, if you love your son, take him and run," Rick barked. There was no pleading in his voice. No entreaty. "You don't want him to see this."

"Rick . . ." Nicole began.

"Now!" he shouted. Behind him he could hear Nicole and Trevor moving away.

"You don't want this, fishbait," sneered Barton. He had stopped just out of Rick's range.

"You're wrong, Slice," Rick said. "You're wrong, Tub. You're wrong, Bandit. I *do* want this."

Barton shook his head. "I see you've put some pieces together," he said. "Bad idea. Stupid idea. Now I *have* to kill you. Before, I only *wanted* to kill you."

"Ain't gonna happen," replied Rick.

Barton laughed again, his voice low. There were still people in the park but at a distance. Barton doubtlessly wanted to take care of business and leave without attracting attention. "This is my family. It's none of your business."

"This is Tiger's family," answered Rick. "It's my business."

Barton drew a knife from the belt at his back. It was a big knife. Rick could only imagine that it was one used by Special Forces soldiers. Barton turned the blade in a sliver of light that shone through the bushes. "This is good-bye to you," he said. "Your brother was smart. You're stupid. He's gone. Where does that leave you?"

"Tell you what, *Tub*," Rick replied, choosing from among all the possible names he could use to address his enemy. "You don't scare me. You're a coward. Always were. You were never good enough to wear a Green Beret. You only made it because Ryan was babysitting you."

Barton was circling to Rick's left, his knife out in front, moving it from hand to hand. He was claiming the open space at his back. Rick pressed up against a huge shrub, higher than his head.

"Nobody will ever know," Barton said. "Cuz you ain't going to tell."

"Tub, I've hated you since I saw you cut a helpless streetie. This is for him. It's for Tiger. It's for Nicole. It's for Trevor. It's for a better world without you."

Barton was slashing his knife from side to side. "Say good-bye, fishbait."

Chapter 81

MIRANDA MARTINEZ STOOD NEXT TO Lieutenant Taylor in a cluster of law enforcement personnel. A squad from SLCPD SWAT had made a silent entry into the park, closing off the paths. When a radio message from a spotter confirmed contact between their suspect and Rick Street, the officers closed off the perimeter road. A plainclothes female officer corralled Nicole and Trevor, moving them to safety. Black-clad figures formed an invisible cordon at a distance around the two combatants.

"It worked," said Miranda. "There he is. The monster."

"The only real evidence we have against Barton is his AWOL status," Taylor briefed the SWAT leader. "We suspect him in at least five killings. Four women and the Diaz murder. He's been smart and elusive. The other man, Street, is wired for sound. We're recording to a van."

Lieutenant Taylor continued, "We'll hold back and get whatever audio evidence we can. If it looks like Street's losing the fight, then we move in. If Barton escapes capture or prosecution as he has in the past, he'll be back on the street. We've got to nail him while we can get our hands on him. At the moment, it's pretty much up to Street."

Chapter 82

RICK MOVED WITH BARTON'S KNIFE. The endless hours of training provided by Danny Komatsu had been spot on.

"Count the rhythm of side-to-side slashes," Komatsu had taught Rick. "An attacker has a rhythm. Even if he's trying to cover it with random moves, when his focus is on you and your moves, he'll forget his disguises and fall into his rhythm. So count."

Rick was counting. He dodged and feinted. His only real challenge was staying away from the edge of the knife.

"I figure you've killed at least six innocent people," said Rick, "maybe seven." He was beginning to feel a little winded by the movement. He needed to go on the offensive, forcing Barton to move more. The big man was breathing heavily, but he could probably move that knife around for hours without tiring much. The fight needed to go full body for Rick to have any advantage.

"Could be," answered Barton with a backhand slash that Rick deftly evaded. "You'll never know."

"One thing I know for sure," said Rick, "is that they were all helpless. You're a coward. Your big problem here is I'm not helpless."

"You'll still be dead either way," replied Barton, making a sudden thrust.

Rick waited an instant until Barton's knife arm was fully extended, then grabbed his wrist with a backhand hold, twisting into the bigger man's body and driving his elbow into Barton's jaw. Barton staggered but held on to the knife.

With his right hand, Rick grabbed the knife wrist and ducked under the arm, twisting backward with both hands. The knife sprang free and clattered onto the asphalt. Before Rick released the arm, he kicked the knife into the grass at the side of the walk.

He didn't have to let Barton's arm go; he could have wrenched it hard, popping the shoulder or breaking a bone, but his work for the evening wasn't finished. Only Rick knew what that work really was.

Barton charged him, grabbing him around the midsection, driving him up the path toward the knife. Rick twisted to let Barton's momentum drive past him on the left side, but Barton's grip held, and he spun Rick away. Rick stumbled onto the grass, his back to his opponent. He didn't fight the fall but let it carry through, propelling him back into a standing position a dozen feet from Barton, who had recovered his knife.

Barton was now breathing audibly.

"You're out of shape, fatso," Rick taunted. "That's why they called you Tub, right?"

Barton was strong, but he wasn't especially agile. His execution of moves was sloppy. He was relying on strength rather than finesse.

Rick moved back within range, drawing the next knife attack. Again, Barton's slashes were regular as they danced in and out of shadows. Rick noted that the rhythm was slightly slower. Barton was already wearing. It was only a matter of time.

At the end of another right-to-left slash, Rick followed with another backhand grab to get the wrist. Barton had learned from his first mistake. This time, he hit Rick in the face with a wicked cross from his left hand and brought the knife back across Rick's chest. Rick could feel the knife dragging on an upper rib and knew he was wounded. The knife was so sharp that the only pain was a burning sensation. Too quickly for Rick to react fully, Barton thrust. The thrust caught Rick on the other side, along the left side of his rib cage.

Rick backed away. "A couple of lucky moves," he taunted.

"You're on your way out, fishbait." Barton grinned.

Chapter 83

MIRANDA WATCHED THE FIGHT FROM a distance through the trees. The intruding foliage made it difficult to see exactly what was happening. It seemed that Rick had been wounded, and Barton was moving in for the kill.

"That's it," Miranda whispered. "Time to go."

Lieutenant Taylor shook his head. "M, why don't you stand away? You shouldn't watch this. It's not over yet."

"Taylor," she whispered in an acid tone, "I don't want Rick dead so you have a murder to pin on Barton."

"We've got to hold," replied Taylor, unruffled by Miranda's accusation.

"I say it's time to stop this." Miranda was raising her voice.

Taylor put his finger to his lips to quiet her. They were at a good distance, but he obviously didn't want to chance tipping Barton off to their presence.

"I'm going in there," said Miranda. "Rick is wounded. This is my fight, not his."

"We're not going to let Street die. He's holding his own. He'll call for help if he needs it. Things are going according to plan," replied Taylor.

"Taylor, he's wounded." Miranda's eyes flashed with anger.

"M, let me remind you that you're no longer a public servant. You're a private citizen. I'm telling you to stand away. If you interfere here, we *will* arrest you for obstructing. Are we clear?"

Miranda turned away and moved into the night. She knew the score, but she would get close. No threat—and no knife—was going to take Rick from her while she still breathed.

Chapter 84

RICK STILL HAD SOME MOVES left in him.

Barton had wounded him twice.

How badly he didn't know. He did know that neither wound had penetrated his rib cage. He would lose blood, but he wasn't going to die.

Rick had been in similar situations before.

No better preparation for a fight than a million fights before it.

He had heard that some animals pretended to be fatally wounded to give their attackers a false sense of superiority before they struck. Rick was doing so now. He let his face show what he considered to be the right amount of anguish as blood flowed freely from wounds on both sides of his upper torso.

Barton moved in for the kill.

With another wicked slash, Barton repeated his earlier left cross. Rick laid his head aside, and the blow glanced off his ear.

Winning a solid grip on the knife wrist, Rick pulled it down with all the force his body weight could generate. He drove it up behind Barton's back, wrenching it as high toward the shoulder blade as he could, even springing off the asphalt walkway to get a slight height advantage.

The knife clattered to the asphalt again.

Barton's shoulder joint popped audibly. The killer groaned. Continuing pressure on the wrenched arm with one hand, Rick grabbed Barton by the chest and drove him backward, bringing him down fully on the flat of his back, wounded arm beneath him.

Barton cried out in pain. The impact on his unprotected head stunned him further. The left arm flailed about aimlessly.

Rick's right hand moved instantly to his opponent's throat. His powerful grip tightened around Barton's windpipe. He squeezed with his might but stopped short of crushing it.

In all his pain, Barton made an effort to reach Rick's head with his left hand. Guessing at the searing pain Barton was enduring from his shoulder, Rick felt a sudden grudging admiration for his opponent's tenacity. Barton was not acting like the cowardly bully Rick had imagined.

Rick increased the pressure on the windpipe. Barton's eyes bulged. "Put that arm down, Tub. The fight's over," Rick panted. "Next thing I do is crush your larynx. It can't be put back together. For the rest of your life, you don't talk. You don't breathe without help. You're gonna be a freak. Better jail than that."

Again, he upped the pressure. Barton was gagging, struggling with his might for air.

Rick's mouth was right next to Barton's ear. "Any last words?" he asked. "Wanna beg?"

Barton shook his head best as he could.

"Confession is good for the soul," Rick hissed. "Don't want to tell me about Grandma Barton's fall? How about Gail Anderson? How about the women you cut down on the street? Tell me about Art Diaz. You killed him to keep things tidy in Miranda's life. Right?"

Barton continued to gag. Tears leaked from the corners of Tub's eyes.

"Tell me about the arrangement you made to get my brother killed so you could have his family. When you killed him, you killed the only real friend you ever had. Then I showed up. That must have been a big disappointment. Come on, Tub." Rick was shouting. "Tell me all about it. You know I'm the only one who cares. Say something. At least give me a reason to feel good about killing you."

Without removing his hand from Barton's windpipe, Rick eased the pressure. Barton stopped struggling, though he writhed in pain. He looked Rick in the eyes. "You think this is the life I wanted, fishbait?" Barton's words were barely audible between gasps for air. The voice startled Rick.

Barton looked away, into the space above them.

Rick had seen Barton be hard, vicious, and unfeeling. Lying there, locked in a death struggle with him, Rick suddenly sensed in the smallest measure Barton's humanity. That's not what he wanted to feel at the moment.

"Why?" Rick screamed into Barton's ear. "Why did you kill Ryan? Why so many women? Why so much destruction?"

Barton's eyes closed. "A deal with the devil," he croaked.

This wasn't the time for philosophical discussion. Even wounded, Barton was dangerous. Rick had reached an impasse. Barton's life was in his hands for the moment, but the balance could shift at any second. Rick wanted a quick, lasting solution for the sake of Nicole, Miranda, and the others.

Barton's knife lay within inches of Rick's left hand. Rick could see it out of the corner of his eye as he spoke in Tub's ear. If he grabbed that knife, he could put an end to the matter. Who would know that he hadn't acted in self-defense?

Rick grasped the knife and moved it to Tub's neck, the razor sharp point next to the carotid artery. It was the only solution that made sense. "It's blood for blood," Rick said. "How will it feel to die by your own knife? Like so many others? Last chance, Tub," he said. "May as well go out with a clear conscience."

"Kill me, and you'll never know," answered Barton.

Rick increased the pressure. The tip of the knife slid through the skin, blood oozing out around the edge.

What are you doing? A familiar voice screamed inside Rick's mind. *This isn't you. This isn't the man you want to be. Do this, and you'll never live with it.*

Rick's hand started to quiver. *What about Tub's parents? Do you want to be the hand that kills their hopes? What about Ryan who protected Tub's life at the cost of his own to give Tub every chance to reform?*

Slowly, Rick withdrew the point of the knife, shaking his head.

Barton seemed to be fading, not from blood loss, but from pain.

"Okay, Tub," said Rick. "You deserve to die. But not by my hand. Not tonight. I just tell you this: if you ever trouble the women in my life again, I'll kill you in a heartbeat."

Rick stood, tossing the knife away.

Barton got slowly to his knees and staggered to his feet. His arm hung useless at his side. His face was a study in pain. He gasped and wheezed for breath.

He didn't look at Rick again. Moving off-balance, twisting in pain, he disappeared into the shadows.

Chapter 85

SUDDENLY EVERYONE AROUND MIRANDA MOVED into action.

"The suspect is moving," radioed the SWAT leader. "Contain him in the park. Move. Move."

"Your boyfriend just turned Barton loose," Lieutenant Taylor said, stepping to Miranda's side.

Shadowy figures emerged from cover in every direction.

Miranda heard voice commands across the park in Rick's direction. She heard the revving of a motorcycle engine, probably Barton's bullet bike.

"Stop, or I'll fire."

Then the scream of rubber on pavement. A short burst of weapons fire. Continued acceleration of the bike. More shouting. Another burst. And another. The sound of impact and crushing metal. The engine of the motorcycle screamed in the distance as though the throttle were stuck.

By the time Miranda reached the paved perimeter path, she could see a cluster of figures gathered just inside a cone of light from a park lamp. Men in body armor and black uniforms mixed with officers from the Detective Division.

"The suspect is down," radioed the SWAT leader.

Miranda raced toward the spot where Rick had fought with Barton. Rounding the shrubbery, she saw him standing motionless, his arms wrapped around himself.

Reaching him and seeing his blood-soaked shirt, she gasped. "Rick, you're wounded." She turned and shouted, "We need medical here."

He looked about in alarm. "Nicole is in the park with Trevor. She was parked down by the south entrance."

"They're okay," Miranda answered softly. "Sit down, Rick. Help will be here soon. You're wounded. Please sit down before you fall."

"It looks worse than it is," Rick replied, still on his feet, still holding his chest.

Miranda shook her head. On impulse, she threw her arms around him—heedless of the blood—then looked up and kissed him.

"I'm so relieved that you're alive," she said. "I love you, Rick. I need you. Please don't leave me."

Looking increasingly faint from exertion and loss of blood, Rick replied, "I love parks. Always have. But lately, seems like every time I go to the park the police are there. Guess I'm not that far from being fish bait after all."

Chapter 86

FALL PASSED QUICKLY, AND THE holidays brought peaceful days and nights. Rick finished the requirements for his degree. After work each day, he bused across town to the university and took afternoon breaks with Miranda.

"You seem happy," he said.

"I'm getting fat and lazy," she told him.

"You look great to me."

"Really? Do I look better in jeans or in dress pants?"

"You make whatever you're wearing look good," he told her.

"I'm starting to worry about you." She wrinkled her brow.

"Why?" asked Rick.

"You're getting to be a little too smooth," Miranda said. "When I first saw you, you were a diamond in the rough. Now you're the real thing—cut, polished, set in silver. I'm afraid it will go to your head at any minute."

With free hours on his hands during the holiday season, Rick made additional visits to the Rescue Mission and continued to volunteer. He was both happy and sad when he saw familiar faces in the homeless community. The visits gave him opportunity to reflect on the mighty changes in his life. They also confirmed his conviction that good people could be found everywhere. Hanging with his old crowd from time to time, the thought struck him that he had been as good a person before his arrest as he hoped he was now. Troubled, unfulfilled, but still a good person.

He went home from each visit determined to build on his new life.

Chapter 87

RICK STREET REACHED THE MATHESON Court House just before the ten o'clock hour on Tuesday, January 14. The weather was lousy for getting around. Snow was blowing horizontally, the temperature just above freezing. The walk across 400 South Street was short, but the lining of his blue windbreaker was no match for a Utah winter. He stamped his feet on the rubber mats just inside the doors of the building's rotunda to dislodge the loose snow from his new shoes.

Rick wore a new outfit that Miranda had helped him pick out at a men's store. Miranda had wanted him to look good for his final court appearance.

"We want the judge to take one look at you and know you've met every condition of your probation," Miranda told him.

The outfit included darkish grey to nearly charcoal slacks pleated in the front, a striped blue dress shirt, bold diagonal bars in his multicolor tie, and a black belt and dress shoes. Rick had never once dressed like this in his twenty-nine years. He couldn't do it now save for Miranda searching through the offerings, nodding her approval or sweeping away the misfit items. Rick let her choose, loving every moment of her attention and closeness.

He had awakened early, straightened his apartment, and visited with Jesus.

He thought again about Jennifer Sopel Franklin, who was also praying for him as she did every day. This morning Rick prayed for her in return and then went to get his hair styled. He told Rachel, the stylist who had been doing his hair for the past year, that he needed something special because he was going to court. She took a little extra care and set his hair with spray that she claimed had a knockout masculine scent.

Rick looked his best. He spied Miranda across the lobby talking to the public defender. This was Rick's third time through the routine. He should be getting accustomed to the butterflies in his stomach, but he knew he never would.

Miranda waved him over. As he approached, he stripped off his windbreaker and nodded at the public defender. Miranda eyed him carefully.

She was dressed to kill. She wore a moderately cut dress of sea-mist blue velour that hung alluringly from her charming frame. Complementary beads and a waist-defining chain belt accented her outfit. Standing on five-inch heels, her slim muscular legs caught Rick's eyes. He couldn't suppress his smile. "Wow, woman. You look great."

"Good morning, Mr. Street." She smiled. "Ready to go to court?"

"No," confessed Rick. Letting his ever-present self-doubts show through, he opened his arms to showcase his attire. "Don't you think I'm overdoing it?"

Miranda laughed. "No, the only danger is that the judge might propose marriage. Wait here a second," she said and hurried away.

Rick glanced at his public defender, who never had anything to say. "How ya doing?" Rick asked.

"Getting late. We should go in." The defender looked at his watch.

You're all personality.

Miranda returned carrying a garment in a plastic bag still on a hanger. She handed her coat to Rick and quickly unhanged the garment.

"Put this on," she ordered.

A navy blazer. Rick slipped it on. It fit him perfectly.

Miranda smiled broadly.

"Did you rent me a costume?" Rick asked, turning so she could view him from all angles.

"No, Mr. Street. That's a gift from your probation counselor."

"How did you know what size to buy?"

Miranda held her arms out in front of her in a circle. "I just told them to make it this big."

Rick smiled. "Thank you—for this and for everything else. I'm going to miss you."

"Got to go," the public defender reminded them. He led the way. Miranda followed, several steps ahead of Rick, who eyed her from behind, appreciating the view.

"Mr. Street, what are you looking at?" she asked, turning her head.

"Think I lost my contact," he said.

"You don't wear contacts. Please get serious," she said.

As they approached the door, the uniformed attendant opened to them. Glancing into the courtroom, Rick could see that the room was packed. His spirits fell immediately and dread swamped him. *Oh no. I was hoping it wouldn't be a busy day.*

He paused at the door, dreading the walk down the aisle. Every seat was occupied. The courtroom hadn't been this full on either of his previous visits.

Miranda, sensing that Rick had fallen behind, turned partially and signaled him to come ahead.

As he stepped into the room, letting the door close slowly behind him, he noticed to his left a group of familiar faces. Members of the street community who Rick had known and recently reconnected with filled two full rows of courtroom seats on that side. Rick recognized most of them. Reverend Marsh of the Rescue Mission, Arch, Dodo, Scotty and Soapy, and several others. There were a few women, including Happy Trails. Rick smiled weakly and tried to wave. Two or three stood and moved within range so they could shake hands with Rick. Others, seeing him stop, also stood to greet him until a small knot of people were reaching their hands through for a touch.

The judge stuck the sound block sharply. "The defendant and counsel will takes your places," came the commanding voice.

Rick turned away from his street friends and hurried to the front. Almost immediately, he saw Trevor Tate break away from his mother's grip and bolt into the aisle in front of him, grasping Rick around the waist. Rick stopped abruptly and bent down to give the boy a hug. "Hi, tiger," he said softly. "Great to see you. Stick around so we can talk when this is over."

Without a word, Trevor loosed his hold and returned to his mother. Rick looked up at Nicole with a smile and saw, lined on her row, the faces of all the Tate family. All smiled their greetings.

Rick hurried on, taking his place beside Miranda.

"So, Mr. Street," said Judge Springer, looking down at him over her reading glasses, "you're in my courtroom once more."

"Yes, Your Honor," replied Rick, looking steadily up at her.

"Two years have passed," continued the judge. "The public defender, with concurrence of the court-appointed probation counselor, has filed a brief before the court claiming that you have met all the conditions of your probation. Have you?"

"I believe so, Your Honor."

"Can the people of the State of Utah be assured that if you are released from probation you will continue to be a responsible citizen? Obeying the laws? Bringing credit to your community? And to all those who obviously value your friendship?" she asked, sweeping her hand across the breadth of the room.

Rick turned his gaze partially on the courtroom crowd. He saw only a few of the faces, but in addition to the Tates and his street community friends, he noticed a cluster of his coworkers from the store, the Komatsus, Father John, and several faculty members from Salt Lake Community College.

"They can, Your Honor," he replied, looking back at Judge Springer.

"And what do you plan to do with your life, Mr. Street?"

"Your Honor, I plan to work in the community, maybe helping some of my friends on the street find their dreams."

"Very admirable," replied the judge. "You realize, of course, that not all of your friends have the same capacity as you. You've become a poster child for the homeless community. Not everyone could do that."

"I know not everyone can have a Miranda Martinez in their life, Your Honor. We're all different, but we all have dreams. There isn't anyone whose life couldn't be better with a little help."

"That's true," said the judge. "You also realize, I hope, that those who give their lives to that kind of service don't become rich from it."

"That's okay, Your Honor. I know how to live on a nickel," replied Rick, using a well-known street aphorism. He heard a round of snickers and muffled cheers from the street people in the rear of the court.

"Don't ever lose your idealism," said Judge Springer, nodding her approval. She turned to the public defender. "Anything else from you, Counselor?"

"No, Your Honor," he replied, shifting from foot to foot.

"And how about you, Ms. Martinez?"

"No, Your Honor," replied Miranda. "Mr. Street can speak for himself."

"He just has," said the judge. She looked at Miranda steadily for a moment. "Ms. Martinez, you get an A+ for your work in Mr. Street's behalf. I'm sure he agrees. If you need an internship while you're in school, please come see me."

"I will, Your Honor. Thank you." Miranda smiled, shaking her head gently so that her rich, radiant hair flowed away from her face.

The judge smiled. "You don't have to be beautiful for me, Ms. Martinez. I'm after your brains."

Miranda laughed. "Yes, Your Honor."

The judge surveyed the courtroom. "I have before me the public defender's brief and the probation counselor's statement. Is there anyone else in the courtroom who wishes to serve as a character witness for the defendant?"

Her question was followed by a brief hush throughout the room.

Nicole Tate stood. A second later, Linda stood, followed by Dennis and then the rest of their row.

Seeing those people stand, members of the street community on the back rows stood almost simultaneously. Father John, Danny and Heiko Komatsu, Rick's coworkers, others, and finally nearly everyone in the room stood, some who had come to witness other hearings.

Judge Springer surveyed the room, and after a long pause and a sigh, she brought her gavel down on the sound block. "You may all be seated," she declared. "The court doesn't have time to hear all your testimonies. There are other defendants in this city beside Mr. Street."

A ripple of laughter coursed through the room.

"However, your message to the court has been duly noted. Richard Harrison Street," she spoke loudly and pontifically, "the court finds you in compliance with all conditions of the aforementioned probation order and terminates that order. Furthermore, in light of your exceptional compliance, this court orders the record of your arrest, conviction, and subsequent probation expunged. Mr. Street, you are a free man. Go from this court and do all the good you can with all the life you've been given. You are dismissed." With that charge, Judge Springer brought down her gavel for the last time in the case again Richard Harrison Street.

The courtroom erupted in applause, crescendoing into whistles and cheers. Judge Springer watched this breach of courtroom etiquette for several long moments, a small smile playing at her lips. Then she struck the block loudly and repeatedly, raising her voice almost to a yell. "Order in the court," she bellowed. "Order in the court."

She struck the block again. "This is a courtroom, not a sports arena. If you want to cheer, go to a basketball game. Now get out of my courtroom. If I hear another outburst like that, you'll all spend a night in jail. It'll give you opportunity to reflect on the decorum of our legal system."

Having restored order, she glanced over at the bailiff, shaking her head, a hint of a smile on her face.

The public defender reached a hand out to Rick perfunctorily and was gone before Rick could thank him.

Those who had come to witness Rick's hearing poured out into lobby.

Chapter 88

As Rick followed the crowd out of the courtroom arm in arm with Miranda, a cheer went up. The next fifteen minutes passed in a round of greetings with the Tates, Danny and Heiko Komatsu, Father John, Miranda's parents, and other well-wishers.

Rick spied Happy Trails. The bashful girl from the Rescue Mission passed with two or three of her companions. Rick called out to her.

"Happy!"

When she looked up, he smiled and waved. She immediately turned crimson and looked away, her hand moving automatically to her chest, her fingers wiggling a barely seen return wave.

Yeah. You see me. And you know I saw you. On the outside, you're afraid to make a show. On the inside, you're thrilled that somebody noticed you, knows your name, thinks enough of you to go public with it. I know you feel it. Let it work in you, girl.

Finally, when everyone's hand was shaken and every hug received, Rick exhaled deeply. He scanned the lobby, searching the faces.

"Who are you looking for?" asked Miranda, who had slipped off one of her heels and was scratching her calf with her stockinged foot.

"Probably nobody," answered Rick. "I really only invited one person to be here today. I'm thinking you've been busy inviting the rest."

Miranda smiled. "How does it feel to have so many friends?"

"You know what?" asked Rick, gazing into the depth of her eyes. "If I had never met you, this would never have happened. You know where I'd be today? Out there on the street. Sitting in some doorway shooting the bull with a buddy. Standing in some line. Waiting for some door to open. Dreaming of my future. No hope. No belief in myself. Afraid to look people in the eye. Afraid to talk. Just plain afraid."

He pulled her close, standing there in the public lobby, people passing on every side. "Thank you. Miranda—Miranda—Miranda. I love the sound of your name. I love you. Thank you."

Miranda said nothing, her face nestled in his neck. She purred ever so slightly. The only place Rick had ever heard the sound before was from a family cat when he was a child. He grinned.

Across the lobby, he saw a woman looking at them, sitting on one of the benches. Rick was suddenly aware of the spectacle he and Miranda were presenting. He felt that old familiar urge to look away. Instead, he maintained the woman's gaze. She also didn't look away.

"Let's step over here," Rick said, softly steering Miranda in that direction. "I think my guest may have come after all."

As they stepped in front of the woman, she stood. She was tall, nearly six feet, attractive, but not glamorous. Her features were refined. She was dressed well.

Rick extended his hand. "Jennifer?" he asked.

"Hello, Rick."

"You came a long way." Rick felt a surge of emotion.

"This has been one of the happiest, most glorious days of a lifetime," Jennifer replied. She extended a hand to Miranda. "My name is Jennifer Franklin," she introduced herself. "No credit to me, but I brought this fine man into the world." Her eyes misted, forming tears that she quickly dabbed away.

"I'm so pleased you came," said Rick. "This has been a glorious day for me, for us, and having a chance to meet you is icing on the cake."

Jennifer reddened slightly, her face showing her warmth. "My husband, Bill, is here as well. He had to step away for a moment but should be right back." She fell quiet. An awkward silence followed.

Rick was determined to make this a sweet moment for them both. He didn't know quite what to say, but saying anything was better than saying nothing. "Are you going to be in town long? Did you come just for this?" he asked.

Jennifer smiled. She looked at him like she couldn't get enough. Rick knew she was braving her personal embarrassment to relish this moment she had dreamed of for nearly thirty years. She appeared to be an intelligent, educated woman. Her manners were refined. She spoke thoughtfully.

It wouldn't have mattered to Rick if she had been as backward and afraid of the world as he had not so long ago. He would still have treasured her kindness in coming to share this happy moment with him.

"As you know," Jennifer said, "my parents live here. So do most of my brothers and sisters. So we have a place to stay. Bill is a faculty member at Portland State. He took a few days off. We came because you were kind enough to invite us, but it also gives us a chance to visit with my family. We can stay as long or short as we wish."

Rick turned to Miranda. "Jennifer was nineteen when Ryan and I barged into her world." To Jennifer, he said, "Incidentally, I don't have the mark on my chest. Ryan did. I confirmed that with his wife, Nicole. So I was the oldest."

He said this boastfully for Miranda's sake. "I rule."

They all laughed.

"Jennifer, I invited you for lots of reasons. Maybe the most important is that I've thought a lot about your prayers for me. I learned to keep a journal from Ryan. Not too long ago, I tried to write down the times that something unexpectedly good has happened in my life."

He looked at Miranda, the greatest miracle in his life. "This woman's name was on the top line. It took me a while, but the more I listed, the more I remembered. In the end the list was long. I could have gone even further. Then a thought came to me out of the blue. The first and greatest miracle in my life was my first breath. And that opportunity was given to me . . ." Rick paused to recapture his composure, which took him a few seconds. "That opportunity was given to me by a frightened, sorrowful nineteen-year-old girl who was doing the best she could. She was trying to do the right thing for me and for my little brother. She could have—" He broke off the thought. "She was trying to do what was best. So I went back to the top of the list and squeezed in above Miranda Martinez the name Jennifer Sopel Franklin."

Tears were pouring from Jennifer's eyes. She was mopping at them furiously.

Rick stepped beside her and put his arm around her shoulder. "Thank you," he said.

Jennifer lost it altogether at that point. She was beginning to recapture her composure when Bill Franklin returned. Perhaps wondering what had transpired in his absence, he looked at his wife inquiringly.

They spoke for a few more minutes, and before they parted, Rick turned to Jennifer. "I'd like to meet the members of your family, your parents especially. Do you think they'd go for that?"

"They would be thrilled," Jennifer replied.

"Do you have a number where I could reach you while you're here?"

Bill Franklin took a business card from his wallet. "Use this cell number." He pointed.

Chapter 89

RICK AND MIRANDA RETRIEVED THEIR coats and faced the outside weather.

"My car's in the underground," Miranda said. "Let's take that."

"Kind of nasty out." Rick nodded.

"That was so nice, what you said to Jennifer." Miranda squeezed his arm. "I like you more all the time."

"Nah," replied Rick. "I'd get on your nerves if you had to be around me very long."

"Is that so? Why is that?"

"Well, I sing while I'm brushing my teeth," he said with a smile. "You can imagine how annoying that would be. And I'm fanatical about keeping my place clean."

"I've noticed that." She laughed.

"No, I'm afraid I wouldn't wear well," he said more seriously.

They stood looking out through the windows of the court building's glass vestibule at the driving snow. Pedestrians hurried toward their destinations. The windshield wipers of passing cars and buses worked hard to keep pace with the accumulation.

"I've taken the day off school," Miranda said softly. "I don't really want to go back."

Rick just nodded.

She looked at him steadily. He could see her gaze, but he looked straight ahead of him out the windows.

"You know what, Mr. Street? I'm not your counselor any longer. But in all honesty, my professional advice to you is to get yourself a wife, settle down, and have a bunch of kids."

Rick laughed.

"You think that's funny?" she challenged.

"It's the kids thing," he answered. "I'm terrible with kids."

"Nope," she replied. "Won't work. I've seen you with Trevor. You were born to be a dad. You think like a kid." It was her turn to gaze out the windows while he looked at her. "Often," she continued, "you act like a kid."

"Hey, watch it," he warned.

"I think you'll be a wonderful dad. Can't you imagine some darling dark-eyed girls and little black-haired boys?"

"What if they're blond?" he asked.

Miranda punched him on the arm. "You'd better mend your ways or you'll never live to have children," she scolded.

"Okay," he said. "I suppose you're right. I've never doubted you so far. That brings us to a question that's been on my mind lately. Where does a Mormon go to marry a Catholic?"

"Are you a Mormon?" Miranda asked.

"I was born one," he replied, "and I feel really good around them. I guess that's something I need to find out."

Miranda was quiet and thoughtful for a few seconds. The pair was in no hurry. They had nowhere to go, and the weather didn't beckon them to rush outside.

"You're right," she finally said. "I've seen some unhappy marriages where neither partner dares to really express religious feelings because they're of different mindsets."

Rick was nodding.

"On the other hand," she continued, "there's a lot to be said for marrying for love." She paused as if deciding what to say next. "Do you love me, Rick?" She looked up at him, the question written on her pretty face.

Rick looked into her eyes.

No looking away this time. No looking away ever again.

"I love you, Miranda."

"I don't mean the way I look," she said. "That will change. Not just your feelings for me at this moment. This moment will pass. Harder times could follow. Will you love me then?"

She was putting him on the spot, but she had a right to do that. She was asking questions that needed to be answered. She was asking him to search his heart. He couldn't let this woman down.

"I like the way you look," he began. "I like your touch, your smell, your taste, your feel. But even more"—he smiled—"I love the way you think. I love the way you talk. I love the ways you're tough and the ways you're tender. I love your dreams and your drive to lift other people." He paused, trying to really get in touch with the truth about Miranda Martinez.

"Miranda, what I really love is your soul. Your goodness. The person you've become by making the choices you've made. I love you, Miranda. You, way down inside those eyes." He pointed at her pupil and looked into her eyes as though trying to peer into her soul. "You, behind the beautiful face and the gorgeous body. I know you're hiding in there somewhere. It's you I love," he called. "Can you hear me in there?"

Miranda laughed. "Marrying me means working out a lot of differences," she said tenderly. "Not just religious differences. Cultural. Maybe political. Parenting too—that's a big one. Can we do that?"

"You make it sound like we would be the first people who ever got married," he said. "Don't make it sound too tough, or I'll run away screaming."

She smiled. "Can we do it, Rick? Really?"

Rick paused, his face now serious. "Can *you* do it?" he asked. "It'd be easy for me. I would be marrying a woman who is beautiful, educated, and accomplished. A woman with a proven track record. A law student, for Pete's sake. You're the one who'd be taking a chance on a former street bum. A reformed binger. A man who knows his way around the inside of a courtroom. All you'd have to bolster your confidence is my solemn word that I'll never let you down. I'll never lie to you. I'll never cheat on you. I'll try never to disappoint you. I'll try to become the man you think I can become. So I'm asking you, Ms. Martinez, can we do it? Really?"

Miranda pointed at the city and county building across the street. "That's where the county clerk's office is," she said. "That's where they issue marriage licenses."

"Wow! You know how to close a sale," Rick replied. "Okay. Let's go."

"Just like that?" she asked.

"Just like that," replied Rick. "Of course, I make it sound like a spur-of-the-moment thing, but you know I've been thinking about this in one way or another since the minute I first saw you. Besides," he continued, looking around them, "the people here are probably tired of watching us make out."

"I doubt it," said Miranda.

"You can't walk over in those." Rick pointed to her spike heels.

"I came prepared," she replied. She reached into her bag and withdrew a pair of sneakers and socks. She turned toward a bench to make the change.

"Those won't cut the mustard either. Not in weather like this." Rick laughed.

"You don't give me enough credit," she said. "I've been out on cold days and cold nights. Are you afraid to go out there?" she asked.

"Are you kidding? I'm a street hound. This is nice weather compared to some days."

Coats and shoes adjusted, Rick Street and Miranda Martinez pushed the door open against the blast of frigid winter wind, walking arm-in-arm away from the building.

As they walked along, bracing against the wind, Rick Street mentally listed the women in his life, all seen and embraced during the morning. Miranda, Linda, Nicole, Jennifer, and others. Before the pedestrian light turned in their favor and they started across the street toward their future together, Rick thought, *God didn't make stupid women.*

About the Author

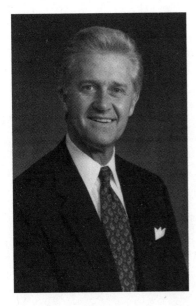

FRANK RICHARDSON IS A FORMER military chaplain, Vietnam veteran, and career administrator for LDS Welfare Services. During his career, Frank became acquainted with many homeless men and women, their challenges, and the agencies that serve them. He holds a PhD in communication from the University of Washington and teaches public speaking at Weber State University in Ogden, Utah.

Frank published two earlier novels: *Where the Sun Rises* (2009) and *Sudden Peril* (2011).